There Is No Death

(A Patrick Brady Mystery)

JASON E. DZEMBO

Patrick Brady Mysteries

Fellow of the Craft

Vices & Superfluities

There Is No Death

And, coming in 2017,
Secrecy & Circumspection

Copyright © 2016 Jason E. Dzembo

All rights reserved.

ISBN: 1530623529
ISBN-13: 978-1530623525

This one is for my family, immediate and extended. The good, the bad and the ugly.

I'll leave it to you to determine who falls into which category.

Chapter One

Family. Those people who share our blood, our genetics, our triumphs and our tragedies. They are the most important people in our lives, and the most irritating. Friends come and go but family never leaves, even if you think you want them to. Not forever. Family always comes back, be it like a fond memory or a bad penny. Still, you *do* for family. In the end, family is everything. Love 'em or hate 'em, but you're stuck with 'em.

My father taught me a lot of things. How to change the oil in the family Impala. How to shoot a rifle and knock over an aluminum can from fifteen paces. How to use a bag of frozen peas as an icepack under your armpit when your father forgets to mention a little thing like recoil. Along with creative accounting, he taught me multi-tiered ethics. It was okay to screw a big corporation once in a while – they'd never feel it – but you don't take advantage of family. Not only will they feel it, but even after it's forgiven, it is rarely forgotten. "If things ever get so bad," he once told me, "that you have nothing left, you still have your family. Me, your mother, Ian. Your aunts, uncles, cousins. They're always here for you. And you'll be there for them."

My father, on the whole, is a good man. More than that he's a good father. I've always hoped that, when my time came, I'd be half the father he was. I grew up looking forward to fatherhood.

Which is why I was devastated to have that chance so abruptly torn from my grasp.

I suppose I should back up just a little. My name is Patrick Brady. I'm thirty-two years old and, for about fourteen months, I've been divorced from my wife of eight years. Shortly after our divorce was finalized Larissa, my ex-wife, dropped the bombshell – she had just given birth to a daughter. To be accurate, she had said that *we* had a daughter.

My silence must have spoken volumes because she laughed nervously into the empty space in the conversation. "No, no," she added, hastily. "I don't mean me and *you*. I meant *George* and I. *We* had a daughter."

"Oh," I replied intelligently. I was still trying to determine how I felt about being a father and now I had to figure out how I felt about *not* being a father. "Are you...are you sure it's his?" I asked.

I felt her hesitation. "Yes," she answered coolly.

I did some quick math in my head and added, "Because I assume you had ... the baby on the 5th, since that's the day I called and your sister said you weren't home." She made a faint murmur of agreement. I continued, "And that means there's a slight possibility that..."

"She is *not* your child," Larissa interrupted emphatically. "That's why I didn't tell you I was pregnant. We decided it would be better to wait until the divorce was finalized. I didn't want to complicate things."

"But," I insisted, "did you ever actually have any tests done to make sure it...*she* is his?" I pinched the bridge of my nose. "Because if I remember those days before we separated correctly, there's a chance that..."

"Patrick, stop," Larissa pleaded. "You're off the hook, okay? You're safe. The whole divorce was amicable. Let's part as friends. Whatever Katie's genetic makeup, we are happy to raise her as our own. You don't have to feel obligated to..."

It was my turn to cut her off. "It's not an obligation!" I barked. "If that child, if *she* is my child, then I want to know. I have a right to know. Did you have any tests done or not?"

A pause. A quiet "No." Another pause. My chance to speak now or forever hold my peace.

"I want a paternity test," I said softly.

"Fine," was Larissa's crisp response. "I'll call you tomorrow to make arrangements. I have to go. *My* daughter is crying." The line went dead.

A few weeks later found me at the doctor's office. The plan was to get a cheek swab for a DNA test. As I chatted with Dr. Garrison, I mentioned the irony that, in eight years of marriage, Larissa had never gotten pregnant until just before we separated. The doctor gave me one of those pensive doctor-type looks, where they suspect something significant is wrong but they are oath-bound not to say anything definitive, at least until they've run more tests. "Perhaps," said Dr. Garrison, "you should have a testicular biopsy to be certain."

If there are two words in the English language that should never, ever go together, they are "testicular" and "biopsy". To anyone out there with testiculars, if your doctor every recommends this procedure, let me give you a brief insight into what you've got coming.

In reality, it's not that bad. They give you enough anesthesia that you won't remember the surgery itself but not enough, apparently, to actually knock you out. The doctor who did my surgery (hereinafter referred to as Dr. The Claw) claims I carried on a conversation with him the whole time. I don't know what it was about. I hope I didn't say anything incriminating. While I was babbling away, they made a small incision in my scrotum, sliced off a tiny piece of one of my…testiculars, and stitched me back up. Physically it wasn't bad – except for resisting the urge to scratch as the scab healed – but the knowledge of what had been done while I was doped up, and rambling on about God knows what, is psychologically wearing.

It was a mixed blessing that, when the results of the biopsy came in a few weeks later, all my concerns about the procedure itself immediately evaporated.

Dr. The Claw's attitude was solemn as he delivered the results. "You don't appear to be producing any sperm."

"I don't understand. I mean, something... comes out..." I gestured descriptively.

"Just seminal fluid," The Claw explained. His tone was neutral, bordering on weary, as if he told people this kind of news every day and it had begun to wear on him. "There are several 'pieces' in the testicles, necessary to reproduce. You're missing a number of them."

"How is that possible?"

A casual shrug. "It's a genetic thing," he said.

I stifled a morbid laugh. "So I inherited a genetic disorder that prevents me from passing that disorder on to my own descendants because this branch of the family tree stops with me?" My voice was laced with irony. If he heard, The Claw ignored it.

"Basically, yes."

"Can it be fixed?" My voice seemed to be rising in pitch. I attributed that to the stress of the news, not to my...deficiency.

The doctor shook his head solemnly. "I'm afraid not. I'm sorry, Mr. Brady, but you're sterile."

And, like that, my dreams of having a family were squashed. On the plus side (I guess) there was no chance Larissa's daughter was mine. On the other hand, no other child ever would be either. Larissa took the news stoically and was kind enough not to say either "I told you so" or "Neener, neener."

Angela Button, my girlfriend of (at the time) about eight months, took it harder. She, too, had been looking forward to someday embracing the joy and misery of parenthood. We had yet to even broach the subject of marriage, never mind having children, but it was always assumed we would someday. The news that we were to be childless brought us both to tears as we sat on my ratty rattan couch and cried.

That had been just over a year ago. Since then, the subject hadn't come up again. In fact, on the topics of marriage, children or the future of our relationship, we had both gone out of our way to avoid any discussion at all. For the last thirteen months, we had been in a holding pattern, trying to focus on the now, in hopes that the later would sort itself out.

Today, as usual, those worries were moved to the

back burner. We had more immediate concerns. And while it didn't seem as broad-reaching or devastating as my sterility, we both were feeling anxious about the next several hours. Despite my own doubts, I did my best to reassure her.

"We will be fine, Angela," I said soothingly, stepping behind her and rubbing her shoulders. As a part time exotic dancer and a full-time returning college student, she had an amazing body. It wasn't the only reason I loved her, of course, but it didn't hurt. "They're good people and they love you. And it's only one day."

"Easy for you to say," my girlfriend sighed heavily. "They aren't your family."

"We had Thanksgiving with my family last year," I reminded her. "We agreed to take turns."

"I know," she moaned. She wriggled her shoulders in my grasp, working a kink loose. "I just didn't expect this year to creep up on us so quickly."

"The holidays have a way of doing that," I agreed drily. "But it will be fine. The four of us had a…fair time last Christmas. And I think your father is really starting to warm up to me."

I had met Angela, in part, through her father. Anthony Button was a member of the same Masonic Lodge as my father and I. Angela and I had actually met before as children, but were never really close. At that point, the six year difference in our ages had been more significant than it was now. No fifteen year old boy wanted a nine year old girl tagging along with him and his friends. Angela and I had become reacquainted almost two years ago when I met her at the gentlemen's club where she danced. I had just joined Acacia Lodge and Tony had asked me to visit the club from time to time and keep an eye on her. Whether he had expected the two of us to fall in love or not, I don't know, but, once we did, he had made it clear that if I ever hurt her, it would go badly for me. I didn't think he was serious…but I couldn't say for sure that he wasn't either. Fortunately, it hadn't been an issue.

"I'm not worried about Daddy," Angela said. "Well, not completely. But he and Mom have been… bickering lately. Plus I talked to Mom last night and it sounds like my brother will be there too."

"Russ?" I was unable to keep the surprise from my voice. Angela twisted to give me a significant look over her shoulders and nodded wordlessly. "I finally get a chance to meet your elusive brother," I murmured.

Angela scowled and turned away again. I resumed the shoulder massage. "Don't get your hopes up," she muttered. "We've all learned not to."

We were silent for a moment. Finally she let out a

long raspberry and stood, crossing the kitchen to take the green bean casserole from the oven. Two serving dishes, containing mashed potatoes and dressing, respectively, already sat on the counter, covered in aluminum foil and ready for the ride to her parents' house.

I watched as she set the hot casserole dish on top of the stove to cool and turned off the oven. "That doesn't sound like you," I remarked. "You've never been one to give up on someone. You are the Queen of Second Chances. I should know; I've been the recipient of one or two of them."

She arched one eyebrow. "At least," she said deadpan. "But Russ is a different story. He's hurt so many people, put my entire family through hell so many times. It's hard to keep giving someone like that chance after chance. Sooner or later you have to say 'No more. You're done breaking my heart.'"

I moved to join her, putting my arms around her. Nearly a full foot shorter than me, she was able to rest her head comfortably against my chest. I stroked her hair, inhaled her scent. "I promise," I murmured, "no matter how many times Russ breaks your heart, you will always have mine."

Angela took a step back and looked up at me. "That may be the corniest thing you've ever said."

"But it made you smile, so it was worth it," I

countered.

"You got me there." She leaned up on her tiptoes and we kissed. As our lips separated, she sighed, glanced at the food on the counter and said, "Okay, let's go get this over with."

Chapter Two

We could hear the yelling before we even walked in the house. As we approached the front door, I could only make out some of the words between Anthony Button and his wife. Words like "unfaithful," and "cheating," and "divorce." I glanced towards Angela. The clench of her jaw told me she'd heard the shouting as well. I shifted the serving tray in my arm and laid a free hand on her shoulder. She looked at me with grim resolution. "I'm fine," she said in a tone that belied the statement. She turned away and rang the doorbell. The shouts subsided.

The delay was long enough that, if we hadn't heard the shouting previously, we might have pressed the bell again. Instead we waited in silence. I held her hand, hoping it gave her some small comfort. She glanced up with a sad smile and mouthed the words, "Thank you."

With the faint squeak of a hinge, the door opened. Tony Button stood there, his face impassive. There was a bead of sweat trickling down his balding head. The air smelled like turkey and sage. "Right on time," he greeted us.

"Hi, Daddy!" Angela said with a sweet, and seemingly genuine, smile. She buzzed her father on the cheek, careful not to spill the large bowl of dressing she carried.

Tony gave her a quick embrace. "Hello, Dumpling!" Over her shoulder, his face briefly lit up, his issues with his wife temporarily replaced by the happiness of seeing his daughter. He glanced up and our eyes met and his stolid mask slid back into place as he stepped back from her and offered me his hand. "Patrick," he said. "Happy Thanksgiving."

"Happy Thanksgiving, Tony," I agreed as we shared a firm handshake, each automatically giving each other the pass grip of Master Mason. "Something smells good."

"I'm glad someone appreciates it!" Regina Button, Angela's mother, entered the foyer behind her husband, wiping her hands on a dish towel. For a woman in her early fifties, she was maintaining herself well. Lean and toned, hair stylish and, I assumed, colored to a chestnut brown. She wore a string of pearls around her neck. She looked composed, but her eyes were still tinted with red. She sounded like she was teasing, but the sidelong glance she gave Tony was icy. She moved past him, gesturing us inside. "Come in, come in! He'll just keep standing here with the door open otherwise."

Angela's father remained silent, but I saw his jaw working as he moved aside and we entered the house.

"I still have to grab the mashed potatoes from the car," I commented. Tony reached for the casserole dish but Regina was just a little faster, taking the glass bowl from me.

"We'll bring these out to the kitchen while you grab them," she said. She turned, heading back through the archway from which she had come. Angela followed her.

I glanced at Tony. "Trouble in paradise?" I asked, trying to lighten the mood with a bit of guy talk.

Tony regarded me with a frown. "Better get those potatoes so I can close the door or we'll never hear the end of it."

Realizing that was probably as close as we were going to come to bonding, I returned to my car. Tony closed the door behind me. The cool air felt good, as did the opportunity to be free from the tension inside. This was going to be a long day. If it didn't mean leaving my girlfriend behind, I might have considered getting in the car and heading home, mashed potatoes and all. For Angela's sake, though, I grabbed the remaining serving dish from the back seat and closed the car door.

As I stood up, a silver Mini Cooper pulled into the driveway. A few years old, it showed some signs of wear and tear. I decided to wait for the occupant, if only to avoid returning to the lion's den.

The car parked beside mine and the engine was killed. The glare on the windshield from the early afternoon sun prevented me from seeing the driver. When the door opened and the man behind the wheel got out, I admit to being momentarily confused.

The man who emerged was wearing work boots, dark blue jeans, a white T-shirt and a blazer. He had thick black hair. His face looked as though he'd recently lost weight, some residual skin hanging loosely around his skull. I could see the family resemblance to Tony and Angela. He had a strong, broad chest. In one hand he held a plastic grocery bag. None of this was what caught my attention. My surprise stemmed from the fact that he was barely over four feet tall.

I didn't think I was staring, but he looked up at me with a bemused scowl. "Someone alert the villagers," he remarked dryly. "The giant is loose."

"I...what?" I asked.

"Sorry, maybe you can't hear me up there," the man said as he came closer. The proximity only emphasized the difference between his stature and my own six-foot-four frame. He raised his voice. "I said, hello! I'm Russell! You can call me Russ, for short. Get it? Because I'm short!" He extended his empty hand. His nails had been bitten back. Along the top of the trapezium bone on his wrist was a short thin red mark.

"Patrick," I said, shaking his hand. "I apologize. I

didn't mean to stare."

"Forget it, giant," Russ said with a dismissive wave. "They never tell anyone. They say it's because they want to treat me like one of you full grown freaks. I think they're embarrassed. I'm their dirty little secret. Pun intended."

I had no response for this brash little man. He seemed amused by that. He nodded. "Big and dumb, huh? No wonder my sister likes you. Come on, Bunyan, let's get inside." He heft the bag and said, "The pie man cometh!" He moved towards the house and I followed along, mincing my stride so as not to overtake him.

Walking into the kitchen, I heard Angela stop in mid-sentence. I hadn't heard what she was saying but from the set of her jaw and the evasiveness of her mother's eyes, I guessed it had something to do with the scene we'd overheard on our arrival. Russ appeared oblivious. "Hey, Ma," he said, "I found this scarecrow hanging out in the driveway. Can we keep him, huh, can we?"

Regina hugged her son and bent to exchange air kisses with him. "I'm so glad you could make it, Russell," she said. She glanced my way with a faint smile and said, "But I think your sister has already called dibs on your new friend."

"True story, bro," Angela agreed. She stepped

forward and hugged her brother tightly. She gave no indication that, an hour earlier, she'd been expressing her doubts about him. They separated and she looked down at him. "You're looking good, Russ," she said seriously. "How are you doing?"

"I been clean two months today, if that's what you're asking, Sis," Russ replied. His jaw went rigid as he spoke, the only outward sign of his defensiveness. "How about you? Still showing off the goods to dirty old men?"

I tensed. Before I could respond, Angela gave her brother a tight smile. "Touché," she conceded. "And, yes, I'm still dancing."

"Much to her father's displeasure," Anthony added, entering the kitchen from the dining room. Father and son faced each other across the linoleum floor and hesitated, each waiting to see who would blink first. Finally Anthony stepped forward. "You shaved," he commented offering his hand.

"Well, yeah, I finally got the hint after all those times you chastised me for showing up all…scruffy, I think was the word you used. Thought it was the least I could do," Russ replied. He regarded his father's outstretched hand, then ignored it. He stepped closer, arms wide, a smirk on his face, daring the older man to deny his son the hug.

Anthony took it in stride, embracing Russ and

patting him on the back twice before pulling back. "The effort's appreciated," he said. Looking over at Regina's back, he added, "Isn't that right, hon?"

Ignoring her husband, Regina turned to Russ and said, "I believe the turkey is just about ready to slice. Would you like to do the honors this year, Russell?"

Russ's gaze passed between his parents suspiciously. "Isn't that usually Dad's job?" he asked.

"Never too late to pass on the tradition," Regina said flatly. "Besides, the mood he's in, I wouldn't trust him with a knife."

"Trouble in paradise?" Russ questioned.

"Nothing we're going to talk about right now," Anthony said firmly, giving his wife an icy stare.

Regina smiled tightly at Russ. "Apparently," she said, "it's nothing we're going to talk about right now."

There was a long awkward pause, one of those pauses that was made longer by its awkwardness, and more awkward by its length, until the pause threatens to drag on into an uncomfortable infinity of silence. Once again, Anthony made the effort, albeit begrudgingly, to break the stalemate.

"Carve the turkey, Russ," he rumbled. "It's time you learned how anyway. Any questions, just ask your mother. Apparently, she knows everything." He left the room without another word. The tension in my shoulders eased a notch.

We didn't see Anthony again until we sat down to eat. Angela and I set the dining room table and brought the food out, taking advantage of those fleeting moments by ourselves to take solace in each other's arms and each other's company.

"This is so much worse than I expected," Angela whispered to me as we stole a moment to share an embrace. She clung to me like a drowning woman to the last life preserver.

"Just bad timing, I'm sure," I assured her. "Dinner just happened to coincide with their argument."

"I've never heard my parents throw around the idea of divorce before. It's just not something they believed in. My mother always joked she'd kill my father before she divorced him."

I attempted a reassuring smile. "Then let's be grateful they're *only* talking about divorce."

She huffed. "At least Russ seems to be doing well. For now anyway."

I smiled wordlessly and gave her arm a squeeze. I'd already determined this was neither the time nor place to mention the track mark I'd seen on his wrist when he first greeted me in the driveway. Though the mark looked relatively fresh, I had little actual experience with drug addicts and couldn't be sure I saw what I thought I saw. I supposed it could be over two months old. There was no reason to unnecessarily upset her further.

We finished setting the table and bringing out the food. My mouth was watering from the smell of the turkey and the gravy and the dressing. On the last trip from the kitchen, Regina and Russ followed us to the dining room. The room had a rustic feel to it, all dark stained wood and kitschy knickknacks. The tablecloth embroidered with lace around the border and the silverware appeared to be ware of actual silver, recently polished for the occasion. The plates were a simply patterned china and the glasses were crystal. Every detail spoke of subtle elegance for the celebration of the holiday. Juxtaposed against the tension that permeated the house since our arrival, the whole effect felt flat, staged, like we were setting out wax food on a cardboard display in a furniture store. The finery was lipstick on the proverbial pig.

At the table, Regina accepted the platter of turkey from Russ without comment, and set it in the center of the table for him. The assistance was automatic, borne from a lifetime of helping Russ reach places his stature might otherwise make difficult. He appeared to have done a good job carving the turkey; meat that had previously been attached to the bird's bones was now laying sliced on the platter. As we took our seats at the table, the only person missing was…

"Tony!" Regina shouted into the adjoining living room. "Dinner's ready. Do you want to join us?" Her tone implied she didn't care whether he joined us or, instead, chose to run to the store for a quart of milk and just never come back.

There was no response but a few moments later, Anthony appeared and slid into his chair at the head of the table. He glanced around the table and remarked, "Everything looks and smells delicious."

"It should," Regina responded tightly. "I've been slaving over it all day."

"And we all appreciate it, Mother," Angela interjected. Her voice rose half an octave, the falsetto highlighting her attempt to try and defuse the situation. "And thank you, Russ, for carving the turkey. It looks wonderful."

Anthony grunted quietly. "Slices are a little thick, but not bad on the whole, son," he remarked.

"Thanks, Dad," Russ replied. "Good to know all those years of culinary school are finally paying off."

"I didn't know you went to culinary school, Russ," I chimed in. "My friend Daniel used to run a restaurant…" I saw no need to add that the restaurant failed and he now owned the strip club where Angela danced. Besides, Russ's bemused glance brought me up short. "And, you were being facetious, weren't you?" I asked.

Russ tapped his broad nose twice with a pudgy finger. "Good call, Bunyan."

"I hate to interrupt this budding bromance, but I'd like to eat before the food gets cold," Regina said, "Let's say grace now please." She held out her hands to either side. Her children, who sat on either side of her place opposite Anthony, took her hands. I took Angela's other hand. It was cool and soft and damp. She squeezed my hand three times, an unspoken signal we'd devised when one of us wanted to leave. I gave her one squeeze back, silently acknowledging her feelings, but indicating that we were helpless to get up and leave right this moment. Anthony and I exchanged a brief glance and he took my left hand with his right. In contrast to Angela, her father's hand was hot, dry and calloused. His grip was strong. I noticed neither he nor Russ made any attempt to complete the circle, probably because Russ was seated too far from his father for their arms to reach.

"Lord, we thank You for the opportunity today to be with our loved ones" – Regina snorted and Tony paused and gave her a hard stare for a moment. She kept her head bowed, pretending not to notice. Her husband continued - "Bless this food to our continued good health, and bless us to Thy service. In Your name, we pray. Amen."

They all murmured "Amen." Not being much of a churchgoer, most of my recent experience with prayers was during the opening and closing of Lodge. Out of habit, I began to give the traditional response, "So mote it be," but caught myself after two words and hurriedly threw in an "Amen" of my own. Tony tilted a slightly amused half-smile in my direction.

We began to fill our plates, passing the various serving bowls and platters around the table clockwise to avoid confusion. "I'm famished!" Russ announced. "I've been starving myself for a day and a half waiting for this!" He finished placing heaping helping of mashed potatoes on his plate and passed the bowl to his mother.

"Everything really does smell delicious, Regina," I ventured. Hopefully my compliment would get a better reception than Anthony's attempt in the kitchen had.

"Thank you, Patrick," she said with a smile that didn't reach her eyes. "I can't take all the credit. You know Angela made a lot of this too."

"Yes, ma'am," I agreed. "And she did an excellent job as well." I gave Angela's thigh a squeeze under the table. If I correctly read the look she gave me in response, it was apparently a highly inappropriate way to touch her while at the table eating dinner with her family. I returned to dishing up a couple slabs of turkey and passed the platter to Tony, who remained silent. I noticed Angela had about half the amount of food on her plate as I had on mine. She poked at it without interest.

"Yeah, good grub," Russ agreed, tucking a forkful of green bean casserole into his cheek. "If that whole dancing thing don't work out, maybe you can become a chef. Maybe get your own television show like whatshername from Lake George." He winked at his sister as he chewed his food.

Angela gave her brother a tight smile. "Maybe, and if that doesn't work, there's always that whole psychology thing that I'm going to college for to fall back on."

Russ swallowed and shrugged. "Yeah, I suppose."

"How's school going?" Regina asked. I noticed that she was studiously avoiding looking at her husband. It was subtle but had to take a concerted effort since he was directly across the table from her. For his part, Anthony stared straight ahead, chewing his food deliberately, ignoring all of us.

"Pretty well," Angela answered. "A few more weeks until finals, but I should make the Dean's List."

"I'd certainly hope so," Tony remarked. He didn't look her way as he spoke. "You're a bright girl."

"How about you, Daddy?" she asked, jumping on the opportunity to include him in an innocuous conversation. "How's work?"

Her father shifted one shoulder in a shrug. Behind his wire-rimmed glasses, his eyes glanced down momentarily as he poked at a piece of white meat with his fork. "Work is work," he said. He put the turkey in his mouth and chewed, resuming his forward glare.

Regina's eyes finally shifted towards her husband and I felt a prickle of icy electricity as their gazes locked. He met her chilled stare with one of stone. "Really, Tony," she said with exaggerated cheerfulness, "do you think you could contribute a little less to the conversation?"

Anthony blinked and glanced at Angela. "Sorry, Dumpling," he rumbled. "I'm a little…preoccupied today." He directed the last comment to his wife.

"Well," Regina retorted, "maybe you could join the rest of us here, in mind and not just body. What do you think?"

"I've apolo-," he started.

Regina slapped a hand down on the table that made Angela and I jump. Russ paused with his mouth full and glanced back and forth between his parents. "Don't. Apologize," Regina hissed, enunciating each word. "You don't mean it anyway. What are you so distracted by anyway? Or should I ask, *who?*"

Anthony set his forked down, dabbed at his

mouth with his napkin and set it next to his plate. His moves were precise. Deliberate. Angela reached over and gripped my leg, digging her nails in. Sure, but when *I* grabbed her thigh it was inappropriate. Whatever. "That's enough, Regina," Anthony said in a low tone. "Let's just eat in peace."

"Too late for that," Russ muttered. Somehow, though, he managed to cram another forkful of cornbread dressing into his mouth.

"Oh, now you want peace," Regina spat. "What's wrong? Don't want your kids finding out your dirty little secret?" Russ opened his mouth to interject but thought better of it and kept eating. "God forbid they find out their father is an adulterer!"

"I said, that's enough!" Anthony roared, standing so abruptly his chair tipped over. He slammed a thick hand down on the table, shaking it. His glass tipped over, white wine soaking the tablecloth. The glass rolled over the edge of the table and shattered as it hit the floor. He ignored it. "You have no right to…"

Regina interrupted. "Oh, don't you *dare* tell me what rights I have, you lying son of a bitch," she howled. She stood as well but with much less damage to her surroundings. "All those times you have to work late? Those phone calls that you take into another room? How fucking stupid do you think I am?" The vulgarity sounded forced, as though her mouth was unfamiliar territory for the word.

Angela stood unexpectedly. I hurried to follow suit, not really sure why. Russ glanced around, shrugged, and got to his feet. "I think we'd better go," Angela said. "Give you two some time alone."

"What?" Russ demanded. "But I brought pie!"

I moaned and glanced at Angela. Attempting to defuse the situation I grinned and said, "I love pie! Please can we stay?" My attempt only netted me a sharp elbow in the kidney.

"I think it's best if you all leave," Tony agreed, not breaking his face-off with his wife. "I'm sorry, kids." Regina grunted at what she no doubt believed to be another false apology.

We said hasty good-byes. There were a couple hugs and handshakes and we were out the door, but not before Regina insisted on sending each of us home with several plastic containers of leftovers. In the driveway, Angela, Russ and I regrouped.

"Well, that sucked," Russ summarized, leaning against his car.

"I don't think I've ever heard Mom swear before," Angela said.

Russ nodded, "And I've only seen the old man that angry a handful of times. Usually at me."

Angela held up her right arm and said, "Look at this, my hands are shaking!"

We were all silent for a minute. "Now what?" I asked finally.

Angela shrugged. She held up a plastic shopping bag full of our share of the food. "Russ, would you like to come over to my place? We've got enough food, maybe we could salvage the meal there."

Russ gave her a crooked smile, his eyes twinkling. "Thanks, sis. I appreciate the offer. I don't think I've been to your place in years." He patted his thighs and glanced around and added, "I'm probably going to decline though. I think I need to go and blow off some steam, you know what I mean?"

"We'd be glad to have you over any time," I said as Angela regarded her brother through narrowed eyes.

"Thanks, Bunyan," the shorter man said. "That's mighty big of you. Pun intended." He turned back to his sister. "Actually, I think I'm gonna go see a guy about a thing. Which reminds me. I don't suppose you got a few bucks I could borrow? You know I hate to ask, but I'm a little short."

I swallowed a snort but not quietly enough to go unobserved. Angela glared at me. Russ nodded with exaggerated patience. "That's right, Bunyan, laugh it up."

"What's the money for, Russ?" Angela asked, staying on topic.

They exchanged a look. "I'm only going to get some pot, Angie, I swear," he said quietly. "I haven't touched an ounce of heroin in six weeks."

"Really?" Angela asked. "Earlier you said it was two months."

"Maybe it was, I lose count of the days," Russ conceded. He glanced away.

Angela reach down and grabbed her brother's hand, turning it to expose his wrist. "And how old's that track mark? Looks fresher than six weeks."

Without answering the question, Russ said, "Angie, honest to God. I'm not planning to shoot up. I've been taking my subs. I'm all good."

Angela remained silent for a moment. Russ shifted his weight from one foot to the other, then threw his hands up. "No, you know what, never mind, forget it. Don't worry about it. I'll be fine, really. I'm sorry I asked." He came over, arm extended. "Bunyan, it's been real. Nice to meet you. Hope to see you again some time." He turned back to Angela, not quite meeting her gaze. "Angie. Stay in touch, huh? I love you, kid." He held out his arms and Angela hugged him. Her full, firm breasts pressed against his forehead. I was glad they were family, or I'd have felt a jab of jealousy. Brother and sister separated and traded sad smiles. Russ started to turn away.

"Russ, hold on," Angela said. He turned back towards her. I thought I caught just a glimpse of a smirk, but I couldn't be sure. Angela rooted in her purse and came out with a couple twenty dollar bills. She held them out.

Her brother looked from the money to his sister. He reached out and took it from her. "Thanks, Angie," he said softly. "I'll pay you back. You know I'm good for it."

"I'll add it to your tab," Angela remarked.

Russ did a quick silent count of the bills and slipped them in his pocket. "I really am just getting some weed, you know. I'm not bullshitting you."

"Whatever," Angela said sullenly. "Just, please be careful, Russ. Please."

"Always am," he said, some of his rakish charm returning to his voice. "Drugs haven't killed me yet."

"Not for lack of trying," Angela pointed out.

Russ neither confirmed or denied the allegation. "Love you, Angie."

"Love you, too, Russ."

Another quick hug between siblings and we were all in our respective cars and heading on our way.

Once we were back on Route 7 and headed toward Angela's apartment in Troy, I glanced at her sidelong. She continued to look out her window as the world whizzed by. The air was cool and the cloudy skies had begun to clear.

"You okay?" I asked gently.

Angela snorted. I was reminded of her mother's derision towards her father. I shifted the focus of my concern. "It was kind of you to help your brother out."

"Kindness had nothing to do with it," she said to the window. "If I didn't give it to him, he'd have found some other way of getting it. If he couldn't borrow it from someone, he'd steal it or sell his medication or just steal something he could sell. He's an addict, Patrick. Seeing my parents fight like that was a trigger. It made him anxious and he needs a fix. So he'll go get it, whatever it takes to do so. So, if I loan it to him, at least it reduces the trouble he can get into. He'll pay me back someday. He has his ups and downs. Next time, he's working and he's staying clean, he'll pay me back."

"How much does he owe you?" I asked.

At first I didn't think she would answer. Finally she said quietly, "About twelve hundred dollars."

Obviously Russ and Angela had danced this dance

before. He knew, when he asked for the money, that she wouldn't let him leave without it. I tried not to think of the lap dances she had given to raise the money he'd wheedled out of her. I decided not to mention the smirk I may or may not have seen. No need for her to feel like he was taking advantage of her any more than she already did. Instead I said, "At least he sounded sincere about only getting pot. Still illegal and not a good thing, of course, but better than heroin."

"Russ is an accomplished liar. Probably because he believes most of his own bullshit. I have no idea what he's going to do with the money. Like I said, all I can do is beg him to be safe and hope he does."

Her body shuddered and, when I glanced over, I could see the tears slipping from her eyes, rolling down her porcelain cheeks and dripping off her chin unheeded. I couldn't think of anything that I could say to make things better. I rested my hand sympathetically on her thigh. She didn't resist this time. We drove the rest of the way to her apartment in silence.

Chapter Three

Nearly two weeks later, I sat in the crowded barroom of the Capital District Masonic Hall. Outside, rain was pouring down and the wind was howling. The storm was expected to continue for several hours, with the possibility of some trailing snow showers overnight. Not a great night to be out, and yet dozens of Freemasons from around the Capital District saw fit to visit my mother Lodge, Acacia No. 43, for tonight's meeting. Acacia met on the first and third Wednesdays of each month and, since November had five Wednesdays this year, it had been three weeks since the Lodge had met. Those extra seven days made it feel like it had been forever.

Behind the bar, Brothers Michael Morse and Jackson Jones, the Lodge's Stewards for the 2011-2012 term, were busily taking orders and ringing up sales in the ancient cash register that sat near me. Having worked the bar last year, during my term as a Steward, I empathized with them. Michael's long blonde hair was drawn back in a ponytail and for tonight's special occasion he, like several of the Lodge officers present, was wearing a tuxedo. He was clean shaven. I almost didn't recognize him without his jeans and denim shirt. Jackson, a young black man, was one of the Lodge's newest members, having just been raised this past spring. He had an easygoing demeanor and a quiet charm. He showed no sign of ill ease, despite being the only black man in the room. One of Freemasonry's dirty little secrets is that we are frequently behind the times and slow to change. Since the colonial days, a type of segregation had existed in Masonry in America. The "regular" Grand Lodge in any given jurisdiction operated independently from the Prince Hall Grand Lodge in the same jurisdiction. By unspoken agreement, the white guys joined the regular Lodges and African Americans joined Prince Hall (named for the African American Freemason, who founded the organization in colonial Massachusetts). It was only in the last couple decades that the two organizations had begun to formally recognize each other's existence. Since then, the unspoken restriction on who joined which type of Lodge had begun to finally dissolve. Jackson was Acacia Lodge's first bold step in a long overdue future.

As I nursed a Diet Pepsi, careful not to spill any on my own tux, my father walked through the door across the way. I raised my plastic cup in his direction. He turned to the man coming through the door. The man was had a round belly and a cherub's face partially obscured by a long thin beard. He was bald and his eyes sparkled mischievously. My father point towards me and the man nodded. The two of them made their way through the bar in my direction, pausing once or twice to be greeted and shake hands with a Brother. "You missed a heck of a dinner," my father said by way of greeting. Tonight, as part of the Official Visit of the District Deputy Grand Master, the officers of the Lodge took the District team out to dinner. It was tradition. Tonight's dinner had been at Verano's, an upscale Italian restaurant in Lansingburgh. My father had encouraged me to attend the dinner, even offered to pay my way. He said it was important for me to know my fellow officers and to "press the flesh" with the District leaders. I'd begged off though. The holidays had left me feeling out of sorts this year. Leaning back in his chair in his office at Balla's, the family construction company, he shrugged and said it was my choice, but his disappointment dripped from the statement like honey.

I gestured to a red stain on his stomach. "Looks like it," I remarked.

Dad grimaced. "I'll never understand why we go out for pasta with red sauce when we're all wearing tuxes."

I didn't point out that the other diners appeared to be stain-free. I tilted back in my seat and held my hand out to the man who was with him. "Hi," I said. "I'm Patrick Brady, Sean's son."

"Nice to meet you, Patrick. David Johnson," the

man said. "Your father's told me a lot about you." He smiled broadly and I noticed he was missing an upper molar.

"You're the Assistant Grand Lecturer," I observed, ignoring my father's knowing smile at my recognition.

"Guilty as charged," David agreed. The AGL, as the name implied, was the assistant to the Grand Lecturer, a Grand Lodge officer whose job it was to oversee the proficiency of the ritual that the various Lodges presented throughout the State. To make that job easier, each District had one or more Assistants, who traveled to their own local Lodges and helped with, as well as critiqued, the performance of their ritual work. As a thespian trapped in a man's body, the ritual of our opening and closing, and especially the work of the three Degrees that were required to become a Mason, was of especial interest to me. My father knew that. He also knew what I was going to say next.

"I want your job," I told the AGL.

David Johnson's smile broadened but he looked momentarily confused. "I'm sorry," he asked.

"Well, not *yours* specifically," I explained. "But I'd love to be AGL someday."

As understanding dawned, David nodded. "I've

only had the position myself since May and I'm already enjoying it. It's been great, traveling around the District, getting to know the Brothers and see them doing their work."

"I would love to do that," I said. "I'm going to be doing the Middle Chamber lecture for the first time next month. I'm really looking forward to it." I was referring to the major lecture of the Second Degree.

Pulling a Blackberry from his jacket pocket, David asked, "When's that?"

"Second meeting in January," I answered, running through my mental calendar. "The 18th, I think."

The AGL tapped at his PDA a couple times. "Looks like I'm free. Maybe I'll come by and watch, give you some pointers," he offered.

"That would be awesome," I said.

"I knew you two would hit it off." My father's amused grin made me realize how star struck I sounded. I gave a self-deprecating chuckle.

"Sounds like he's going to be a chip off the old block," David remarked.

"Nah," my father said as Jackson came over to take his drink order. "He'll be better."

I felt myself flush at the unexpected compliment but let it slide. Nodding towards the bartender, I asked

David, "What are you drinking, Right Worshipful?"

"Jack Daniels, please," David told Jackson. "Two ice cubes."

My father ordered a gin and tonic, which surprised me just a little. I didn't often see my father drink. I tossed ten dollars on the bar to cover the cost of the two drinks.

Turning back to me, David Johnson said, "By the way, I'm only a Very Worshipful, not a Right Worshipful."

"Why's that?" I asked. I hadn't heard of a Very Worshipful title before.

"The Right Worshipful title is given to members of Grand Lodge who are appointed by the Grand Master. The Grand Lecturer appoints his assistants, with the Grand Master's approval of course, but since we aren't directly appointed by the Grand Master, we are considered Very Worshipfuls instead," David explained.

"That doesn't seem right," I mused. "I imagine you work as hard in the District as the DD or the Staff Officer. You deserve the same recognition."

"Just the way it is," David shrugged. "When you're Grand Master someday, maybe you can change that." We both laughed. Jackson delivered the drinks and took the ten dollar bill.

As we sipped our respective beverages, I asked David. "Which Lodge are you from?"

"Webb Lodge number two thirty-seven, down in Albany," David answered. "I was raised there about nine years ago."

"And you're already the Assistant Grand Lecturer?" I asked.

My father scoffed and remarked, "With our membership on the decline, people rise to higher positions a lot more quickly than they used to." With a nod to David he added, "Not that the honor isn't well-deserved, Dave. I just mean that, back when we had twenty Lodges in the District, there was some genuine competition for positions. Now we're done to half that number, and as often than not the powers that be are scrambling to find someone to fill the chairs rather than the other way around." He raised his glass and added, "At least they made a good choice where you're concerned." David clinked glasses with him and they sipped.

"Gentlemen!" a sonorous voice sliced through the hubbub of the Brothers there assembled. Stuart Humphrey, the current Worshipful Master, stood in the center of the room, raising his hands for silence. About the same height as my own 6'4", he loomed over those around him as he made his announcement. "I hate to cut our fraternal fellowship short, but the hour is upon us. I need all the officers of Acacia Lodge upstairs to open. Visitors, if you would please assemble in the lobby. Brothers Stapler and Anderson will be lining up the delegations." He smiled and added, "We'll see everyone upstairs!"

There was the general murmur and shuffling of chairs as people finished their drinks and moved to their respective locations. I shook hands with David. "It was nice to meet you."

"And you," he agreed with a smile. "I look forward to your Middle Chamber next month. But no pressure!" We laughed and my father and I made our way through the thinning crowd and headed for the Lodge room. As Assistant Grand Lecturer, Very Worshipful David Johnson would be among one of the delegations formally escorted into the Lodge room and was free to stay behind for now.

"Glad to see you two hit off," my father murmured as we made our way out of the bar and through the lobby of the building. The room was done in shades of brown. A folding table had been set up opposite the front door and Marc Stapler and Sebastian Anderson, two of our Past Masters, sat there with an array of signed visitors cards in front of them. They were sorting them into piles, representing the various delegations of visiting Brothers. Catching Marc's eye, I gave him a nod as we walked by.

"Yeah, he seems like a nice guy." I replied.

"He is," my father agreed. "More than that, he's a good person for you to know if you ever want to advance in the Craft, outside of the Lodge. You really should have come to dinner. Would have done you some good to press the flesh with the DD and Staff Officer, too."

"Next year," I promised. Dad nodded.

We crossed the lobby and ascended the stairs to the second floor. Anthony Button was there, speaking to Jerry Wight, the Lodge Secretary. It wasn't uncommon to see the two men together, since Tony was the Treasurer of the Lodge. I hadn't seen or spoken to him since the aborted attempt at Thanksgiving dinner. When he saw me, he held up a finger, quickly concluding his conversation with Jerry, and nodding his head towards me. Jerry glanced in my direction and said to Tony, "Okay, yeah. I'll make sure we get that voucher to you tonight then, okay. And we can, you know, cut the check and get the order in to Grand Lodge." He gave my father and I a nod, not quite meeting our eyes, and slipped into the Lodge room.

Tony approached me. My father clapped me on the shoulder. "See you inside, kid," he said. He gave Anthony's hand a quick shake and followed Jerry into the Lodge room.

Angela's father guided me out of the flow of traffic and lowered his voice. "Patrick, I just wanted to apologize for the scene at Thanksgiving. It was totally uncalled for. I hope Angie isn't too upset."

"She was, but I think she's getting over it," I said. "Things have quieted down for you and Regina, I hope?"

Anthony sighed, glanced around. "I don't know. I guess. We aren't really talking right now. Which is better than screaming baseless accusations at each other across the dinner table." His eyes locked back to mine abruptly and he added firmly, "And they *were* baseless. I hope you and Angela realize that."

"We both find it difficult to believe that you would cheat on Regina," I said diplomatically.

"Good, there's that at least." The older man breathed a sigh of relief. He removed his glasses, pinching the bridge of his nose. "I don't suppose either of you have heard from Russell?"

I shook my head. "Not since that night," I replied.

Anthony clucked his tongue. "His mother gets worried when he's out of touch for too long. Usually means he's up to something no good." I didn't mention that it seemed to me that Regina wasn't the only one worrying about their son. He shrugged off the thought and said, "Well, again, I just wanted to apologize. Maybe we can have you kids over sometime soon for a do over."

We entered the Lodge room, which was fuller than normal. The Official Visit of the District Deputy was an annual event at each Lodge and often brought members out of the woodwork who we normally didn't see. There were a number of Brothers, mostly older men, that I recognized by sight. I scanned the crowd. I spotted Cliff Everett, also known as the Chief, sitting in the back row idly chatting with my father. As a Lodge trustee, my father had no specific seat in the room and could sit wherever he wanted. I, on the other hand, had my assigned seat. As Senior Master of Ceremony, my spot was to the right of, and a little in front of, the Senior Warden on the west end of the Lodge, near the outer door, through which we had entered. Don Florence, the Senior Warden was already seated in his throne-like chair and gave me a solemn head nod. He took the sanctity of the Lodge room very seriously for someone who was only in his mid-twenties. On his left side, mirroring my own seat, was Jared Lawson, the Junior Master of Ceremony. He was a quiet man, self-conscious, as though he wasn't quite comfortable in his own skin. Even though he had been a Mason about a year longer than I had, his attendance had been sporadic. Because of that, Stu had decided to bump me ahead of him in line, making me Senior Master of Ceremony to his Junior. This was the first time I had seen him since Lodge started up in September.

At 7:30 precisely, the Worshipful Master gave a sharp rap with his gavel, and the remaining straggling officers and Brothers scurried to their places. Caleb Wells, Past Master and long-time Tiler, closed the outer door. I shook my head silently. Our ritual books, which contained a cipher of all of the work we did for degrees, as well as the opening and closing our Lodge, also included copious stage directions and one of them very clearly stated that the outer door was supposed to remain open at the start, to be closed later at the appropriate time. It was just one example, but, as much as I loved our ritual, I couldn't understand why people couldn't be bothered to fully read and understand their roles.

The Master and senior officers went through the opening ritual with relative proficiency. I sat silently, toying with the fringe on my apron. One strand had come unfurled and hung lower than the rest. It offended me. Probably because, otherwise, I felt I looked pretty sharp tonight.

Once Lodge was opened in due form, Worshipful Humphrey dispensed with the reading of the previous meeting's minutes and asked if there were any reports of sickness or distress. The Secretary had one report. "Worshipful Master, um, yeah, I have a message from Brother Richard McAlistair, okay? He sends his regards and, um, yeah, his regrets. Says he wants to be here tonight, okay, but he's been having some respiratory problems lately. He hopes to see everyone soon. So. Yeah."

I nodded regretfully. I liked the older man, admired his careful precision in everything he did. The respiratory problems were concerning but, since his doctors expected him to be dead two years ago, it would be hard to complain. I made a mental note to give Richard a call.

Worshipful Humphrey made quick work of any business we had to bring before the Lodge. The main issue was that we needed to place an order with Grand Lodge for white aprons and other supplies for the Degrees we had coming up. The expense was approved by a vote of the Lodge and the Secretary promised to get a voucher to the Treasurer and place the order.

There was an expectant pause. The Worshipful Master conferred with the man on his left, Worshipful Phil Ballard, Chaplain and immediate Past Master. It was a custom in Acacia, and other Lodges, that the outgoing Master be appointed as Chaplain so that, from his place beside the new Master, he could be available to prompt and advise. From the far end of the room I couldn't hear the conversation.

Finally, the Worshipful Master turned towards the

room again and addressed Harvey Mann, the Junior Deacon, who sat just inside the outer door, keeping us safe from intrusion. "Brother Junior Deacon," he said, deep voice resonating off the wood paneled walls, "would you please check with the Tiler and see if our delegations are ready."

After a moment of back and forth, Brother Mann reported that the delegations were ready to enter and sat down. Almost immediately there were three sharp raps at the door. He stood up again, came to the sign of fidelity and announced the alarm. The Worshipful Mastered ordered him determine the cause and, after conferring with the Tiler, he announced that a delegation of Officers and Brothers wised to enter. The Worshipful Master ordered them admitted.

When the outer door was opened, Right Worshipful Thomas Mann, Harvey's uncle, entered. He stood to the right of a Brother I didn't recognize and escorted him, and the line of ten or twelve Brothers behind them, to the center of the Lodge. "Worshipful Master," he said in his thin reedy voice, "I present the following delegation of officers and Brothers." He referred to the stack of visitors cards that he held and began to identify each Brother in turn. As their name was read, the Brother took a step forward, greeted Worshipful Humphrey, was acknowledged and stepped back into the line. After the introductions, the Master directed that they be brought to the East to be greeted personally. Right Worshipful Mann led the group up the north side of the Lodge and, as the delegation took turns shaking hands with the Master, he returned to the altar at the center of the room. When the delegation had been received and they were settling into chairs around the room's perimeter, Mann saluted the Master appropriately and left the room.

A couple moments later, the process was repeated, this time with a delegation of officers and Brothers from Hiram-Austin Lodge No. 91. Hiram-Austin shared the Capital District Masonic Hall with Acacia, as well as a couple other appellate Masonic groups. In terms of numbers and finances, Hiram-Austin dwarfed Acacia, although I wasn't privy to the details of each category. I always felt a sense of superiority radiating from its members. In theory, all Masons were on an equal level. But, as *Animal Farm* taught us, some were more equal than others. I recognized Victor Van Rensselaer and David Whalen from my brief time tending bar last year, as well as Scott Tisdale. Scott and I had initially butt heads but I had grown to find him to be intelligent. He always had a reason for his actions. Any disagreements between us were over different viewpoints on the reasons, rather than the actions. We had developed a mutual grudging respect for each other. After the Hiram-Austin delegation was introduced and welcomed, they sat.

Right Worshipful Mann took a seat near his nephew's post.

Next came a delegation of Past and Present Grand Lodge Officers, men from around the District who had served Grand Lodge in one capacity or another, all wearing their aprons trimmed with purple and gold, some more aged than others. The Lodge was raised and we gave them the special form of applause known as Grand Honors as they were received.

The following was a delegation of one – Very Worshipful David Henry Johnson, Assistant Grand Lecturer – escorted by Right Worshipful Nicholas Goodell (himself a past AGL). Grand honors were given and Very Worshipful Johnson was offered, and accepted, a seat on the Master's dais in the East.

Yet another rap at the door. I was having flashbacks to my Episcopalian upbringing with all the standing and sitting we'd been doing as the delegations were received. This time it was the Staff Officer. Grand Director of Ceremonies, Right Worshipful Luke Grey, was escorted by our Secretary's father, Right Worshipful Joseph Wight. He received his Grand Honors and took a seat on the Master's immediate right.

The final entrant was the main attraction. Unlike with previous delegations, it was announced that the District Deputy Grand Master, Right Worshipful

Randall Simmons, was about to enter. Since he outranked the Master of the Lodge, he didn't need to wait for permission to enter. The DD strode into the room confidently, escorted again by Right Worshipful Wight. I caught a whiff of vodka and stale cigar smoke as they passed. He saluted at the altar and immediately went to the East. He thanked his escort and ascended the dais, where he received his Grand Honors.

"Right Worshipful District Deputy, it's a pleasure to have you here this evening," Worshipful Humphrey intoned. He handed him the gavel and added, "The Lodge is yours." The chaplain shifted one seat to the left and Worshipful Humphrey followed suit, leaving the District Deputy in charge of the meeting and Lodge, as protocol required.

With a rap of the gavel, the DD sat the Lodge. As he settled into the Master's chair, he asked the Staff Officer to take roll call. One by one Right Worshipful Grey read out the names of the Lodges and its members stood. Some Brothers stood for more than one Lodge, if they were dual members. In the end, Hiram-Austin had the best attendance and were awarded the Traveling Trowel, a symbolic award our District used as incentive to encourage Lodges to bring as many members as possible to the District Deputy visits. There was no formal presentation of the award since Hiram-Austin had won it at the previous visit as well and, confident of their victory this evening, their

Master hadn't bothered to bring it with him to pass on. Of the ten Lodges in the Capital District, eight had at least one member present.

The next fifteen minutes were taken up with Lodge announcements. One by one the Masters, or other representatives, of each Lodge stood and announced upcoming events – Degrees, holiday parties and so on. Worshipful Humphrey reminded everyone that Acacia Lodge would be holding a First Degree in two weeks, for two candidates. After that came committee reports. Going down his list, Right Worshipful Simmons called on the chairmen of the District committees on such topics as Awards, Communications, Charity, Family Involvement, Retention and Youth. When they finished, the floor was turned over to Very Worshipful Johnson, who reminded everyone of the importance of our ritual and his own willingness and availability to assist the Lodges and Brothers however he could, and then to the Staff Officer, who announced that masonic education courses would soon be scheduled for the spring and that he would get an email out.

With all other business dispensed with, the District Deputy climbed to his feet. His salt and pepper beard had more of the former than the latter, and that highlighted his vodka-induced florid cheeks. He smiled in a manner that he probably thought was ingratiating. When he spoke, his voice had an accent I couldn't quite distinguish. Brooklyn, maybe? Jersey? It definitely sounded like something from down that way at any rate. There was just the slightest of slurring to his speech. "My Brothers," he said, spreading his arms to visually encompass all of us in that category, "I want to thank Acacia Lodge for the excellent meal and the hospitality they showed myself and the rest of the District Team tonight. I have had an opportunity to review their books and have found them in order." Worshipful Humphrey wiped his forehead in an exaggerated display of relief. To him, Right Worshipful Simmons added, "Worshipful Master, I am presenting your Lodge with a copy of the Grand Master's annual message, to be spread upon the minutes of the Lodge." He handed the Master a thin booklet. After brief glimpse, the Master passed it to the Chaplain who, in turn, passed it the Secretary.

The District Deputy continued his speech, "Thank you to all of those who made reports tonight. And, most importantly, I want to thank you all for being here on this dreadful evening." He gestured towards the curtain covered windows. Outside the rain was battering the building. "You know, as I was getting ready to leave tonight, my wife said to me, 'I don't understand why you're going out tonight. It's not fit for man nor beast out there.' And I said to her, 'Because we are neither men nor beasts. We are *Masons.*'" He paused and walked down the three steps of the dais to the floor level as we all reflected for a moment on the sentiment. Careful not to cross between the East and the altar, Right Worshipful Simmons began to walk the room as he spoke.

"My Brothers, one of the key points of the Grand Master's message this year has been Brotherhood. I'm sure each of us looked out the window or at the weather forecast and, at least for a moment, considered staying home tonight. And yet, here we are. Why is that? I'm sure some of us are here out of a sense of obligation." He paused by the Junior Master of Ceremony's chair and rest a brief hand on Jared's shoulder. "We have offices to fill or reports to give, we *have* to attend. Well, that's certainly true. It certainly wouldn't have been much of a District Deputy visit if *I* had stayed home." A few men chuckled. He resumed his idle walk, passing in front of me. I kept my face carefully neutral as the wave of cigar fumes washed over me. He nodded at the Senior Warden and then at me as he passed. "Most of us, though," he continued, "are probably here for our love for the Fraternity, for the camaraderie. For the opportunity to fellowship and share the Brotherly love that comes with being Freemasons. You know, there are Masons in every part of the world? In some countries, of course, they are more reclusive or hidden than here in America, but they are there. And those Masons, in England, or in Spain, or Africa or China? They, too, are our Brothers.

Think about that for a moment. Each of you in this room is part of a Masonic family that encompasses the globe." He paused allowing those assembled to consider the point. I saw my father smirk and whisper something to the Chief, who pointed to his ear and shrugged helplessly. My father nodded.

"Is there anyone in this room who would hesitate to help a Brother in need?" the District Deputy asked as he continued around the room. Passing near the Junior Warden, he glanced at my father, who smiled innocently and returned gaze placidly. No one raised their hand. Right Worshipful Simmons nodded knowingly and said, "I'm glad to hear that. Because, my Brothers, you may not realize it, but we are *all* in need of something. We are in need of stronger Brotherhood, a stronger connection between one Mason and another, between one Lodge and another, even between one District or jurisdiction and another. When it comes down to it, those are all just administrative roles. In reality, we are all part of *one* Fraternity. Sometimes we get wrapped up in the concerns of our own Lodge, and we forget the big picture." He reached the Secretary's desk, turned, lingered and began to retrace his slow steady pace clockwise around the room.

"Even in our own District, we have Brothers in need, Lodges in need. Like most Districts, we have a mixture. Most of our Lodges are somewhere in the middle, but we have a couple strong Lodges and we have three or four that are...less so. It was not that long ago that we had eleven Lodges in this District, until Sand Lake Lodge closed down a couple years back. I won't name names, but I can think of at least one more Lodge, maybe two, that are probably in seriously jeopardy of closing in the next five years." He paused near the Junior Deacon and turned back towards the East, addressing Worshipful Humphrey. "Worshipful Master, please understand I mean no disrespect and I'm not casting dispersions or blame, but..." He returned his attention to the entire group, "I was concerned when reviewing the books for Acacia Lodge. I'm not a member here and, from the outside, I would have thought that Acacia was doing well, was holding their own. Their ritual is good, they're bringing in new members. But their finances are in trouble."

I glanced towards my father and saw his jaw tighten. His placid gaze took on a razor's edge. Uh oh.

"This being my second year as District Deputy," Right Worshipful Simmons continued, "I was able to see a decline from 2010. It wasn't major, but it was concerning. By my estimation, this Lodge could have as little as ten years' worth of operating capital left." He held up his hands defensively and tilted his head to one side. For a moment he looked like Pentacostal parishioner praising the Lord. "Don't get me wrong! I know we are not in this for the money. But the sad fact is that money *is* one of the factors to having a successful Lodge. Fortunately, Acacia is not yet in dire straits. As I said, they're bringing in new Brothers and that helps. There's time to examine their budget, to see where expenses can be cut. Perhaps dues need to be raised. Your trustees should examine your investments and ensure they are still what's right for your Lodge." It felt like he was studiously avoiding my father's intensifying glare. Dad, together with Right Worshipfuls Goodell and Wight, were the Lodge's three trustees. None of them appeared too happy with the direction of the District Deputy's monologue.

"Perhaps," he continued, seemingly unaware of the reaction he was provoking, "you might begin considering the dreaded C-word." My eyes widened slightly, but it turned out not to be the word I was thinking of. "Consolidation. Right now you share a facility with one of the strongest Lodges in the District. You already do some work with them. I know you do a joint summer picnic, for example. I'm not saying you *need* to merge. But, perhaps it should be considered." Throughout this part of the speech, the District Deputy, perhaps by intent, was idling north along the west side of the room, primarily facing empty seats. After he and his accompanying miasma sidled past, I glanced again at my father. I couldn't make out the words but he and Cliff were talking in a heated whisper, loud enough that nearby Brothers were glancing uncomfortably in their direction.

The solemn part of his speech concluded, Right Worshipful Simmons smiled broadly again as he continued. His manner was one that said, "See, look at me. I'm your friend and Brother! How could you possibly take anything else I've said personally? I'm just like you!" He spoke for a few minutes more about the importance of Lodges helping Lodges, Brothers aiding Brothers. I don't know if anyone was really listening.

Returning to the dais, he concluded, "Brothers, please drive safely on your way home this evening. May the Great Architect of the Universe watch over us and our loved ones. God bless America and God bless our beloved Fraternity. Thank you." En masse, most of the assembled rose to their feet and afforded him with polite applause. My father stood last, clapping as slowly as he could while still appearing respectful. His glare was unchanged.

The District Deputy returned the gavel, and control of the Lodge, to the Worshipful Master, who summoned the Senior Warden to join them in the East. Brother Florence removed his jewel and left it on the chair and began to cross the room. My father rose and strode over towards the vacated seat, having been tapped prior to the meeting to fill in for the closing of Lodge. As he passed me, we exchanged a glance.

"Interesting," I murmured.

"It's a crock of shit," he retorted. He climbed the two steps to the Senior Warden's chair and donned the medallion that had been left for him without elaborating.

The Worshipful Master accompanied the District Deputy, Staff Officer and Assistant Grand Lecturer from the room as we all stood and applauded again. Once things had settled down, Brother Florence granted permission for anyone to leave who so desired, except for those necessary for the closing of Lodge. Most of the guests took advantage of the opportunity. The minutes were read and the Lodge was closed in due form and, with the exception of the Senior Warden pro-tem, harmony. Outside, the rain continued to hammer against the windows.

Chapter Four

Dad's mood was only marginally better the next morning at work. My position at R. J. Balla & Sons, named for my father's mother's father's father's father's father, was supposed to be temporary, following my unexpected divorce from Larissa and subsequent return from California to New York. That had been almost two years ago, and I had begun to settle in. My father had expressed his hopes that, in the next ten years, my brother Ian and I would be able to run the business together ourselves and he could retire. I had to admit the idea had its allure. Ian, who headed up one of our two two-man work crews, certainly had the mechanical knowledge, and I had begun to get the hang of the business side of things over the last twenty-two months or so. Douglas Adams once wrote "I may not have gone where I planned to go, but I have ended up where I needed to be." That seemed to apply in this case.

Working with family is a dual edged sword. Generally, the atmosphere is a lot more casual. I was given more leeway when I made mistakes, as I'd been more wont to do earlier in my career. And though we didn't accrue vacation time per se, on those rare occasions when I took time off I could just ask, secure in the knowledge that, if my request was denied, a quick call to my mother (who, of course, was sleeping with my boss) would rectify things. The downside of that casual atmosphere, though, was that, because Ian and my father and I were family, we were less inclined to adopt professional personas while at work. So, when my father came storming into the small lobby of the office at 7:55 the next morning, I could tell from the way that he wiped the mud from the parking lot off his shoes onto the welcome mat that he was still in a foul mood.

Ian and I were already sitting and chatting in the adjoining room at what we called the conference table, because we thought that sounded businessy. It was a badly scraped old oak table that had been salvaged from a job a few years back and, with six mismatched chairs, it took up most of the room. One wall was mostly windows looking out into the parking lot and at the traffic that went by on Route 32. Opposite that was a whiteboard where we tracked ongoing and upcoming jobs. At the far end of the room was a wood burning stove for cold damp mornings such as this. I had made a point to get in a little early today and make sure the fire was going. Dad breezed past the conference room, convenience store tea in one hand, banana in the other, and into his office. The door shut solidly behind him. Ian glanced at me. I shrugged. "Masonic stuff," I remarked.

"Oh," Ian grunted, "that again."

I nodded. "So, what were you saying?"

"Just that women suck." He took a drag from his cigarette and gazed out the window as I stoked the fire.

"Ali broke your heart, huh?" I asked sympathetically.

"My heart wasn't the organ I was concerned about," my brother responded sullenly. "But I thought we were having fun together. Apparently she didn't feel the same."

"You know," I said, taking my seat across from him, "you're twenty-six. Almost twenty-seven. Maybe it's time to stop playing the field and look for something a little more serious."

Ian glanced at me. At least I think he did. It was hard to see his eyes behind the dark sunglasses he habitually wore. "Serious," he asked, "like you and Larissa?"

I remained silent for a moment, stung. "I was thinking something more like me and Angela," I said.

He relented. "Sorry, man, that was uncalled for. I didn't mean to step on your dick like that. All I meant was if a straight laced conservative guy like you can't stay married, what kind of chance do I got?"

"I'm not so straight laced anymore," I said. "I go to a strip club pretty regularly now. I even drink sometimes."

"Hard cider hardly counts as drinking," Ian countered, "and your girlfriend works at the club and your best friend owns it. So you're not really making a lotta points here."

"Fine. Regardless, don't sell yourself short. You're a good looking guy, you've got some kind of rakish charm that the women seem to adore. I'm sure you could find a woman to settle down with."

Ian shrugged. "Too early to be so sappy," he muttered. His sullen deflection of my comments was enough proof for me that I'd hit my mark. Though hesitant to take the compliment, it had nonetheless been received. Changing the topic, Ian asked, "The old man said anything about getting a new wet saw yet? We're gonna need it when we start that bathroom at RCCC next week."

"Not yet," I answered. "He's going into belt-tightening mode. Winter is coming."

"He can tighten his belt all he wants," Ian countered, "but we still need the equipment to do the job."

"I think he's still hoping Rusty can get the old one working."

Ian snorted. "Rusty's already declared it a lost cause."

I spread my hands helplessly. "I'm sure Dad will think of something. I'm just middle management."

Rocky and Rusty McLoughlin walked in and, a moment later, Mike "Mickey" Taylor joined us. Rusty was Rocky's uncle and they two of them formed our second construction crew. Mickey was Ian's crewman. As everyone settled in, I went and tapped on my father's office door, peeking my head in. He was taking a bite of banana, slathered with peanut butter, with one hand and jabbing one-fingeredly at his computer keyboard with the other.

"Everyone's here for the morning debrief," I said.

Without looking up from his screen, my father rumbled, "You handle it. Should be a quick one."

I tilted my head and backed out, pulling the door closed behind me. Returning to the conference room, I explained that the boss was on a phone call. Rusty reported that they were continuing their demolition in the library at Rensselaer County Community College and would need a check for the dump. Ian said he and Mickey were set with the project they were working on. Watervliet had recently received a grant to assist senior citizens with making their homes more energy efficient and Balla's had managed to secure a handful of the projects. Ian and Mickey were currently installing insulated vinyl replacement windows in one such house. The project was not going as smoothly as it should. As one of my first, rare forays into the field, I had been sent to take the measurements for the windows. Somehow I'd managed to come up half an inch short on the height of all ten windows. Since they were custom sizes, they couldn't just be returned to the manufacturer and replaced, so Mickey and Ian were forced to build out each frame to make the windows fit. It was a pain in the ass, or so Ian was fond of reminding me when he returned to the office at the end of each day.

As we wrapped up, I stepped into my office off the conference room. It had formerly been a utility closet. Panel boxes still hung on the back wall and the push broom, rolling mop pail and vacuum still rested in one corner, but I'd managed to carve out a decent enough area for a small desk and a single four-drawer filing cabinet. Current accounts payable, accounts receivable, construction projects and employee records were stored here. As the drawers filled up, the overflow from previous years was cycled to the cabinets in Dad's office. I opened my middle drawer, took out a sheet of three printer-ready checks and tore off the top one. Made it out to the landfill and signed my name with a flourish. Rusty was waiting by my door and I handed it to him, reminding him to bring back a receipt so I could account for it. Past him, through the conference window, I could see Ian and Mickey pulling out of the parking lot, the white Balla's van spitting gravel from its back tires as they left.

I considered letting my father know the meeting was over, but decided it was best to avoid him until the storm had passed. Let him finish his breakfast and crossword puzzle first.

Shortly after 11:30, I heard the front door open and close. I waited and listened to see if it was a customer. Footsteps across the hardwood floor, a rap at my father's door and then the guest entered his office. The lunch crew had begun to arrive. Normally I would have set everything aside and joined them in his office, sitting back and kibitzing as we waxed Masonic. I hadn't talked to Dad all morning and I wasn't sure how his mood was yet. Better to let someone else take the brunt. I continued working until I heard a second guest arrive. I turned off my computer screen, pulled the door closed behind me and walked around to my father's office, entering without knocking.

Thursday lunches had been a weekly tradition around Balla's for nearly twenty years. The year before he became Master of the Lodge, my father started having lunch with his best friend, John Emanuele, every Thursday. As well as being my godfather, John was also a new member of the Lodge at the time. Often they discussed the business of the meeting the night before. On off weeks, the discussion was usually less Masonic and more diverse. Over the years, the size and members of the lunch crew had fluctuated. After John had died last year, my father kept the tradition going.

When I entered the office, Cliff was already settled comfortably into the good visitors chair. Scott Tisdale, the most recent addition to the group, stood beside my father's desk with a folder in his hand. He was looking over Dad's shoulder as he read something off the computer screen. He nodded as he read, murmuring, "Yeah, okay. That looks right to me." He frowned. I sat on the hard wooden bench along the wall and greeted the Chief. While my father and Scott finished reviewing whatever they were looking at, Cliff and I chatted idly. I found his Southern drawl soothing.

A couple minutes before noon, Marc Stapler arrived, completing our crew. We all got up and headed for the door. "Calavicci's?" my father asked. I nodded agreement. It was my turn to buy. When I first returned home and started working at Balla's, money was tight. I'd initially had to pay for lunch with the company credit card and have a quarter of the cost taken out of my paycheck each week. In recent months, though, I'd finally gotten onto some stable footing and it still felt good to be able to cover the cost of our lunches on my own like a real grown up.

Calavicci's was a quaint hole in the wall about a

quarter mile from Balla's. We occasionally ate somewhere else, especially if it was Tisdale's turn to buy, but we were here often enough to be considered regulars. When we entered, two small square tables had already been pushed together in the center of the dining room to seat six, just in case we'd brought some fresh meat with us. With a nod to the hostess, the five of us took our usual seats. None of us needed menus.

As we settled in, Deidre came by, squeezing through the narrow gaps between the tables with practiced grace. The maneuver was that much more impressive as she was now about four months pregnant with her and her boyfriend's second child. She placed our drinks in front of us, already knowing what we'd be having. Diet Pepsi for my father and I. Root beer for Marc. Seltzer for Scott and a cold glass of milk for the Chief.

"How's mah favorite girl?" Cliff asked with a smile. He reached out and gave her rounded belly a rub. Deidre laughed and tossed her thick black hair back over her shoulder. I wondered how old I had to be before women considered me a cute, harmless old man who could say or do anything they wanted.

"We're doing very well," she said proudly, cupping her stomach. "I've got an ultrasound next month and I can't wait to find out the sex. I'm hoping for a girl this time, but Rich wants another boy."

"We shall keep our fingers crossed, then, mah dear," Cliff said. Deidre kissed him on his balding forehead. I decided I probably had to be at least sixty-five. Maybe seventy.

Deidre took our orders. Three bowls of chowder, two salads, one with blue cheese, one with Russian, to start. Two deluxe double cheeseburgers, one veal parm, one shrimp scampi and a senior tuna platter. As she headed to the computer at the bar to place our order, I took the opportunity to admire her legs, still looking fantastic despite the pregnancy.

When my wandering attention returned to the table, I immediately noticed the shift in atmosphere. My father sat at one end, casually looking across to Cliff at the other. Cliff returned his gaze with glistening eyes and a placid smile. Scott was frowning. Marc's face seemed to mirror my own uncertainty.

"So," the Chief drawled, "an interesting meeting last night." He dragged the word 'interesting' to its full four syllables.

"It was," my father agreed.

Silence.

Marc Stapler innocently broke the silence with *the* question half a moment before I could. "Is the Lodge really in such dire straits?"

All eyes turned to towards my father. His jaw

twitched. He glanced toward Scott Tisdale and nodded slightly. Scott began to distribute single pages from the folder he held. "By my calculations," my father said evenly, "the Lodge will be out of money in about eight years." He accepted a paper from Scott without looking at it. "There was some creative accounting involved in the report to the District Deputy, giving a slightly rosier impression and leading him to the conclusion that we had ten years left."

I looked down at the paper, if only to hide my surprise at the news and at the tone in my father's voice. Was it regret? Disappointment? Possibly even shame? I realized with a start that he was blaming himself for the Lodge's plight. On the page was a spreadsheet and a graph indicating income and expenses over the last three years and carrying that projection into the future. Shortly after the beginning of 2019, the Lodge finances sunk into negative territory. More than likely, the Lodge itself would sink along with them.

"So the DD was right?" I asked. "We should consolidate?"

"No," my father said emphatically. "We can still pull out of this."

"How?" Cliff asked. It was a simply stated question loaded with significance.

"We raise the dues," my father said, beginning to

tick off options on his fingers, "we can trim the fat out of the budget. Follow up on our delinquent members or NPD them. Put together a couple fundraisers each year, dinners and the like. And, yes, maybe tweak the investments."

"And how long does that buy us?" Cliff asked.

My father shrugged. "Minimum five years, but really, there's no reason it couldn't go on in perpetuity. Finances always fluctuate. As long as we stay on top of everything, there's no reason we can't ride out this lull."

I saw Scott nod. The Chief smiled with sympathy. "You sound like me, twenty years ago."

"And you managed to keep the Lodge afloat so that we could be here twenty years later," my father pointed out. "There's no reason we couldn't be as successful this time."

Deidre arrived with a large round tray and distributed drinks, soups, salads and smiles. We all thanked her. When she left Cliff was nodding thoughtfully at my father's remarks. "Quite true. But our circumstances weren't quite as bad. And Ah acted quickly. *And* it took several years of concerted efforts on the part of several people to make it work." He smiled, showing off a full set of dentures. and pointed his soup spoon at my father. "Including you young guys."

Dad smiled as he crumbled oyster crackers into his chowder. "I remember."

"Think you still have that kind of energy to do fundraisers all the time?" Cliff asked.

"Probably not," Dad conceded, "but we have a new batch of energetic young guys to do the heavy lifting."

Cliff made a clucking sound, blew on his chowder, ate a thoughtful spoonful. "Problem is, the Lodge is a lot smaller now. And with a smaller pool of Brothers to draw from, that will lead to people burning out sooner. You may not be able to maintain it indefinitely."

"Maybe not," Dad agreed. "But every year that we keep the Lodge afloat is another small victory. Increasing our income, reducing the outflow will slow the bleeding. Anything we can do to bring in funds over and above that only helps."

Marc and I watched the conversation like a tennis match. Scott had been listening attentively and finally weighed in. "I think the question you need to answer is what is the drop dead point? How low do your Lodge's finances need to get before you *do* decide that you need to either merge or fold? You can't wait until you're out of money. Like most things with Masonry, it takes time to consolidate Lodges. I wouldn't recommend going much lower than fifteen, twenty thousand before you pull the pin and start the process."

A glance at the spreadsheet, some quick calculations. I came to the same answer as my father said, "So, at the rate we're going, we would reach that tipping point in about five years." He glanced around the table. "Plenty of time to turn the ship around, I think."

I nodded. Scott agreed. Cliff said nothing. After a pause, Marc stuck his neck out again. "Playing devil's advocate here. What is the downside if we *did* decide to consolidate?"

"We lose our identity," my father replied. "Acacia Lodge is over a hundred and seventy-five years old. We have a long rich history. Our members have included local politicians, entrepreneurs, and several Grand Lodge members, including one Grand Master. I hate the thought of that history being lost in a consolidation."

"Wouldn't that history just get roiled into the history of the new Lodge?" Marc asked.

My father sighed. "Probably," he admitted. "But it wouldn't be the same." He took a couple bites of his cracker-thickened chowder and said, "Normally I would say we wouldn't want to lose control of our money, but obviously that's not a factor in this case."

"So…?" Marc asked.

Scott said, "One of the first steps would be finding a Lodge willing to merge. Hiram-Austin may seem like a logical choice, but there's no guarantee they would go along with it." The implication hung in the air for a moment as we finished our soups and salads.

"You mean," I asked around a cheek full of lettuce and blue cheese, "Hiram-Austin doesn't want Acacia to merge with them?"

"I mean," Scott replied, "*I* personally don't think it's a good idea. I would vote against it and encourage others to do the same. The vote might still pass, but it wouldn't be unanimous."

"Why would you oppose it?" I asked. I felt myself bristle, a reaction Scott Tisdale often aroused in me.

"To protect the Association," my father answered me while looking at Scott. Tisdale tipped his head in acknowledgement. My father elaborated, "Acacia and H-A are the two major bodies that meet in the building. They are the Temple Association's prime source of income. If they merged, the Association, who is responsible for maintaining the facility, would end up bearing the burden of that expense. As president of the Association, that would weigh heavily on Scott, I'm sure."

"So, again, it all comes down to money," Marc commented.

"Unfortunately, yes," my father agreed. "It takes money to operate a Lodge, just like any other business."

Deidre came and cleared our dishes, returned with our meals. Conversation flagged while we ate.

"It sounds like," I said eventually, "we don't need to panic yet. Minimum, we have four years before the finances are bad enough that we should explore consolidation. If we start taking steps now, we can hold that off." I glanced deference at Cliff and added, "Maybe not indefinitely. But perhaps long enough for our finances to take a turn for the better."

Everyone nodded their consent at my summary of the situation. The discussion moved on to less contentious topics.

"Why didn't you escort the District Deputy in last night?" Marc asked Cliff. "Wouldn't you traditionally do that, as the senior Right Worshipful in the Lodge?"

"They asked me if Ah wanted to," Cliff acknowledged, "but mah arthritis was acting up something fierce, 'specially with all that rain, so Ah declined. Joe *graciously* filled in." There was a touch of ironic humor mixed with the word 'graciously.'

After lunch we returned to Balla's and said our

good-byes. I headed for my office, but my father asked me to join him for a moment. We went into his office instead. I sat across the desk from him. "I've asked Scott to get us a couple petitions for membership."

"Aren't we already members?" I asked bemused.

"This petition isn't for initiation. It's for affiliation."

"Meaning?"

"Meaning we would become members of a second Lodge. In this case, Hiram-Austin."

My eyebrows crept up my forehead in question.

"With the DD rattling his saber," my father explained, "things will probably come to a head quicker than we would like. Yes, we could last several years, but the Master may not wait. Scott will have an uphill battle getting Hiram-Austin to vote against it. When the time comes…you and I will be there to add our votes to the mix."

Chapter Five

Business was slow that Saturday night at Danny's Place. But it was early still, barely 8:30. Things would pick up as the night wore on.

I sat at my usual table. It set off to one side, towards the back, so as not to take up prime real estate near the main flow of traffic. From this vantage I could see the heavy velvet curtain that separated the entrance from the main club, a good slice of the DJ's booth and, if I twisted a little in my seat, I could look back over towards the small bar where Daisy was pouring non-alcoholic drinks with a crop top and a smile. The staircase over the DJ's booth wound its way up the balcony above me and to the bathrooms and private show rooms upstairs. At the end of that hallway was the office of Daniel Lanolin, owner and operator of the family-friendliest gentlemen's club in the greater Capital District. He was also my best friend from high school, with whom I'd reconnected after my return home. Friendship had its privileges; I was given carte blanche in the club, free to come and go and drink all the free Diet Pepsi I wanted. Which, at three dollars a can, was a pretty good deal, I thought. Was it any wonder I visited here at least once a week?

Complimentary beverages aside, the club had one other draw for me. She was currently sitting on my lap, scantily clad in a ruby red number and thigh high mock leather boots with blocky six inch heels. In the time that Angela and I had been together, our sex life had been quite satisfying, thank you, and you don't need to know all the juicy details. Yet on the nights I came to watch her dance at Danny's, there was always this little extra je ne se quois about her. I'd seen her totally naked in the privacy of each of our apartments, become intimately acquainted with every inch of her body. Yet here she seemed like a different woman. Almost as though the woman I knew was just a mask and only here, in this strip club, was she able to shed that mask (along with everything else) and be free. I suppose it was possible, even preferable, that the club persona was the mask.

Aside from the two of us, there were two kids from one of the local colleges sitting at the rail watching a new girl whose name I hadn't caught yet, and a couple, about five years younger than me, sitting off to one side, getting a dance from Georgia.

I traced lazy circles along Angela's back, savoring the feel of her baby soft skin against my fingertips. Daniel was sitting with us, his idle chatter belied by his sharp gaze, keeping an eye on all aspects of his business simultaneously. From his perch on the edge of the chair, I knew he knew exactly how many Diet

Pepsis Daisy had behind the bar, the next three dancers in the rotation and how much cash, to the dollar, that Vlad had in the register out front.

"Where's Jane tonight?" I asked. Jane was Daniel's business partner and two times ex-wife.

Daniel's constantly moving eyes lighted on me for a moment. "She went out to Buffalo to visit her parents for the weekend. She figured she'd take advantage of the lack of snow to get out there and get back without actually having to spend Christmas with them."

"Sounds like an excuse to me," I said. "The weathermen are already saying it'll be a green Christmas."

Daniel shrugged, glancing around the room. Georgia had moved from the male portion of the couple to the female and the male portion was watching intently as his girlfriend received a dance. I found myself holding Angela just a shade tighter. *Eat your heart out, buddy,* I thought.

"I suppose I can understand not wanting to be with her family for the holiday," I added. Angela and I exchanged a knowing glance.

Daniel returned his gaze to me. There was a hint of a smile in his eyes. "Who says she's not?"

I looked confused but Angela picked up the

implication first. She grinned and punched Daniel in the arm. "Oh my God!" she declared, "You two are dating again!"

Daniel scowled and shushed her. The music was loud as always, but Angela's squeal pierced the thumping bass easily. "Kinda sorta, yeah," he agreed. "We're not giving it a name. It's just dinner once in a while. Sex a couple times a week. That's it. No expectations, no obligations."

"So you're dating?" I asked.

"Shut up," Daniel grumbled. After a pause he added, "We're comfortable together, that's all. We aren't rushing back into a third marriage or anything. We're just enjoying each other's company."

"Well, I'm happy for both of you, Danny," Angela said. She leaned over and gave my friend a hug. Jealousy swelled, but I quietly subdued the green-eyed monster.

As they parted, a movement by the velvet curtain caught Daniel's eye. He smiled with amusement and glanced my way. "Well," he remarked, "*this* should be interesting."

I followed his gaze to find out what was so entertaining. My brother had just entered the club and was heading our way. It took my brain a moment to parse the information, like a kid seeing his teacher at the supermarket. I knew the person and I knew the location but, to my knowledge, the two had never overlapped. I became sharply aware of Angela's weight on my lap and the reason for Danny's amusement became clear.

Daniel was already on his feet, hand extended to greet Ian. They shook, patted each other on the back. "As I live and breathe," Daniel said, "Ian, I don't think I've seen you in ten years. Christ we were kids back then. How the hell are you?"

Ian spread his hands, tilted his head. "Hey, you know, every day's a new day. How about you?" He glanced around and said, "Nice place you got here."

"Well, one does one's best," Daniel smiled. "Sit, join us. What are you drinking?" He gestured to Daisy and she made her way over from the bar. In her early twenties, Daisy was the only employee I'd never seen naked. She spent her time behind the bar instead of on stage. Shame, I thought, she had the body for it.

"No alcohol?" Ian asked.

"Not if I wanted to have a fully nude club," Daniel agreed. "We got some O'Doul's though."

Ian made a face. "Nah, what's the point of non-alcoholic beer? That's like paying a hooker to give you a lap dance." He paused and actually looked embarrassed for a moment.

Daniel's laugh put him at ease. "If they did that, I might be out of business," my friend said, smoothly reassuring my brother.

"I'll take a root beer," Ian told Daisy. She nodded with a smile and went to retrieve the drink. He sat down beside me, clapping a big calloused hand on my shoulder and giving me a shake. "Hey, bro! What's good?" Before I could respond, he looked at Angela, his eyes doing a slow once-over. "Angela," he said with a grin, "even more of a delight than usual to see you."

"Always the charmer," Angela said. She leaned in and gave him a hug. Apparently hugs were in high demand tonight. Ian's hand momentarily overlapped mine as he returned the embrace. He kept it mercifully brief.

Ian reached for his wallet as Daisy returned with his soda and a glass. Daniel held up his hand, telling Daisy, "No charge." Well, hell, first he hugs my girlfriend, now my little brother was muscling in on my free beverage deal. Ian nodded his thanks, toasting Daniel with his can of root beer before taking a swig.

"What are you doing here?" I finally managed to ask. Perhaps too sharply, judging from the looks I got from Angela and Daniel. Ian rolled with it, as if anticipating my reaction.

"I heard they had naked women here," he

responded with a broad grin. He waggled his eyebrows. "I *like* naked women."

I glanced sidelong at Angela then retuned my gaze significantly to Ian. "There are other strip clubs," I pointed out.

"Hey!" Daniel demanded, "Don't go discouraging my clientele."

"Don't worry about it," Ian said, "He's always talking this place up. So I figured I had to give it a go."

"Well I, for one, am glad you did," Daniel said.

"You don't think it might be awkward?" I asked. I nudged the top of my head towards Angela.

"You got something wrong with your neck?" Angela asked coolly.

"I'm just not comfortable with him seeing you…here," I said. I could almost hear the sound of the shovel hitting the dirt as I continued to dig myself deeper.

"Oh?" Angela asked, arching an eyebrow. "Are you embarrassed that I'm a stripper?" We'd had similar conversations before. They rarely ended well. Before I could answer she turned to Ian and asked with mock sincerity, "You *do* know I'm a stripper, right, Ian?"

Straight face Ian replied, "I'd heard rumors."

Angela nodded and returned the focus of her

budding ire to me. "Just because I love you, Patrick, doesn't give you the right to control my every move. You *know* what I do for a living. I take off my clothes and grind on guys for their enjoyment." I winced. "If you have a problem with it, you should have thought of that a long time ago. Hell, I seem to remember that's how *we* met."

I swallowed, willing myself to remain silent and just let the storm fizzle out. I failed. "I'm okay with you doing your job…"

"Well! Thank you for your permission!" Angela huffed. Ian let out a low amused whistle.

"…but," I continued doggedly, "it's different when it's someone I know. Especially my brother! I mean, come on, you think Christmas dinner is going to be the same once he sees you…you know…?"

Time hiccupped and took a moment to settle back into its normal flow as Angela stared icily at me for several long seconds. Then she turned towards Ian and, in one smooth practiced move, gripped the bottom of her red halter top and lifted her arms over her head, removing the garment in one gesture.

Her bare back to me, Angela glanced over her shoulder and said, "I guess we'll find out."

Ian continued to stare for several seconds, blinking three times and running his tongue across his upper lip. It was not a lewd gesture but more of a contemplative one as he decided how to respond. Finally he raised his eyes to Angela's face and said, "Very nice."

"Thank you, Ian," Angela said. With the same practiced skill, she quickly donned her top again. It was against the unwritten protocol to be naked, or partially so, if you weren't on stage at the time.

To me, Ian said, "You should keep picking a fight with her. Let's see how far this goes."

I raised my hands in surrender. "Fine, forget it. Points made. I'll stop being such a prude. Besides, it doesn't matter who sees what. At the end of the night, you're still going home with me." A pause. "Right?"

Angela let me hang for another second or two before slipping me a conciliatory smirk. "Of course, you fucking idiot," she said. I found the response oddly reassuring.

Daniel stood and said, "Well, I've got a few things to do upstairs before we start getting busy. You guys have fun. If you end up fighting over a girl, Ian, don't hurt him too badly."

"I'll do my best," Ian assured him. I gave them a single syllable bark of laughter.

"See you guys in a while." Daniel made his way upstairs.

Having finished with the couple, Georgia sidled towards our table. For a change, her heels were not ridiculously high and her shorter stature became apparent. She exchanged a glance with Angela, who nodded and Ian. "Patrick's all mine, but you can have him. That's Ian, Patrick's brother."

"Oh," Georgia purred as she slid up to Ian and ran a long silver fingernail up his chest and neck. "Hello, Ian, Patrick's brother. How are you tonight?"

"Much better now," Ian replied with a smirk. Georgia chuckled throatily.

"Care for a dance?"

"I thought you'd never ask." Ian smiled up at her. Georgia was curvy but a little plain of face. The blonde ponytail that fell between her shoulder blades was real. She leaned into my brother, her face close to his as she ran a hand over his shoulder, shifting her weight so her bare leg began to rub its way up his thigh.

"Hey, you," a husky voice whispered in my ear, breaking my attention. I turned to Angela who was watching me with something akin to amusement. "Hypocrite much?" she asked.

"What do you mean?"

"I mean I'm supposed to dress like a nun around your brother, but you can ogle another dancer while I'm sitting right here on your lap? And I noticed you checking out Daisy, too, in case you think you got away with that."

Her logic was sound. I dipped my head in acknowledgement. "You're right. I'll try not to be such a stick in the mud."

"You better," she said. She leaned in and gave me a lingering kiss. That made everything better. "I'll be back," she said, standing. "I'm up next."

A moment or two later, my brother and I sat there alone. "Georgia didn't invite you upstairs?" I asked.

"She did," Ian answered, "but I figured I'd bide my time. The night is young."

I nodded.

"I didn't mean to cause any problems," Ian said. "I figured you'd get your panties in a twist but I thought it would be good for a laugh."

"It's fine," I said grudgingly. "I'm *not* ashamed of her or what she does." I chuckled and said, "Besides, who would have thought that, between the two of us, *I'd* be the one who ended up dating a stripper?"

"Heard," Ian acknowledged. We toasted with our soda cans and relaxed a little.

The little redheaded number on stage was naked now and had finished her set. She was picking up the outfit she had strewn across the stage floor and blew a kiss to the two college guys sitting by the rail. The only reason I was sure she was at least eighteen years old is because I knew Daniel wouldn't knowingly hire anyone underage. Still, I found myself looking at her and feeling like a dirty old man. I really needed to find somewhere better to hang out.

"Say good-bye to Crystal, ladies and gentlemen!" the DJ's voice boomed from the overhead speaker. "She'll be making her way around to greet you all personally. Remember to be generous. These ladies work for your tips and your tips alone! Coming to the stage now is our own little slice of Heaven. Here's Angel!"

Pink's *Raise Your Glass* began to play over the speaker as Angela emerged from the dressing room and mounted the three steps to the stage. One of the kids whistled. I looked at Ian. He looked at me, with a slow smile, and set his root beer on the table. "I'm going to step out for a smoke," he said, standing, "I'll be back in about six minutes."

I did some quick elementary math. "Make it seven. Or eight."

"You got it."

"Hey, kid," I said as he started to turn away. He paused and looked back at me, his eyes resting only momentarily on the stage. I smiled and said, "Thanks."

"Got your back, Jack," Ian assured me and stepped outside while Angela did her set.

Watching Angela dance always stirred something in me. She seemed to be so in her element. I don't know if she was the most talented dancer in the place, or the most graceful. But she was confident and beautiful and those qualities served her well. It didn't hurt that I was madly in love with her. Early on, I made a point of tipping her big when she danced but she had eventually assured me it wasn't necessary. She knew I enjoyed the show and told me I could show her my appreciation in other ways after hours.

Angela was topless and giving one of the college guys an up close view while the second song in her set – another Pink classic, *So What* – played. I saw Danny coming down the stairs. He glanced at the stage, then at me, and took up a position leaning against the railing at the bottom of the stairs and watched Angela dance. He frowned.

As her dance was winding up, he raised his hand to me and gestured me over. Angela and I reached him at the same time and he gestured for us to precede him into the dressing room. It wasn't my first visit behind the scenes, but I always felt a little smug walking into the inner sanctum sanctorum while all the rubes watched and wondered what made me so special. In reality the dressing room was nothing special. Bare cinderblock walls with a row of makeup tables on one wall and a row of dented metal lockers on the other. A rack of random outfits stood in one corner. The room smelled of heady perfume, sweat and old cigarette smoke. It was cold. There was a back door that led to a small, isolated patio, only accessible through the changing room, where the women could go and smoke or get a fresh of breath air when the weather allowed. One of the strippers was smoking outside, probably Heather, and had left the door ajar letting in the cold air. Daniel crossed, held up a finger to Heather asking her to wait a moment, and closed the door, turning to us. His anxiety had already rubbed off on both of us as Angela, still naked, stood beside me and looked at him. "What's wrong?" I asked.

"Angela," Danny said, stepping forward and taking her hands in his. He seemed oblivious to her nudity. "A call just came in for you. Your mother is in the hospital. Your father says someone shot her."

Chapter Six

St. Luke's Hospital stood a couple blocks off Hoosick Street, one of the main east-west thoroughfares through Troy. It towered over the downtown area, a benevolent place of healing and recovery. Whatever horrors and atrocities the denizens of the inner city inflicted upon each other, St. Luke's stood ready to patch them up and send them back into the fray. Or to hold on to their remains until the funeral home could retrieve them. It was also the closest hospital to the rural Raymertown home of Anthony and Regina Button.

I dropped Angela at the door to the emergency room before pulling into the parking garage. Upon hearing the news, she had hurriedly thrown on her street clothes – a pair of black yoga pants and an oversized grey sweatshirt – and, after giving Ian a single sentence explanation, we drove to the hospital from Latham as quickly as I could, while maintaining relative safety and a minimal likelihood of getting stopped for speeding. She managed to remove most of her heavy makeup in the car, en route. I was glad it gave her something to focus on, although she kept whispering, "Oh God, oh my God. Patrick, what am I going to do? Can't you drive faster? Oh my God," and things of that ilk. Her mascara was still darker than average and the occasional sparkle of glitter still flashed on her face and neck, but she most of the vestiges of her job were obliterated by the time she walked through the sliding glass doors and into the emergency room of the hospital.

By the time I got inside from the parking garage, she was speaking to a nurse and waiting impatiently for me to arrive so we could be buzzed in past a locked door and into the emergency room proper. "Room 4, down the hall on the right," the desk nurse reminded her before the door closed behind us. I followed two steps behind as Angela sped down the hall. She almost missed the room and I staggered as she stopped short and turned to the right.

The room was small and packed with medical equipment. The bed was gone but Anthony Button was sitting in a hard plastic chair, hands clasped between his knees, head hanging down, eyes closed. He remained that way for a moment after we entered. Angela softly said, "Daddy?" He opened his eyes startled and looked up at us. He stood, opening his arms. Angela embraced him and began to cry. He held for a moment, and nodded a greeting at me over her shoulder. Finally Angela stepped back, sniffling and shaking herself, regaining her composure. "Daddy, what happened?"

"We had gone out Christmas shopping," Tony

explained. His voice was tired and flat. He had no doubt told the story to the police once, probably more than that. "Things have been getting better in the last week or so. We've been talking about our issues and had agreed to go to couple's counseling." He shrugged listlessly. "I guess that's not important now. Anyway, we got back to the house and were carrying in bags. We were *laughing*." He paused, ground his teeth and looked away, keeping his composure by sheer force of will. Angela squeezed his hand. After a deep breath, he continued, "We were talking and laughing and, for a moment, it was like old times, walking close, shoulders touching. She stopped suddenly and turned towards me, hugging me. And then there was this sound. Two quick pops. Gunshots, I guess. They both hit her. She tried to speak, but she couldn't. My God, though, the fear and pain in her eyes…" He trailed off, voice shuddering. His daughter hugged him again and they took strength from each other. When the embrace ended again, Tony spread his hands helplessly. "Anyway," he concluded, "they're operating on her now. Removing the bullets. She didn't wake up the entire ride here. I drove her in myself, carried her to the car, put her in the passenger's seat. We didn't have time to wait for an ambulance." Another steadying breath and he stopped speaking.

"What about the shooter?" I asked. Anthony looked at me in bewilderment. "Did you see them?" I prompted.

"I...no," he answered. "All I thought about was Regina and she was hurt and I had to get her here. I didn't even think to try and see where the shots came from or anything. I guess...I just panicked. Hell, I think the bags from the store are still laying on the ground where we dropped them. I couldn't even tell you where they came from, if the shooter was in the house or the woods or where. God, I hate this feeling."

I gave him a sympathetic nod. "You were in shock," I said, "you were on autopilot while your brain tried to make sense of it all. Try to take some comfort from knowing that your first instinct was to save your wife."

Anthony nodded thoughtfully. Angela was wringing her hands and looking out towards the nurse's station, centrally located in the center of the emergency room. "How long has she been in surgery? When will we hear something?"

"It could be a couple more hours, they said."

"What about Russ? Did you call him and let him know?"

"I tried," Tony said. His voice took on a harsh edge as he added, "It just went to voice mail so I left him a message. No way of knowing if he got it. Or if he's already passed out for the night somewhere. I also called..." He was cut off by a low buzzing from his breast pocket. "Maybe that's him now," he commented. He pulled out his cell phone and checked the caller ID. He glanced at the two of us and frowned. "Excuse me," he said and stepped away, crossing the three steps to the far side of the room. Snapping open his phone he said in a low voice. "Now's not really a good time. Can I call...?" He stopped midsentence, listening. "Yes, but..." Another pause. Another glance at us. Putting his hand over the phone speaker he said, "I'm going to step outside for some fresh air while I take this. If you hear anything, come get me." Without waiting for a response, he left the room at a brisk pace.

I watched him go, thoughts of Regina's Thanksgiving accusations ringing in my ears. Angela seemed less concerned about her father's departure. "What am I going to do, Patrick? I can't lose my mother."

I guided her to the chair that Anthony had vacated and sat her down. She rested her head against my stomach and I stroked her hair. I didn't have any answers for her.

There was a rap at the door, quiet but firm. We looked up. The middle aged man standing there wore a State Police uniform. He held his wide-brimmed hat in his hand, revealing a closely-cropped head of dark red hair. A tint of grey was beginning to show at the temples. His brown eyes were alert, his jaw set. Angela stood, wiping tears from her eyes with the back of her hand. "Come in," she said. "I'm sorry, my father just stepped out to take a phone call. I'm Angela Button."

"Detective James Finley," he said as he entered. "I saw your father outside. He said you were here. I figured I would speak with you while he finishes his call."

"I'm not sure what I can tell you," Angela said. "We just got here. I was at work when it happened. All I know is what my father's told me so far."

"Can you think of anyone who may have wanted to attack Mrs. Button?" Finley asked. His gaze was unwavering. He seemed to blink less than most people. The effect was unsettling.

Angela shook her head, frowning. "You mean like, does she have any enemies? I didn't know police actually asked that question. I can't think of anyone. She might be able to tell you after her surgery, though."

"That is the hope," Finley agreed. "When did you see her last?"

"Thanksgiving," Angela answered. She gave a short laugh. "If this had happened then, I might have suspected my father. The two of them had a huge fight that day. We ended up cutting the whole thing short." Finley nodded. Angela's eyes widened slightly and she added hastily, "I'm not saying he did it, though! It was just an argument. Everyone has them!"

"I understand," Finley said with no trace of empathy. "You say you were at work this evening?"

"Yes, sir."

"And where is that?"

Angela hesitated just a moment. "Danny's Place, in Latham."

Finley blinked. "The gentlemen's club?"

"Yes sir."

He nodded. Though he hadn't written anything down, I could tell all the pertinent information had been filed away in his head. He turned to me. "Are you the son?"

"No, sir," I answered. "Patrick Brady. I'm Angela's boyfriend."

One eyebrow arched an entire eighth of an inch. "You got anything to add that might help?"

"No," I replied. "Although if there's anything I can do to help, I'd be happy to."

A faint furrow creased Finley's brow. "Brady? You the Patrick Brady that stopped that killer year ago last spring?"

I tipped my chin modestly. "The same."

Finley grunted. "I know Derek Beckham, the chief over here. He mentioned you."

"I didn't really do much. It was more self-defense than anything," I said.

"That's what I told him," Finley agreed. "Try to keep your nose clean on this one. I don't want you getting involved while you're still a suspect."

It was my turn to blink. "I'm a suspect?"

Angela's father returned, his face expressionless. Glancing at him, Finley responded, "Until I have reason to think otherwise, anyone connected with the family is suspect. I mean it. Stay out of my way." He turned to Anthony. "Any luck getting in touch with your son?" he asked.

Tony shook his head. "He's probably asleep. Won't get the message until tomorrow."

Finley looked at his watch. "We can track him down in the morning. Hopefully we can get some answers when your wife is out of surgery. I'm headed back to the barracks now. You have my card. Call me if anything comes up. I'll come by in the morning and speak to your wife." He nodded his head at us and departed.

"Any word?" Anthony asked. Angela shook her head.

"It's going to be a couple hours," her father sighed. "If you guys want to go home, get some sleep, I can give you a call when she's out of surgery."

"No," Angela said firmly, without even consulting me. "We'll stay here with you." She rested a hand on his shoulder as he settled into the chair again. He patted it and smiled at her.

"Thanks, Dumpling. You're a good girl."

There didn't seem to be much else to say at that point. I managed to find two more unused hard plastic chairs from other rooms and brought them in so Angela and I could sit. I rested a hand on her thigh. She held her father's hand.

Around 10:15, there was a knock on the door. I awoke with a start, having not even noticed I'd fallen asleep. The man who entered was around fifty. He had a head of dark hair in need of a trim and beginning to thin. He had a paunch as though he'd swallowed a volleyball but his arms were strong. His eyes reminded me of Angela. "Tony," he said as he entered the room. More hesitantly, he added, "Angie."

Angela was the first one to speak, her voice like ice. "What the fuck are you doing here?" she croaked. I blinked, not sure I'd heard correctly. She was on her feet, eyes wide like a terrified horse. Tension crackled throughout her body, a snake ready to strike...or flee.

Anthony put his hand out and touched her arm. She flinched and pulled away, from her father, from the man at the door, even from me. Her eyes darted around the room, seeking an escape or a corner in which to cower. "Angie, it's okay. I called him."

"You called *him*?" Her voice began to rise in volume and pitch. "*You* called him? Why, Daddy?"

"I *am* her brother," the man answered softly.

"You're a fucking monster," Angela hissed, saliva flying from her lips as she spat the word. The new arrival winced at the word. She gathered up her jacket and her purse. "I'm going to take you up on that offer to go home and sleep, Daddy," she said. "Call me when Mom is awake...and *he's* gone." She gave her father a quick perfunctory buzz on the cheek and squeezed out the door, staying as far from the man as possible. He took a step back to make it easier for her. She didn't look back to see if I followed.

I exchanged a glance with the two men. Anthony sighed heavily. "Go with her, Patrick," he said. "And be patient with her. She's going to need time."

I hurried after Angela, catching up with her as she breezed out the main door of the hospital, barely waiting for it to slide open. She was forcing her arms into her long mohair coat. Her entire body was trembling. I came up behind her and tried to help her with her coat. "Get off me!" she screamed, pulling away and whirling to face me. Her eyes were wide, wet and haunted. Her chest rose and fell in heavy breaths. "I'm sorry," she said with effort. "Just…just don't touch me right now. Okay? Please."

"No problem," I agreed. "Do you really want to leave?"

"I can't stay here with him," she said. "I won't. Where'd you park?"

I led her to the car in silence. As we pulled out of the garage, she turned the heat all the way up, cranked the blower and rolled her window down, looking out into the night. I drove towards her house, turning onto Hoosick Street and heading downtown.

"Can we go to your place?" she asked softly. "I don't want to be alone."

"Of course," I agreed.

"Better, just drive around. I won't be able to sleep anyway."

At the bottom of Hoosick, I turned and followed the river north through Lansingburgh. The dark water of the Hudson flowed beside us, occasionally visible between the buildings on that side of the road. At the far end of the city, I meandered to Route 40, heading north into Melrose. Eventually she spoke again.

"His name is Wayne Novello," she said. "He's my mother's brother."

"Your uncle?" I asked.

"My mother's brother," she said firmly. "Just shut up and listen. This is hard enough." I nodded and made a point of zippering my lips closed. She ignored me. She paused, long enough that I thought she must have decided to stop talking. We came out the other side of Melrose and the roadside opened up into fields and outcroppings of dark, barren trees. The only light came from the dashboard. In the darkness, Angela finally took a long, shuddering breath and whispered, "When I was ten years old, he raped me."

Chapter Seven

Surprised by Angela's revelation, it was easy to obey her earlier admonition. I remained silent and let her continue in her own time. Before we reached Schaghticoke, I turned left onto Route 67. Sometimes, when driving to my parents cabin in the Adirondacks, if I wanted to avoid the traffic on the Northway, we would take this "back way." I was tempted to continue heading north, but we'd already meandered too far from the hospital and I wanted to be nearby when Anthony called. Though now I wondered if that really was the best strategy.

Angela began to tell her story, a couple sentences at a time, her voice soft and toneless. She continued to stare out the window into a night at least as dark as the memories she recounted.

"I was ten," she repeated. "So he was probably thirty-two, thirty-three. He was living with us at the time. He and my aunt eventually got a divorce, but I don't know if it had happened by then or not. It was June 15, 1995. My parent's fifteenth wedding anniversary. Since he was staying there, they had a built in babysitter. I thought it would be fun. He was 'Uncle Wayne' back then, the typical fun uncle. Made me laugh a lot, snuck me cookies when my parents weren't looking. You know what I mean?"

I nodded silently. She didn't see it.

"He'd never given anyone any reason to think I couldn't be left alone with him. So my parents went out to dinner and a movie. Probably some dancing, too. They still liked to dance together back then. Russ was spending the night at a friend's house. Wayne made English muffin pizzas for dinner. I used to love them! And we watched *Animaniacs* while we ate. My parents didn't like me to eat in front of the television, but Uncle Wayne...but *he* used to let me. He said it would be our little *secret!*" She bit the word off like a piece of rotten fruit.

"My bedtime was eight o'clock," she continued. "I had to take a bath before bed. I was old enough to do it myself, of course, and he didn't try to bathe me or anything." She hugged herself tighter. "He did check on me once or twice, to make sure I was okay, not splashing water around, to let me know I had to get out in five minutes, whatever. Maybe just to...see me. I don't know. I was *ten*, for Chrissake! Fucking *ten*! I hadn't hit puberty yet, I wasn't starting to develop, I was a *child*." He voice edged upward approaching hysteria levels. I kept my own breathing steady, counted to ten, resisted the burning urge to try and touch her to comfort her. She cried quietly for several minutes.

I had seen pictures of Angela around that age, with her long straight auburn hair and big brown eyes. She was a beautiful child but her point was valid; she was *only* a child. The pictures I'd seen had never done anything for me on a physical level. I gripped the steering wheel tighter. A knot was forming in my sour stomach. I drove across the bridge into the town of Mechanicville and turned south on Main Street. Eventually it connected with Routes 4 and 32. When we left the lights of the small downtown behind and were safely ensconced in darkness again, she resumed her story.

"I took my bath. He…checked on me a couple times. Afterward, I got dried off and put on a nightshirt. It was just a long T-shirt with Hello Kitty on it. I had a pair of underwear on too. I remember the way he patted the couch cushion next to him and told me I could stay up until 8:30 to watch some funniest video show with him. It was a school night but it was almost the end of the year. And, again, he was the 'fun uncle.'" She made bitter air quotes, her tone full of contempt.

"At one point during the show there was a video and we laughed hard and he clapped once or twice and, when he put his hands back down, he rested one of them on my leg. It seemed like a natural, innocent thing. He was always patting my arm or my hair or something." This time I shuddered. "So I didn't think anything of it. He kept it there for the rest of the show, squeezing occasionally when some other funny video came on. He even put his head on my shoulder briefly while we were laughing. Seemed a little odd but we were laughing and having fun. I never noticed that, by the end of the show, our legs and hips were pressed up against each other. When the show was over he patted my leg and said, 'Okay, young lady, bed time.' He always called me 'young lady,' never 'little girl.' Maybe that helped him justify it somehow. So he walked me to my bedroom."

We were just reaching the outskirts of Waterford. I silently prayed that, under the lights of the town, she would stop speaking again. But she was getting into the meat of the story and seemed grudgingly determined to bring it to its inevitable conclusion.

"He had his hand on my lower back when we got to the bedroom," Angela continued. "He started talking about how I was his favorite niece. I laughed because I was his only niece. He agreed but said that he felt we had a special bond. He asked if I loved him and, of course, I said yes. In my room he asked if he could get a hug before bed. I hugged him. He kissed my cheek." My stomach was roiling, my knuckles white on the steering wheel. Angela's voice was completely emotionless and steady. She had relived this scene hundreds of times since then, maybe thousands. A piece of her had died each time she relived it and now there was no life left in the memory. Only pain and fear and tragedy.

"He asked if I could keep a secret and I said yes. He said he had always wanted to be closer to me. Like big girls and boys, like mommies and daddies."

We had passed through the town and were following Route 32 over the canal. "Angela," I whispered, "you don't have to…"

"I didn't know what he meant," she continued, ignoring me. Just past the rural cemetery, I turned onto the side roads, delaying our inevitable return to my apartment. "He said he wanted to *make love* to me but he didn't think anyone would understand how he felt, so we had to keep it a secret. Like staying up late or eating in front of the television. It was fun having our little secrets and I *did* love him. I said okay. He warned me it might hurt and I was nervous but he said he'd try to be gentle. I didn't know what he meant and he said we could start slow and just kiss and he kissed me on the mouth. I'd never kissed anyone like that except maybe a fleeting good night kiss to my mother or father before. It tickled and I remember laughing when he did it. He laughed too. Then he told me I should take off my nightshirt."

The side streets were not nearly as dark as her uncle's soul. Still, only the occasional streetlight or porch light broke the gloom. I wondered if she'd stop the story when we got to my place. I decided to make a beeline for the building, even though I doubted it.

"I got scared but he asked if I trusted him. Of course I did. He asked if I knew about boy parts and girl parts and I told him my friends had said that boys had a 'wiener'. That's what we called it. A wiener. Like a hot dog. He asked if I wanted to see his." She took a long shuddering breath. Her voice remained flat. We pulled into the parking space in front of the two story building I called home. Well, technically, only one apartment upstairs was home. The others were rented by other people. She glanced around as if realizing where we were for the first time. She sighed.

"Anyway, I said yes and I remember thinking how funny it looked when he pulled it out. But it wasn't funny when he told me what he wanted to do with it but he told me that was how grown-ups made love. And he kissed me some more. His hands were on my skin and it didn't seem to scary, even when he told me I could touch…it. We got in the bed and he…kissed my body. I remember the way his lips felt on every single part they touched. He worked his way down…"

"Angela," I pleaded. I didn't need the gory details. I was ready to throw up.

She glanced at me, then looked at her hands in her lap. "That's why I've never liked when you try to…," she whispered and gestured vaguely towards her lap. I nodded my understanding. "From there, things proceeded as you can imagine. We…did it like mommies and daddies. It hurt at first. A lot! But he kept his word and tried to be gentle. I was scared but he tried to be soothing and eventually the pain went away and my body felt…weird. And he…finished. I think I did too. And, when it was done and he was lying next to me, sweaty and breathing hard, he reminded me again, *begged* me, not to tell anyone. It was our secret, he said. And I agreed, but I felt so different. It didn't seem right. If it was okay for mommies and daddies why was he so nervous, so afraid I'd tell someone. And I bled, of course. Maybe if he'd noticed that and thought to change my sheets, maybe things would have been much different. But he didn't. He just kissed me good night and tucked me in and called me young lady and turned off the light and closed the door behind him. And I lay there in the dark, feeling sore and happy and scared and weird and empty and wet and cold." I left the car running as we sat in front of my building, trying to absorb all the heat blasting from the dashboard, hoping it would remove the chill from my bones.

"My mother saw the blood when she washed my sheets a couple days later and she asked me about it. I hadn't planned on telling anyone. But she must have thought maybe I was getting my first period. And, honestly, I just somehow felt that this was a different kind of secret than staying up late or eating in the living room. So I told her. She asked me a lot of questions. I don't know if she believed me. She didn't want to, that was clear. I felt worse after I told her, as if confessing to what had happened was worse than the deed itself. Like it was my fault. I was sent to my room until my father got home and she and he talked in harsh whispers and then they both confronted… him in a lot louder voices and that night he packed his things and left. I never saw him, they wouldn't let me see him. They kept me in my room until he was gone. And the whole time I stayed there, I was trying to figure out what I'd done wrong, what I had done to make my parents mad. Why *I* was being punished and kept in my room. By the time the let me out, I'd already decided I must have been to blame for what had happened."

"Oh, God," I whispered.

"We didn't talk about it, or him, again. Not for a long time and, if we did, his name was always mentioned in hushed tones. It was always referred to as 'that incident with Uncle Wayne'. I didn't go to counseling or therapy or anything, not at first. We just kind of buried it. I don't know if I was traumatized or if I just thought I was supposed to be traumatized, but the effect was the same." She gave a bitter bark of laughter. "I slept around in high school. And now I'm a stripper. Stereotypical story, I guess."

"Not at all," I said, hoping it was reassuring. She gave me a small sad smile of appreciation at my feeble attempt. I risked taking her hand. She jerked at my touch, but didn't pull away.

"Eventually things went back to normal. Or as normal as possible. Like I said, he got a divorce. I don't know if it was because of this or not, but he has a daughter that's a year younger than me and I'm sure there were questions about whether or not she was safe. She and I have talked since then and I don't think he ever touched her. But he moved to Newburgh and we really haven't seen much of him since. No one was that concerned that he was gone, I guess, though Mom cried for a while after he left the house."

She was quiet. "Thank you for telling me all this," I said at last. "I'm so sorry that happened to you. I never imagined."

She shook her head faintly, brushing off my remarks. She took a shuddering breath. "There's one more thing, kind of related, that you may as well know since I'm telling you all my dirty little secrets tonight." I wasn't sure I could take anything else.

"What happened to me...affected me," she said slowly. Where earlier she had spoken steadily and without emotion, she now picked her words carefully. This part of the tale had not been shared as much and was not so well rehearsed.

"I would imagine you were incredibly traumatized," I said.

"Just shush," she said brusquely. She pulled her hand away and frowned out the window. "It wasn't just that," she continued, after a pause. "Of course I was traumatized. It's been sixteen years and you saw how I reacted in the hospital. I was lucky I didn't wet my pants. But I'm talking about something else. Something...I don't know...different."

She gestured with her hands vaguely for a moment, trying and failing to find the right words. "After all that happened and after it was swept under the rug like it was, I became very...sensitive. Very *aware*, I guess you could say. Of when things were...not quite right, I guess?" She seemed unsure of the definition, but shrugged it off. "I guess that's as close as anything else. It's like I developed a sixth sense that alerted me to danger or...significant situations."

"You mean you became psychic?" I asked. Despite my best efforts, my skepticism was plain.

She shook her head vehemently. "No, see, that's not it. There's not a word, I don't think, to describe it really. It's like, having been hurt like I was, I became more sensitive to things that had potential to hurt me again. It doesn't happen all the time. I can't predict the future or anything. I don't get visions or any of that nonsense. Just kind of a gut feeling that something's off. Not always dangerous, just…well, off. I'm not describing it well." She shook her head in frustration.

I risked taking her hand again. She let me. "It's okay, Angela. I think I get the idea."

"Maybe," she said. She brightened for a moment, turning towards me. "Okay, here's an example. Remember Becky?"

"Delaney?" I asked, eyebrows rising. About six months into my relationship with Angela, I'd come into the crosshairs of what one might commonly refer to as a psycho bitch. She'd almost cost us our relationship. My life as well, for that matter.

"Remember when I brought you the papers that I found in her locker?"

I nodded, then understanding dawned. "You mean you had a…I don't know what you want to call it. A feeling?"

"That works as well as anything," she agreed. "I just felt that I should bring them to you right then. And it's a good thing I did."

"I could have stopped her myself," I said, a touch defensively.

For a moment, my old Angela was back, eyes twinkling as she patted my leg and said, "Sure, babe. Keep telling yourself that." She sighed. "At any rate, the feelings come less now than they did as a child. Pretty rarely. I don't know why. Maybe I'm not as afraid anymore. Or maybe it's because I'm more cynical as a grown up and don't expect everything to be safe or happy all the time. Maybe it's just because I've outgrown a belief in magic." She shook her head again. In a whisper she added, "I just wish I'd been able to help my mother."

"Maybe you didn't sense anything about her because she's going to be fine." She gave me a sad smile and another pat. I felt patronized.

"I've never told anyone about those...feelings," she said at last. "I eventually went through more than my share of therapists about the...the rape. Most days I'm okay. I can go long stretches being okay. But then something will trigger a memory. Some detail from that night will show up, like English muffin pizzas, and I'll panic and I'll have flashbacks and nightmares for a couple days. I can only imagine how the next few days are going to be for me, having actually seen him in the flesh again. But, like I said, I've dealt with that for sixteen years. I'll manage. But my...feelings that I get, you're the only one who knows about that."

"I'm flattered," I said softly.

"Don't be," she said. "It's as much a curse as a blessing. Misery loves company. And I know I've hit you with both barrels of misery tonight. Can you handle it?" She looked at me, eyes damp and full of concern.

I smiled gently. "I love you, Angela," I told her. "Whatever happened in the past is just that – past. It all contributed to the woman you are today, the woman that I can't imagine being without. You bet your sweet ass I can handle it."

A bubble of nervous laughter percolated up and out of her mouth and she leaned over and hugged me, clinging to me. I rubbed her back with the palm of my hand, kissed her ear through her hair, still fragrant with her perfume from the club. "I love you, Patrick," she whispered.

We locked the car and went inside, climbing the stairs to my apartment in companionable silence. We went to bed. I stripped down completely. She left her sweatshirt and underwear on. I didn't question her need to not be naked right then, when all her old fears had been stirred up. We lay in the bed and she let me hold her as we spooned. Her body was rigid, her breathing regular and deep. I fell asleep. She didn't.

When the phone woke me two hours later, it was dark and I was alone in the bed. The living room light was on, the faint glow making its way to a slice of my bedroom wall. I heard Angela speaking softly into the phone. When she came and knocked on the bedroom doorframe, I was already on the edge of the bed, getting dressed. "My mother's out of surgery," she said. "My father says we should come back. He sounds scared."

Chapter Eight

It was nearly one-thirty in the morning when we returned to the hospital. My brief sleep had done little to refresh me. Angela's father had given us a room number and let us know that his brother-in-law had left for the night.

"He apologized for making things uncomfortable when he arrived," Tony added, his voice sounding tinny on Angela's speaker phone as I pulled into the hospital's parking garage.

"I don't care," Angela said tersely. "He can go do to himself what he did to me sixteen years ago." There was a long, awkward silence. "Anyway, Daddy, we're here. I'll see you in a few minutes." She hung up as we parked. We walked into the hospital holding hands. Hers were cold and clammy.

Regina was in a private room. She was unconscious, her breath slow, rhythmic and a little wheezy. Not that I was a doctor. A number of tubes and wires had been attached or otherwise inserted in her, some mimicking the various functions necessary to keep a body alive, and others tracking the progress of the first group. Her vitals looked normal to me but, again, not a doctor. All I knew is there weren't alarms going off or frantic medical staff running around yelling about stat this or code that. I took that as a good sign.

Tony was as pale and drawn as I've ever seen him. When he stood, one knee buckled. He caught himself as Angela came to his side and eased him back into the rigid square chair beside the bed. "Daddy," she declared, "you're exhausted. You need to go home and get some sleep. Patrick and I will stay here with Mommy."

Oh really? I thought. I was smart enough, though, not to let it fall out of my mouth.

Tony squeezed his daughter's hand and shook his head. "No, Dumpling, it's okay. I'm fine. Just tired. The nurses are going to bring me a recliner pretty soon. They say I'm welcome to stay as long as I want. They've been very kind." He sighed, glancing at his wife before looking back at Angela. "I guess I really should have let you stay home in bed," he added. "I could have told you this over the phone. She came through surgery okay. They think she may recover. But she...well, Angie, she's in a coma. And they *aren't* sure she's going to wake up any time soon. Or...or ever." His voice broke and Angela began to cry, hugging her father tightly. I stood behind her, gangly and awkward and rested my hand on her shoulder, face solemn. I wondered if the nurses had two recliners.

After a time, Angela sniffled and stood up and rubbed her father's shoulder and took a couple steps away to speak with me in private. She dabbed at her reddened eyes. "Go home, love," she told me. "I'll stay here tonight with Daddy. He can't be alone right now. You can come by and get me after work tomorrow."

"Are you going to be okay?" I asked. "What about your…mother's brother?"

"I'll be fine," she said resolutely. "I want to talk to the doctor directly tomorrow, understand exactly what's going on, what there is that we can do, if anything. As for *him*, I was caught off guard earlier. Now that I know he's coming, my emotional and mental walls are up. Soon as he gets here, I'll go to the cafeteria and wait for him to leave again. I'm not a helpless little girl anymore. I can take care of myself." Her eyes burned fiercely, her tone determined.

I brushed her hair with my fingers and smiled at her. "You call me if you need anything. Day or night." I looked past her and raised my voice a little. "Same with you, Anthony. If you need anything, you call me."

"Grazie, figlio," Tony said with a nod.

I kissed Angela. Tender, lingering, hand resting lightly on the back of her head. "Love you, love," I whispered.

"Love you, love," she agreed.

The ride home was quiet, lonely. I trudged up the stairs of my building and managed to get my shoes off before collapsing into the bed. I slept in my clothes.

It was daylight when I awoke again, still face down on the bed, still dressed, an undignified puddle of drool pooled in a divot on the sheet beneath me. I wiped my mouth with the back of my hand and crawled out of bed. I felt like a truck had run me over during the night. Tired as I was, I probably would have slept through that, too.

It was almost nine when I got to work. I called Angela from the car. She had managed to get some sleep and, though I wouldn't call her perky, she seemed to have regained some semblance of life. It may have been a ploy to keep her father's spirits up.

There was a rusting red pickup truck in the parking lot of Balla's when I arrived. A blue tarp covered the bed, secured to the truck body with bungee cords. One section had been undone and folded back and the tailgate was down. As I walked by, I glanced into the open space. At a glance there were three or four new pieces of construction equipment, still in boxes, in the back of the truck.

In the foyer there was another box. It had been opened and contained a wet saw, used for cutting ceramic tile. Just like what we would need for working on the bathroom that we were going to start remodeling at Rensselaer County Community College later this week. How fortuitous.

"You're late," my father said. He and Gene Hickock were standing beside the box. Gene always rubbed me the wrong way. He was…slimy. I always knew when he was lying because his lips were moving. In addition he was a thief. He had once gloated about a time he stole two full pallets of rock salt from Home Depot. It had taken two trips and they even helped him load it.

Gene looked like he was in his mid-fifties, but I suspected he was younger and that his lifestyle had prematurely aged him. He had a thick rat's nest of light brown hair, a nose that had been broken a couple times and a pockmarked face that should have been shaved two days ago. His eyes glittered when he saw me. "Hey, Patty," he said, with a voice abused by years of cigarettes and who knew what else. "How ya been? I ain't seen you since that time in lockup."

Oh, yeah. And Gene and I had shared a jail cell for a night earlier in the year. It was a misunderstanding, but at the time I'd been scared and out of my element. Having probably spent a good third of his life in jail, Gene was able to show me the ropes. He and me three cellmates had actually done okay, helping me get me through unscathed. I resented him for that, since it forced me to say nice things about him.

"What's this?" I asked, nudging the box with my toe.

"Gene was able to procure us a new wet saw," my father answered, giving me a level gaze.

I glanced at Gene, who was grinning just a little too widely. Yeah, I thought, he's a regular procurement specialist. He should have business cards made up. Out loud, I just said, "You're a hell of a guy, Gene."

"I've been called worse." Gene beamed proudly. Idiot.

"There's some paperwork on your desk I need you to take care of," my father said. "When I'm done here, we'll talk," Dad said. It was probably supposed to sound like a suggestion. It didn't but I was glad to get away anyway.

When my father came into my office about fifteen minutes later, I glanced up. "So we're buying stolen merchandise now?"

"You don't know that it was stolen," my father cautioned.

"It came from Gene, which means it must have belonged to someone else at some point."

Dad shrugged dismissively. "I don't ask where it came from. He doesn't volunteer the information. All I know is we have a new wet saw that we needed, and it cost half the price of buying it at the store. Everyone wins."

"Except the store he...procured it from," I pointed out.

"Our little operation here does a couple thousand dollars' worth of business worth of business with Home Depot each month. They won't miss one wet saw. *If* that's even where it came from. And I don't have to remind you that, if we can't keep costs down any other way, we may have to lay someone else off. And you know who's next on the chopping block." He gave me a significant look. My father was a strong proponent of multi-tiered ethics. It didn't help that his logic was sound. It would take a *lot* of wet saws for a big box store like Home Depot to feel the pinch. But our new toy was top of the line and the amount he probably saved would be enough to keep me employed for another week.

"I know nothing," I grumbled.

"That's the spirit," my father said. He clapped me on the shoulder and added, "And, when you get a chance, I'd like you to bring the saw down to Room 8 and dirty it up a little. There should a can of spray paint down there. Mark it like our other tools so no one walks off with it." Room 8 was a storeroom in the darkest recesses of the building's cellar, where most of the expensive equipment was stored. It was a fat pain in the ass lugging equipment up and down the stairs, but it helped prevent it from being "reprocured" by the likes of Gene Hickock. Another precaution was that all of Balla's equipment had a pair of red lines painted across them so they could be identified if they did suddenly grow legs and hop in someone else's truck. "You can burn the box, save us some firewood." He didn't add that it would also destroy any evidence of the saw's origin.

"Yeah, ok," I agreed. I didn't like being a part of it, but I could play dumb with the best of them.

"So, where were you this morning?" Dad asked.

I gave him a brief rundown of the events of the last twelve hours. I left out Angela's revelation about her uncle, focusing instead on the fact that her mother was in a coma in the hospital.

"Damn," my father said with genuine concern. "They're good people. It's a shame. I'll give Stu a call and let him know. We'll get a card out from the Lodge and see if there's anything else we can do. Still no information on the shooter?"

I shook my head. "Not that I've heard. It was probably just a random incident." It was a sad commentary on the state of world today that I could say that so casually.

My father hummed. "I hope you're right." I

watched as he weighed something in his mind. Finally he added, "There was a rumor, years ago, that Tony had…'connections'. Like with the mob. I've never given them any credence though."

"You think Tony put out a hit on his wife?" I asked, incredulous.

"Not at all," Dad said emphatically. "But if he rubbed someone the wrong way, perhaps…there may have been retaliation."

It was hard for me to picture Tony as a gangster. Not impossible, mind you. I'd entertained the same suspicions myself sometimes, but I always dismissed them as outrageous. "I'm sure if there's any connection, the State police will find it," I said. "I was given very clear instructions to stay out of it."

There was a rap on my doorframe and we turned. Scott Tisdale stood there, a manila envelope in his hand. "Good morning, gentlemen," he said. "I have those petitions you asked about."

My father accepted the envelope. "We'll get these filled out today so you can present them to Hiram-Austin on Wednesday." He peeked into the envelope and nodded. "You filled out yours for Acacia already."

Scott shrugged his broad shoulders. "Figured there was no point in waiting."

To me my father explained, "I think we should be

able to control Acacia; I'm not the only one who took umbrage with the District Deputy's remarks. Just to hedge our bets, though, Scott is affiliating. You never know when we might need one more vote."

"This feels kind of shady," I said. It must have been the punchline to a joke my father and Scott shared a healthy laugh at my apparent naiveté.

"Sorry, kid," my father said. "Sometimes I forget you're pretty new to the Fraternity. Yeah, sure, we have a lot of moral standards and common beliefs that we all abide by. That's what makes us all Brothers and what bonds us together. But the day-to-day stuff, the business end of administrating the organization? That's all politics just like anywhere else. In each Lodge it's different; it depends on how many members you have and the personalities involved. It gets worse, the higher up you go in the chain. The personalities get stronger and I think the air actually gets thinner."

"But isn't it still…I don't know…unfair, to try and stack the deck like you're talking about?"

Scott stepped in. "In Acacia, maybe. Like your father said, I think most of Acacia is of one mind on the issue. But Hiram-Austin is split. Honestly, I think both sides believe they are acting in the best interest of the Lodge this time. That isn't always the case; sometimes there are power hungry people who try to manipulate things to increase their own power."

I glanced at my father. "I can't imagine," I murmured. He gave me a broad toothy grin.

"So in this case," Scott continued, "it really is nothing but a difference of opinion. And the vote will be close. And I guarantee you that the people in favor of a merge are doing the same things. We'll start seeing old members and past masters that we haven't seen in years showing up again for meetings, just so they can weigh in if a vote occurs. So, if it helps, don't look at it as we're stacking the deck. Look at it as we are rebalancing the scales."

Scott's somewhat paranoid logic aside, I didn't feel up to arguing semantics with him. In the end, he was right. Based on all I'd heard so far, the Lodges didn't need to be merged at this time. It only made sense to support that position however I could. Even if that meant affiliating with Hiram-Austin Lodge to…nudge their vote in our favor. "Fair enough," I said.

To my father, Scott asked, "Any luck with Ian yet?"

"I'm speaking to him this afternoon," Dad answered.

"What's going on with Ian?" I asked.

"I'm going to…press him a little harder, see if I can persuade him to join Acacia," Dad explained. It had long been the practice of Freemasons not to solicit new members, but to require them to come to us first seeking admission into the Fraternity. The cold hard light of reality and our dwindling numbers – estimates were that, at least in New York, our membership had declined by nearly ninety percent in the last century – had prompted some people to start testing the boundary of this tradition. With Freemasonry showing up more and more in popular culture, now was the time to invite men in to see what we were really all about. The old timers still frowned on actively soliciting members but it was gaining ground.

I considered. "Now is probably as good a time as any to approach him about it," I mused. "He's between relationships, looking for something to give him some fulfillment. Kind of like where I was a couple years ago when you gave me my petition. It's not a bad idea to strike while the iron is hot."

Dad tipped his head towards me and said to Scott, "We'll make a master manipulator out of this kid yet." He made it sound like a good thing.

When the conversation ended, my father walked Scott out to his car, petitions still in hand. I lifted our new wet saw with a grunt and carried it down to the cellar for its new paint job.

Chapter Nine

By the next day things had begun to settle into a routine. I worked during the day. Angela sat at the hospital with her father, by her mother's side. In the evening, she and I got together and she told me about her day. Wayne Novello would sit with his sister and his brother-in-law after Angela had left. Last night, Tony had managed to go home and sleep, leaving the hospital for the first time in the forty-eight hours since Regina had been brought in. It wasn't clear if he planned to go home again tonight or not. Meanwhile, Angela and I were spending Tuesday night at my apartment. She sat in the living room, on the rattan couch that had come with the apartment, taking large glugs of Bud Light from the bottle. The lights were dimmed and she put head back, closed her eyes and let the peace of not being beside a hospital bed wash over her. That peace was no doubt accented by the sounds and smells of me cooking in the adjoining kitchen.

I decided to go with a simple stir fry and some fried rice. As the white rice was simmering and fluffing, I sliced up half an onion and tossed it in one pan with some sesame oil. The other half of the onion got diced up and tossed in a second pan. Vegetable oil was fine for those. Next came some red and green peppers similarly divided. The pans began to sizzle and I stirred them briskly, a wooden spoon in each hand, as the oniony aroma wafted over me. I glanced back through the archway to the living room to see if Angela noticed how cool I looked stirring two pans at once. Her eyes were still closed. Her loss. The stir fry pan got some broccoli from the freezer and some pea pods I'd just picked up today. Feeling adventurous, I pulled a can of bamboo shoots form the back of the cupboard, confirmed that they hadn't expired too long ago and, after draining them, I tossed them in too. Diced up a leftover chicken breast that had not yet turned green and put half in each pan before doing my double stirring trick again. Added the white rice, cooled almost to room temperature, to the appropriate pan with some soy sauce. A couple herbs and a other secret ingredients to truly make the dish my own and, in fifteen minutes, I was done cooking. I fixed us each a plate and carried them to the living room, setting them on the glass topped coffee table in front of her. The rattan frame of the table matched the couch. I hated them both. One more trip to the kitchen for napkins, silverware and an Angry Orchard for me and dinner was served.

Hearing the clink of the utensils on the table, Angela's eyes fluttered open and she smiled wearily. "That smells delicious, baby," she murmured. "I didn't realize how hungry I was until just now."

"Or how tired," I suggested.

Her smile was wan as she sat up and picked up her fork. "Oh, no. I was pretty sure about that."

"No changes?" I asked. I tried the chicken stir fry. Damn, my culinary expertise knew no bounds.

Angela took a couple bites, made some yum noises, then said, "She had a slight fever when I left. The nurse said they'd monitor her but it was probably nothing to worry about." She shrugged. "I'm almost as worried about my father. He's going to make himself sick. I have to force him to eat and take care of himself."

"I know how that can be," I remarked, watching her toy with her food. She saw me watching her and took a big, purposeful forkful. I gave her a wink. "Do they have any thoughts when she might wake up?"

She shook her head and her eyes glistened. "They don't know when…or if."

I gave her hand a squeeze. She took another lackluster bite then put her fork down and leaned against me, her head on my shoulder and cried softly. I held her and said nothing, letting her feel what she needed to feel in the moment.

In time she sat back, blew her nose in her napkin and we continued eating in silence for a few minutes. "Detective Finley came by today," Angela said as she poked at some broccoli.

My eyebrows slid up. I would have thought that would be the headline. "Have they caught the guy?" I asked.

She shook her head again. "No. They're following leads." She made quotation marks with her fingers as she commented. "But he really grilled my father. Tried to make it sound casual, like he was reviewing the information, but I really think he was trying to trip him up. Kept asking what time they got home from shopping, who drove, where my father was in relation to my mother when the shots happened, was he *sure* he didn't see anything. Things like that."

"I'm sure he was just being thorough," I said. "He seems confident in their ability to find the gunman."

"I'm just afraid he's going to think he has. Don't they always suspect the spouse first?"

"That's a good guideline, but every case is different. If there's nothing to make them suspicious of your father, they'll follow other leads. They aren't going to arrest him just because he's an easy target."

We were silent for a few more minutes.

"Patrick," she said, her voice questioning. My Spidey senses began to tingle, confirmed a moment later as she continued, "I know you aren't supposed to get involved, but can you investigate? Maybe just ask around, make sure Daddy isn't a suspect, so my mind is at ease?"

"I was told to stay away from it," I hedged. "Finley considers me a suspect too."

"Baby, please," Angela asked looking at me with deep soulful eyes that grabbed my heart and squeezed. "They're my parents for God's sake. I can't lose them both!"

I tried to hold my ground. "I don't know, love. I…"

She leaned in close to me, making sure her squishy bits touched me in just the right way, in just the right places. "If you do," she whispered in my ear, her warm husky breath tickling me, "I'll be…very grateful."

"Really?" I asked, "I thought you only used your feminine wiles for good."

She gave me a solemn smile. "This is for good. What could be better than clearing my father's name and finding the person who attacked my mother?" Her smile became more playful. Some of the anxiety left her eyes. She added, "Besides, I *like* being 'grateful' with you. In fact, I could use some 'grateful' right now, to help me forget all that's going on for a little while."

I am a gentleman, after all, and if a damsel in distress asks me to help distract her, what am I to do?

I took her hand and we went to the bedroom, leaving the rest of our dinner uneaten. And at 9:00 the next morning, I was sitting in a small anteroom at the State Police barracks, waiting for Detective Finley.

There was an electronic buzz, a click and the sealed door to the station's interior swung outward. Finley caught my eye and gestured for me to follow him. He had a desk off to one side of the main room. The room was abuzz with activity, some of it no doubt police related, though a lot of it seemed to be centered around a box of doughnuts someone had placed on a filing cabinet near the door. Cliché, I felt. They should have gone with bagels.

"What can I do for you, Mr. Brady?" Finley asked, taking a sip from a large Cumberland Farms coffee cup. "I assume you're here about the Button case."

"I am," I agreed.

"Come to confess? Make my job easier?" he asked with a dim smile. He seemed as willing to play it off as a joke as he was to slap the cuffs on me right there, depending on my response.

"I'm afraid not," I said, spreading my hands apologetically "Actually, I was hoping that, on behalf of the family, I could find out the current status of the case."

"Absolutely," Finley replied. "The status is as it's

been all along. Under investigation." He stared at me impassively with those unblinking brown eyes.

I smiled good-naturedly. Lots of teeth. "I guess I was hoping for a little more than that."

"It's good to have hope," Finley assured me. He took a long sip of his coffee, staring steadily at me over the rim of the insulated cup.

I tried a different tactic. "The family is in distress, as you can well imagine. I'm just trying to set their minds at ease."

"I can imagine they *are* distressed," Finley agreed. "Mrs. Button's coma is getting worse. There's probably someone out there that's very distressed by that. Very possibly someone in the family. If she dies, the charges go from attempted murder to murder."

I hadn't spoken to Angela since she left for the hospital that morning; news that Regina was getting worse was a surprise to me. Though, given Finley's disposition, it could just as easily be a ploy to get me to admit something. I was relieved I wasn't actually guilty. At least in this case.

"Detective, I've been asked by the family to do my own investigating. I was hoping we could work in tandem."

Finley looked at me with his steady gaze that felt like he was looking into me, evaluating me. Finally he said, "There's that hope again. Was I too vague at the hospital? I thought I made it clear, and you appear to be of at least average intelligence. But let me spell it out again. You are close to the family. You are a suspect. You are *not* to get involved in this investigation. If you do, I'll have you arrested for interfering. Any questions?"

I sighed. "Just one. Do you have a wife or girlfriend?"

As rarely as Finley blinked, that he did so now was an indication of his surprise at my response. "Perhaps. I'd rather not elaborate."

I accepted his reluctance with a tip of my head and continued, "Assume that *someone* close to you experienced a tragedy that was causing them pain, and you had the ability to bring them comfort. And they begged you to do anything you could to help. Wouldn't you?"

He tapped a thoughtful finger on the side of his cup for a moment. An ounce of humanity crept into Finley's voice and his smile seemed genuine. "Mr. Brady, I understand your intentions are good and that you are under pressure, probably form the family and from yourself, to solve this case. I empathize with your position. But you are too close to this. You aren't a cop or even a licensed PI in this state. I know you've helped catch a killer or two, not just here but during your time in California…" He paused long enough to register my own surprise with a smirk. "Oh, yes, I've looked into you. I spoke with Chief Beckham in Troy and I called California. And the fact of the matter is, if you weren't involved with the family, I might welcome your input on the case. But until I can be sure you weren't involved, I don't want you near it."

I nodded. "I appreciate your candor, Detective," I said.

"Good," Finley said, his professional tone returning. He casually glanced from side to side. About eight feet away, another officer sat at his desk taking a statement from a prim elderly lady with sharp eyes. She had a large purse on her lap and was clutching the handles as though, even here in the heart of the State Police barracks, she feared it may be snatched away. She glanced our way, her keen eyes picking up Detective Finley's own slight movement. I couldn't hear their conversation but I thought she had a faint English accent. She turned her attention to the officer questioning her. Finley looked back at me and lowered his voice a notch. "Here's some more candor for you. You can't investigate. You are a suspect, but I will grant that you are an unlikely one. So, *in the course of routine conversations with the family*, it would be natural for you to ask questions, discuss theories, that sort of thing. And with your record, you might just knock loose something resembling a clue along the way. You ask, you listen and you bring me anything you find, and, as long as you aren't impeding my investigation, I'll assume you came across the information by accident. You get me?"

I felt a smile twitch at my lips but met his impassivity with my own. "I'll be sure to stay touch. Thank you, Detective."

"Happy hunting, Mr. Brady."

I stood and offered him my hand. He glanced at it with a smirk and a slight shake of his head and took another sip of his coffee. I put the hand back in my pocket and left the station.

Chapter Ten

I called my parents that evening. It was something I really should do more often, not just when I needed something. I was sure my mother would appreciate it. I promised to put it on my list of resolutions for 2012.

Mom answered the phone on the third ring. "Hi, honey. How are you?" Her voice dropped almost to a whisper as she asked, "Anything new with Angela's mother?"

"She's about the same," I said. I had confirmed this with Angela after leaving the police barracks. Finley's suggestion that she was getting worse had not been a ruse, per se. Every day that Regina remained in her coma, chances of a full recovery diminished. "I'll let you know if anything changes. How are you?"

Mom seemed delighted that I asked and proceeded to tell me about a bone spur on her left foot. She'd been to a doctor and they had an X-ray planned and she might need an outpatient procedure to have it fixed. I murmured acknowledgements as she spoke, eying the refrigerator from across the kitchen. I had some turkey left from Thanksgiving. Maybe half a cup of stuffing. Ooo, and gravy! Salivating like Pavlov's pooch, I tucked the cell phone between my shoulder and my ear and crossed the room, placing the desired foodstuffs on the counter. The turkey smelled…interesting, but appeared salvageable. Gravy fixes a cornucopia of ills, I reasoned. I found a clean plate in the cabinet beside the sink and dumped all the food on it, popping the whole thing into the microwave.

I gradually became aware that my mother had stopped speaking and I froze. Dimly, I had the impression that she had asked me a question, but I had no idea about what. Something to do with her bone spur, maybe? "Nnnooo?" I answered hesitantly.

"Really?" she asked, sounding surprised. "You called just to talk to me?"

"Of course," I said, hoping the smile in my voice covered my backpedaling. "I always enjoy our talks!" Mom made a humming sound that sounded unconvinced. "Though," I added, "if Dad's around, I probably should say hi to him too."

"I'll put him on," my mother said mildly. "He's in the living room, hold on." As she carried the phone to my father she asked, "Obviously you can't really plan yet, but are you and Angela still coming for Christmas dinner?"

"That's the plan, as far as I know. Like you said, can't really plan at this point. I'll let you know."

"I appreciate it," she said. "Here's your father."

"Thanks, Mom," I said, quickly adding, "I hope your foot feels better. Love you."

"Love you, too, honey," my mother replied, her own voice smiling.

"Yeah?" my father asked a moment later.

"Hey, Dad," I said.

"Ian," my father replied.

I smiled. "Swing and a miss," I responded.

"Eh, fifty-fifty chance. What's up, Pat?"

"Angela's asked me to poke around a little into the attack on her mother. I probably need to take a couple days off to do so."

"You clear it with that detective?" Dad asked.

"Finley, yeah," I said. I gave him a brief synopsis of my visit to the State police. "I'm just going to touch base with the family, see if I can stir anything up. I don't know if it will lead anywhere, but maybe it will make them feel a little better."

"Yeah, maybe," my father conceded. "Just watch your step. You're close to the family and you have a tendency to be a bull in a china shop sometimes. Don't go screwing things up with Angela or her family in the process."

"I will be the epitome of discretion and empathy," I assured him.

His hum of response was as devoid of belief as my mother's had been. "Just watch your step, kid," he said.

"Always," I agreed. After a pause, I asked, "So…that time off?"

"That's fine by me. Save the company some money," he said dismissively. I frowned. I hadn't thought of that. But I supposed I had enough in the bank to skate by for now. "I'm surprised you didn't ask sooner."

"What can I say? My commitment to the family business knows no bounds." I grinned.

"Uh huh. That all you need?"

"That's it."

"Alright. Be careful. Stay in touch. Let me know if you need anything."

"Will do. Bye, Dad."

"See ya, kid." The line went dead and my microwave beeped. As I ate dinner, I considered my approach. There really only seemed one way to start.

The next morning I sat vigil with Anthony and Angela at Regina's bedside. They were on a first name basis with Megan, a hefty woman in her thirties with short-cropped blonde hair and a pleasant smile. She'd been Regina's nurse for the two days she had been in the hospital so far. Nurses are often underappreciated, not only for all that they do within their job description, but for the extra steps they take to make the hospital stay a little less sucky for the patients and their families. Megan's smile brightened the room and, from what I could tell, comforted my girlfriend and her father.

About mid-morning, Anthony groaned and climbed to his feet. I glanced up from the Agatha Christie book I was reading. Angela was doing a crossword. In pen. Brave woman, she. "I'm going to stretch my legs for a bit," Tony announced. "Patrick, why don't you come with me?" Angela gave me a nod and I stood and followed her father from the room, ducking my head instinctively as we passed through the door. It was tall enough to accommodate my height but its width gave the illusion of being shorter. And I've banged my head enough over the years.

We paused by the nurse's station to let Megan know we'd be back in a few minutes and continued on to the elevator lobby. There was a backless bench with naugahyde seats by a window looking out over the parking lot. Three vending machines – one soda, one chips and candy, and one "frozen treats" – hummed softly along the wall opposite the elevators. The lobby was empty. Anthony pushed the down button.

"Angie says you got the go ahead to look into the attack," he said, leveling his gaze at me. He looked tired, older than he had a few days before. Though he had been home to shower and change, I suspected sleep had eluded him.

"In a way," I acknowledged. I didn't feel comfortable elaborating, and suddenly I had a glimmer of Finley's point of view – the cold truth was Tony was a reasonable suspect. Playing my cards close to the vest seemed appropriate, in spite of my relationship with his daughter and my friendship with him. My stomach tasted sour at the circumspection nonetheless. "I'm allowed to investigate within reason."

"Well, feel free to ask me anything you want. You can't ask me anything the police already haven't. I know the spouse is always the main suspect, and they seem convinced I had something to do with it." The elevator dinged and the doors opened. A woman in her forties was standing in the corner of the car, wiping her eyes with a tissue as the man beside her held her stoically. I gave him a grim nod of acknowledgement as we boarded. We rode the three floors to the lobby in silence.

From there I allowed Anthony to lead the way down the hall towards the cafeteria and continued the conversation. "Can you walk me through that night again?" I asked. I tried not to sound apologetic, but it crept into my voice anyway. "I know you've told it a few times already but, now that you've had a few days to let it sink in, maybe you'll remember some detail you hadn't before."

Tony's tone was neutral as he explained, "Not much to tell. We got home from shopping and were carrying the bags into the house. We were talking and laughing and she was about to hug me when she was shot twice."

"And you still don't remember anything about the shooter?"

He shrugged. "I remember hearing the shots, and I think I heard him running away afterward. I have the impression it was someone pretty solid, probably dressed in black, but I never looked at him directly really. I was focused on Regina. I think he must have been hiding in the cluster of pine trees between our house and the neighbor."

"I'm sure the police have talked to your neighbors already."

"Probably," Tony agreed. "They haven't really given me an update." We were moving casually through the administrative section of the hospital now. Offices for billing agents, health care advocates and meeting rooms. I pictured teams of doctors in white coats using the whiteboard at the front of the meeting room to diagnose a critically ill patient. It was possible I watched too much television. The rooms were probably used for meetings with insurance agents and pharmaceutical reps. The cafeteria was ahead and that seemed to be our destination.

"You didn't happen to notice anyone following you while you were shopping, or on the way home? Anything suspicious?" I asked.

"Everything seemed perfectly normal," Tony assured me. "At least until the shots were fired."

I made a clucking sounds with my tongue. "And you say Regina was getting ready to hug you?"

"Yeah," Anthony replied. He smiled wistfully. It was a disturbing look on the ruddy face of a man who intimidated me. "Things had been going better for us for a few days. We had been joking about something stupid and when she stopped abruptly and turned in front of me putting her arms around me. For no reason. Just like we sometimes did when we were young and in love." His voice rumbled.

"I know that feeling," I smiled. Tony nodded. When the moment passed, I asked more seriously. "It makes me wonder, though. I don't know how to ask this delicately but…is there any chance that you were the intended target?"

Tony stopped walking and looked at me. The cafeteria was a few paces away. From here it looked closed. "What do you mean?" he asked, his voice sharp as broken glass.

"Just that. Maybe someone was gunning for you and Regina stepped in front of you at just the wrong moment."

Tony was silent as he stared at me, but I could tell he was rolling the idea around in his mind. He frowned and continued walking. I fell into step beside him. We reached the cafeteria. It *was* closed between breakfast and lunch. We continued walking. The hallway ahead of us was deserted, as though the cafeteria was the last rest stop on a long and desolate road. Finally Tony spoke. "Patrick, you and I share a fraternal bond. Masonically, we are Brothers, bound by our obligations to the Craft. Do you remember those obligations?"

I didn't let the apparent change in topic throw me. I nodded. "For the most part. Maybe not verbatim. Though I'm getting better with the ritual."

"Do you remember the part in the Third Degree obligation, about keeping the secrets of a Brother when communicated as such?" he asked.

"I do," I replied. I wasn't sure I liked where this was going. "I believe that only applies to non-criminal activity though, if that's where you're getting at." The hallway was only dimly lit. Every other light was out. At the far end of the hall was a fire exit door leading outside, the wintry light illuminating that end of the hall. But here, we were in partial darkness.

"Don't worry," he said. "I'm not confessing to a crime." A grunt. "At least not this one, I guess. In all honesty, it's probably irrelevant. And, if it *is* relevant, it'll probably come out anyway. I just don't want it coming from you."

"If it has nothing to do with the case, I promise it will be like I never heard it," I assured him.

He scowled, his face hidden in the hallway's shadows. Finally he shrugged. "That'll have to be good enough," he said. "You're practically family, and I trust your discretion."

We reached the end of the hall. There was a small waiting room and an abandoned reception desk that bore a sign directing errant patients to the information desk in the main lobby, down the hall through which we had just passed. The room was lit solely by the pale glow seeping in from outside and the illuminated exit sign over the door. He sat in a hard plastic chair and I sat across from him.

"I've come a long way from where I started as a boy, growing up in the city," Tony explained. "My parents were good people, first generation immigrants from the old country, eager to make a better future for their family. And for the most part, they succeeded. I went to college at nineteen and eventually settled up here. But for a while in my youth I ran with some…connected people." He had been looking down at his hands as he spoke. He raised his eyes to me.

"Connected?" I asked.

He sighed. "Do I need to spell it out for you, Patrick?" I shrugged. "They were party of the family." I continued to give him a blank stare. I remembered my father's suggestion, but I needed to hear the words for myself. "The *Mafioso*?" he finally said with a testy tone.

I nodded, keeping my face and tone non-judgmental. "Not an uncommon choice in that situation," I granted him.

"I was never really involved deep with anything serious. Rode along a bit. More often than not, I had to sit in the car, be a lookout. It was only a couple years, between the age of fifteen and when I left for school. Towards the end I got to do a little more…hands on enforcement stuff. And I found I didn't have a taste for it. I liked the *idea* of the adventure more than the activity itself, I guess." He sat back, folded his hands behind his head, spoke to the ceiling. "At any rate I was a real low-level player, never even got close to anyone important. Which, in retrospect, is a good thing, Made it easier to get out. But I have…stayed in touch with one of the guys I ran with. A guy who may still be actively involved."

"Someone who, for some reason, may have

wanted you or Regina out of the picture?" I asked. I wondered if Angela knew any of this. It was a moot point. I'd promised my silence and I would honor that. We all did foolish things when we were younger; all that really matters is who we are today. Though this was bigger than shoplifting a pack of gum or getting high behind the school, I still knew Anthony to be a good man. I reminded myself of that like a mantra.

He shook his head. "That's the thing. I don't believe so. Really, it's just one guy. Vito Denato. And I only talk to him once in a great while and I can't imagine I've given him any reason to turn on me. We usually talk about baseball, for crying out loud. He's a Yankees fan. I like the Mets. I keep hoping for another Subway Series so we can get a rematch after 2000. So, I mean, there's no reason for this to be relevant."

The hesitation in his voice was palpable. "Then why bring it up?" I asked quietly.

"Because he called me two days ago," Tony replied, shifting in his seat. "Not long after you and Angie got to the hospital, right after Regina's attack. He said that he was…in town. On business."

My eyebrows slid up my forehead. "Oh? Well, that's a bit of a coincidence."

"My thoughts exactly."

"What was the conversation about? Did Vito

sound threatening?" I asked, though I really hoped that, if he had, Tony would have brought this up to the police before now.

"Not at all. Wanted to know if I wanted to grab dinner. It was late but you know these guys from New York. It's the city that never sleeps. I told him about Regina and he seemed genuinely surprised and expressed his sympathies."

"Had he met her?" I asked.

Tony shook his head. "No. Didn't really want those worlds to cross, you know what I mean? But I'd told him all about her."

"Anything else from the conversation?"

"Nothing I remember. He expressed his sympathy." A smile fleeted across Tony's face. "He offered to stay in town for a few days and help 'take care of' the guy who did it. I told him that wasn't necessary."

"Good choice," I agreed. "So really, it's just the timing of the call that's suspicious. Far as you know there's no reason to believe he was involved."

"I can't think of one, no," Tony agreed.

I considered. "Coincidence or not, it sounds pretty unlikely. I'll keep him in mind if nothing else pans out but I don't think I need to mention him to the police at this point." I knew I was walking a fine line. Finley would want any lead I found, regardless of how unlikely. "Maybe I should talk to him, though? Just to be sure."

Anthony gave a curt shake of his head. "Out of the question. If he didn't do it, there's no reason for him to know I gave up his name, or even considered him a suspect. And if he *did* do it, well..." He clapped me on the shoulder and said with a half-smile, "I'm sure you can take care of yourself, Patrick. But not against a professional. Vito wouldn't hesitate to put two in you, too, to keep you silent. I wouldn't want that on my conscience."

I gave him an understanding nod. "I'll keep him in mind but I won't speak to him unless it appears to be absolutely necessary." Even as I said it, I knew I'd need to cover all my bases. But I wasn't comfortable telling him that. Circumspection.

It didn't help that, between the next two topics, I couldn't decide which was going to be more awkward. I took a breath and plunged forward.

"I appreciate you trusting me with that information, Tony. And I promise as much discretion as I can muster. In the same spirit of discretion, I need to ask this. At Thanksgiving, Regina seemed pretty convinced that you were having an affair." He stared at me. "Was there any truth to that?"

Tony's jaw clenched. I saw his chin waggle as he

ground his teeth. Finally, he said, "The police asked me about the argument we had. I didn't tell them the full gist of it. I left out Regina's allegations."

"But, were they true?" I pressed.

Slowly he nodded and said, "At the time…yes." He held up his hands defensively and quickly added, "But it's over, I assure you. It was a brief and stupid fling and I broke it off about a week before the attack."

I frowned. Against my will, I found my respect for the man diminishing. I knew as well as anyone the temptations that were out there and I was certainly in no position to judge. He seemed more human, less intimidating, as I was exposed to his imperfections. Perhaps, as my girlfriend's father, I'd simply built his pedestal a smidge too tall.

"I should talk to her," I said.

"No!" Tony was emphatic. It was starting to become a pattern – give me a lead and then prohibit me from following it! "I did enough damage to her, I won't have her dragged into this."

I clasped my hands in front of me and lowered my voice, speaking to him mildly. It was a tactic Angela had taught me, which she'd picked up from a psychology class. Defuse the argument, force the other person to remain calm by remaining calm yourself.

"Tony," I said reasonably, "think for a moment. You broke it off with her a week before your wife was shot. You said yourself you couldn't identify the shooter. We're just assuming it was a man. There's no reason it couldn't have been a jilted lover."

Tony's eyes widened. He seriously hadn't considered that. I continued, "And when it comes down to it, if she's not involved, who would you rather have talking to her? Me? Or Detective Finley?"

Tony wanted to dispute my case. I saw him wrestle with it internally. But in the end he conceded with a bowed head, looking down at the floor. I felt like dirt for reducing this proud man to such a humbled state and had to remind myself that it was his actions, not my words, that had led to this.

"Sarah," he muttered. "Sarah Ooi." He gave me her phone number and explained, "She's the receptionist at my doctor's office. Just...just be kind to her, would you? She was hurt when I broke it off."

I assured him I'd be as gentle as a summer breeze. I was touched by his compassion for her.

"One more awkward topic," I told him, "and I think we can be done after that."

"Thank God for that," Tony said with a weak smile. I empathized. This was harder than either of us chose to admit out loud.

"I doubt this has any bearing on the shooting," I said, "but….what happened with Wayne and Angela?"

Tony's wide, usually ruddy face, paled. I found it telling that we had spoken of his past with the mob and his illicit affair, but neither of those subjects had caused him to react so extremely.

"You're right," Tony said tonelessly. "It has nothing to do with the shooting."

"I'd still like to hear it," I said.

"It's a family matter, Patrick. And, contrary to what I said earlier, you aren't *really* family yet. We don't talk about it." His determination appeared as strong as mine on the matter. Maybe stronger. Perhaps it was good that I'd already weakened him with the other topics.

"Maybe," I said, my voice so neutral that my implication was clear, "that's not the best course of action, given your daughter's current profession."

I had not been aware that Tony could move as quickly as he did but he was out of his seat and towering over me in the blink of an eye. "You're out of line, buddy!" he hissed at me. "I don't care what relationship you have with my daughter, or what fraternal bonds we have! You have no right to blame me for what happened! You understand me? No. Fucking. Right!" He stabbed me in the chest with a thick index finger to emphasize each of his last words.

Angela's advice on defusing a tense discussion had worked well before. But I wasn't having it this time. I got to my feet, forcing him to step back just by standing. At my full height I had a good six or seven inches on him. I stared down at him with a confidence I didn't entirely feel. "I'm not blaming you for what he did to her," I growled back at him. "But I am for what happened *after* that. No treatment, no counseling. Do you know she blamed herself for what happened? For all that time? Because *you* wouldn't talk to her? It just got swept under the rug!"

I heard my voice rising, in pitch and volume. When Angela had told me her tale, I'd absorbed it without much reaction, careful not to give her reason to stop. But it had continued to gnaw at me and, now that I'd broached the topic, I found myself reacting a lot more viscerally than I had expected. Emotions weren't my strong suit and the ones boiling to the surface now startled and scared me.

"We tried!" Anthony shouted at me. At the back of my mind I was thankful this section of the hospital was deserted. Security would have had to escort us out of the building. "Don't you think we tried? I tried talking to her. Regina tried to talk to her. But she just shut down. She wouldn't give us any details. She would just apologize. My God, all she would do was apologize! Like it was her fault!" He stopped, breathing hard, spittle hanging from his lips as he stared at me wide-eyed, perhaps hearing his own words and, for the first time in sixteen years, realizing what they meant. His beefy lips quivered. "It wasn't her fault," he whispered hoarsely. "We got bits and pieces over the years, enough to figure out most of what happened but, by God, it wasn't her fault. We tried to explain that to her. We wanted her to understand. But we barely understood it ourselves!"

He slumped back into a chair. I remained standing, but allowed my shoulders to relax.

"As a man, as a father and a husband," he said, his voice a low and phlegmy, "you're supposed to take care of your family. Provide for them, protect them." He took a deep shuddering breath. "And I failed her. I left her alone with a man I thought we could trust and he…he…"

"He raped her," I said quietly. It pained me to see my friend too broken to say the words.

Tony nodded. "And I felt so powerless. I couldn't take away her pain, her guilt, her shame. And Regina. God, Regina, for all her great characteristics, has always been such a private person. I let her talk me out of sending Angie to therapy. The classic 'what will the neighbors think' argument. Maybe if I'd pressed the issue, if we'd sent her sooner. Maybe she…" He shrugged and looked up at me. His eyes were bloodshot but I couldn't tell if he'd actually shed a tear. "Maybe she wouldn't be a stripper now," he conceded.

I relented, resting a hand on the man's shoulder. "For what it's worth, she's an excellent dancer and the industry hasn't hurt her at all. And, don't forget. If she wasn't dancing, she and I would never have met."

Tony gave a snort and a nod. "Then we probably wouldn't be having this conversation."

"Probably not," I agreed. I sat beside him again and we commiserated in silence for a few minutes about the young woman we both adored more than life itself.

"The trauma shaped her," he said at last. "It made her stronger. It could just as easily have broken her. Maybe it did inside. I'm sure she has insecurities. But she's shown so much resilience. As though she came to realize that, if she survived that, she could survive anything."

It was the flip side of the story Angela had relayed to me. I guess it was all a matter of perspective. Truth, at least about squishy topics that are open to interpretation, is often dependent upon one's perspective.

"And you and Regina haven't had any contact with Wayne since…it happened?" I asked. "That must have been difficult on her. He *is* her brother."

"There's been some occasional contact. We made a point of keeping him and Angela separated so she wouldn't be subjected to it, but Regina talked to him every six months or so. She'd go visit or we would meet him for dinner once in a great while. It's not that we didn't believe what had happened or that we excused what he had done. But he's her only brother. She forgave him sooner than I did. I don't think either of us ever forgot it though. Also, he has a daughter, Tanya, about a year younger than Angie. They were closer when they were younger, before everything happened. So we'd let her come up and stay for a week or two during the summers, or take her on vacation with us. But no, for the most part he was kept at arm's length."

"She seemed surprised to see him when he first came to the hospital," I acknowledged.

"Yeah. I should have given her a head's up but everything was such a blur that night." Tony let out a long, lip-vibrating sigh. "It's not easy being a father, Patrick," he said. "You'll find out some day, I'm sure." Obviously, he was not yet aware of my reproductive insufficiencies. "Daughters are especially difficult. Russell presented his own challenges, of course. Still does. But women are a complete mystery to me. My own wife and daughter included."

"Heard," I agreed with a nod of the head.

"You try to do right by your children. You give them everything you can, you love them through all the excruciating crap they put your through growing up, you sacrifice for them. And they take it for granted. It's not appreciated. They don't understand you anymore than you understand them." To my surprise, he smiled. "Then one day, something happens. They aren't a child anymore. They've grown up, matured. They start to get it, start to recognize that you were always there for them. And that's a great feeling as a parent. Knowing that, whatever happened over the last twenty plus years, somehow you got them all through and they turned out okay."

He continued to lean forward on his knees, but he turned his head to look at me. "I've had that feeling with Angie for a while now. Since you convinced her to start talking to us again last year. I don't like her dancing, but I understand it better and I understand her decisions are not always going to be the same as what I would choose. But I can relate to her now, on a personal level. I don't know if we were right or wrong to keep her out of therapy after she was…raped." It was an effort, but a victorious one, for him to squeeze out the word. "But, maybe, in the long run those decisions balance out. She's smart, talented, strong, and she will be successful in her career. She turned out okay."

"Yes, she did," I agreed. "You and Regina did a great job." I didn't wholly agreed with his perspective. Angela had fled her mother's hospital room in fear when she saw Wayne. There were obviously some maladjusted aspects to her personality still, which may have been smoothed out with some help when she was younger. But he was seeking absolution. Or at least forgiveness and compassion. And he had a point. She was all the things he described and more.

Turning back to business, I said, "Why don't you head back to Regina's room, spend some time with your daughter? I'll give Sarah Ooi a call and see if I can stop by this afternoon."

Tony nodded and we stood. He shook my hand with a firm grasp. "Thank you, Patrick," he said, "for everything you're doing, and have done, for my family."

"I wouldn't have it any other way," I assured him. He departed, disappearing down the dimly lit hallway and I made my call.

Chapter Eleven

Sarah Ooi's voice was laced with doubt as I explained who I was and what I wanted but she grudgingly agreed to see me that afternoon. Since I had some time, I decided to drive to Raymertown first and take a quick look around the scene of the crime.

I'm not sure what I expected to find. Shell casings with the attacker's fingerprints? A cigarette stub tainted with his DNA? A receipt from a convenience store down the road, perhaps, where the clerk would be able to provide a video of the assailant buying a Snickers™ bar? No doubt the police had already done their due diligence. But I needed to feel as though I was doing something.

I parked in the long driveway of the Button's house, got out of my car and glanced around. The house sat back from the road about a hundred feet or so and was separated from the houses on either side by two rows of tall pine trees with interlocking branches. There was the flagstone path that led from the driveway to the front door. We hadn't had much snow this year yet, and today was already in the forties, so the ground was damp and muddy with just a smattering of snow and ice in the more shaded areas. The entire front yard, including the walkway, had been surrounded by a barrier of yellow police tape. The lawn was crisscrossed with footprints from the police investigation. I wondered if there had been enough snow on the night of the attack that the gunman had left traceable footprints. If that was the case, hopefully the police followed up on it, because any trace had been obliterated by now.

I stepped over the tape, wondering whether or not I could justify my presence within the barrier to Detective Finley, if I needed to. I was pretty sure he'd be pissed. I glanced around, didn't see any witnesses and walked slowly along the flagstone path, keeping an eye on the trees across the lawn. When I reached the place that I estimated Regina had stood when she was shot, I stopped and scanned the tree line. A few of the trees had disappeared behind the corner of the house. I identified the ones that still had a clear line of sight and made a mental note before crouching down and examining the ground. There was not much to see. Melting ice, mud, dirty footprints and one piece of the path that was tarnished a dark rusty color, no doubt from the blood that had been spilled here. I grabbed an orange traffic cone I had borrowed from Balla's out of the trunk of my car and placed it in the spot where Regina had been shot. Then I crossed to the tree line.

At the edge of the trees I turned and confirmed I could still see the cone. I tilted my head, crouched down and duckwalked my way under the hanging branches, taking up a position in the mulch beside the nearest trunk and looked back at the path again. At full height, even for a normal sized person, the low hanging branches would have obscured the line of sight, making the shot more difficult. The same to be true for the other five or six trees in the row. The shooter, then, must have been crouched, perhaps braced by a trunk. I'm sure the police had reached that same conclusion. Hopefully it helped them more than it did me.

Much of the foot traffic was centered around the third tree from the road. I don't know how they determined that this is where the shooter had stood – probably something to do with trajectories and trigonometry. No doubt the ground had been picked clean of anything resembling evidence.

My back was beginning to ache from all the crouching and squatting I had to do to avoid getting conked on the head by a branch. Looking up to make sure the coast was clear, I slowly stood to my full height. My back thanked me.

I don't know how I saw it. There was virtually no direct sunlight under the boughs, only the diffuse kind, filtered through what must be millions of pine needles. The hair was almost the same color brown as the rough bark in which it was lodged. If I hadn't happened to look right at the tree trunk as I stood, I never would have noticed the three hairs stuck to the tree. There was no way of knowing whose hair it was; it could just as easily have belonged to one of the investigating officers. But it was still worth looking into. I slip slided across the muddy yard to my car and found an empty plastic sandwich bag. There were times I was grateful that I was remiss in cleaning out my car once in a while. At the tree again, I carefully inverted the bag over my hand, plucked the hairs free from the bark, and returned the bag to normal, sealing the hairs, untouched by my hands, inside.

"Excuse me, young man? Are you with the police?" a voice asked behind me. I spun, startled, nearly clocking myself in the forehead with a branch. I crouched and made my way out from under the tree, to the opposite side of the tree line, where an elderly woman was standing, leaning on a wooden cane that was slowly sinking into the muddy ground. She had a head of white hair under a wool hat, piercing blue eyes and faint English accent. She gazed at me placidly as I extracted myself from the pines.

"Actually," I confessed, "not exactly. I'm Angela Button's boyfriend." I tilted my head and said, "In fact, I think we've met. Miss Elpram, if I remember?"

She gave me a knowing smile and said, "Yes, of course, I recognize you, Mr. Brady. Now that you aren't hiding behind so many branches." We smiled at each other benignly. "But what in Heaven's name were you doing under there?"

"I was just poking around, hoping maybe I could find something the police overlooked," I explained. I had casually stuck the baggie in my pocket on the way out of the trees. "Angela's worried the police might go after her father. I guess I was hoping to find something to point them in the right direction."

"Well," Miss Elpram said, "if they suspect him, I hope you are successful. I don't believe Mr. Button would ever lay a hand on her. He's such a good-hearted man, even if he isn't the most loyal husband. But, if anything, I would have thought she'd attack him, not the other way around."

"Oh?" I asked. I never would have expected either of them to attack the other.

"Well, she's always had a temper, you see," Miss Elpram said, pursing her lips and looking away. "But, here, listen to me gossiping." Her eyes twinkled at me as she added, "You know, I suppose, that he had a…a mistress? If the police learn that, it will only make him look worse in their eyes." She gave me a long, penetrating gaze.

"In fact, I'm going to speak with her this afternoon," I agreed. "And yes, it would not be in his best interest for the police to find out. May I ask how you know about it?"

"Oh, he keeps odd hours. And my daughter's friend Rhonda saw him laughing and talking with a young Asian woman last Halloween. She mentioned it to me at church that weekend." Where would the world be without the gossip mills of elderly women?

"Well, like you said, I don't believe Anthony would have done this. Hopefully we can prove his innocence before the police find out about the affair."

Miss Elpram smiled and said, "They shan't hear it from me."

I glanced at my watch and said, "If you'll excuse me, Miss Elpram, I better get going for my meeting with the woman in question."

"Good luck, Mr. Brady," she told me. I thanked her, walked around the line of trees and across the Buttons' yard to my car. When I pulled out of the driveway and down the road, Miss Elpram was still standing in her yard, watching me go.

Sarah Ooi lived in a housing community in Cohoes comprised of twisty, winding roads, cul-de-sacs and crowded townhouses with shared lawns. I rang the bell and stood on the stoop, hands in my pockets, face turned towards the sun with my eyes closed. I knew man-made global warming was a myth, but if I could have winters like this all the time, I was willing to pump chlorofluorocarbons into the air as fast as possible, polar bears be damned.

I was just debating taking off my lightweight jacket when the door opened, bringing me back to the present.

The woman before me was a hair over five feet tall, slim with dark hair and almond shaped eyes that were startlingly green. She was obviously not full-blooded Asian. I guessed her to be around her mid-thirties. Her gaze was not openly hostile, but her eyes were cold as jade.

"Ms. Ooi?" I asked, giving her a bright ingratiating smile.

"It's Miss," she said sullenly, "but call me Sarah. I assume you're Patrick?"

I confirmed that and she let me in, leading me the kitchen where she gestured to a stool beside an island with a laminate top. She offered me a cup of tea, but the offer didn't sound sincere and I declined. She shrugged, poured one for herself and took the stool across the island from me.

"Thank you for seeing me," I said.

She held up a well-manicured hand. "I'm doing it for Tony," she answered. Her voice was like broken glass wrapped in silk. "He said to expect your call and asked me to cooperate." I hid my surprise. He must have called her immediately after leaving me at the hospital. Either that or her called her before we spoke, in which case he knew he would be giving me her name and his resistance was only for show. "I don't owe him anything, but I don't need to be a bitch about it either. Go ahead, ask what you need to."

I blinked, grateful for her directness. I wouldn't have to tiptoe around the elephant in the room. "I've heard that you and Tony had a...relationship?"

She gave a single sharp laugh. "I suppose you could call it that," she said. "I think I was in more of a relationship than he was. To his credit, his family always came first. But if they didn't have plans on a given night, or he was able to get away for a few hours, he made the effort to see me. We had fun together. He didn't want to go out in public at first, but eventually he agreed to the occasional dinner or movie, usually somewhere out of the immediate area. And, yes, we had sex." She gave a sly smile and reiterated, "A *lot* of sex."

"Probably more detail than I need," I murmured trying to scrub the mental image from my brain. "How did you meet?"

She gave a sigh, tilted her head back reminiscing. "I work at his doctor's office. Last summer he was having some blood pressure issues and was coming in about once every week or two to have his pressure monitored and tracked. We spoke and laughed during his visits and, when asked about any outside stressors, he mentioned his marital problems, how he felt Regina was growing distant. He also was having issues with his kids. I sympathized. Nothing would have come of it, though, if we hadn't bumped in to each other at the gas station about a month later. We got talking. He seemed pretty down. When he invited me for coffee, I accepted. She called during our visit and he told her he was grabbing a beer with some friends. As far as I know, that was the first lie he told her about us. We ended up at one of those pay-by-the-hour motels in Latham. When he left, I knew that we would be together again. And that I'd always be his "other' woman."

She sipped her tea for a reflective moment before turning her eyes toward me, awaiting the next question.

"How long were you together?"

The amused smile twisted and she set her teacup down with a faint clink. "Just short of four months," she answered dully. "It ended almost like it began. We went for coffee and he explained that Regina had gone after him at Thanksgiving." Her eyes slid towards mine. "I guess you were probably there for that. Part of it anyway. Anyway, he was overcome with guilt. Our...dalliance aside, he's always been a good man and his family will always come first to him. He told me he was going to try and make things work out with her. And to do that he couldn't afford any other distractions." Another bitter bark of laughter. "That's all I really was to him, I think. A distraction."

"That must have been painful," I said compassionately.

She shrugged brusquely. "I knew what I was getting into. Married men are always going to have their attention divided. That's one reason I've never gotten married myself; I need my space. A married man has to go home at night and I can recapture my solitude. But Tony...I have to admit, I really felt something with him."

"So then this wasn't the first time you've been, forgive me, the other woman?"

She pinned me with an emerald stare. "I don't believe that's relevant."

I let it slide. "I suppose I should ask. Where were you Saturday night?"

"You mean, was I taking jealous potshots at my ex-lover's wife?" she asked. "No."

I didn't sincerely suspect her of being the shooter. Her hair didn't match the ones in my pocket, either in length or color. And it seemed as though, if she wanted to attack Regina, she would have done so in a much more direct fashion. And, glancing around her Spartan apartment, I doubted she had the means to hire someone to do the job for her. Nevertheless, I wanted more than just her denial. I waited, watching her patiently.

"If you must know," she continued after a moment, "I was out on the town. I cared about Tony, but I'm not the type to sit home and cry over a man. I put myself back out there."

"I see," I answered drily. "And was anyone there to confirm your story?"

"A lady never kisses and tells, Patrick," Sarah murmured. With a smirk she added, "But I'm not exactly a lady. I did meet a nice man whose wife was out of town last weekend. We went to his place, a cute little apartment in downtown Troy."

She stopped and I asked, "Do you have his name?"

"I wish I did," she said, "but we weren't looking for anything long-term." She regarded me with mischievous eyes as she took a long sip from her cup.

It was a weak alibi but I let it slide. If need be, the police could canvass the bars to get confirmation of her presence. She was an unlikely suspect and it wasn't a good use of my time to pursue her alibi.

"Did you ever meet Regina Button?" I asked.

"I never had the pleasure," she said.

"Have you seen or talked to Tony since you split up?"

"Only when he called this morning to let me know you'd be contacting me."

"And I don't suppose you have any idea who the shooter might be?"

"I haven't a clue," she confirmed.

I stood. I thanked her for her time. She remained seated, holding her cup with both hands, deterring me from attempting to shake hands. I saw myself out. She watched me go.

On my way back to the hospital, I stopped by the State Police barracks. Detective Finley was just walking out as I arrived. He glanced at his watch and gestured me inside irritably.

At his desk, he said, "I've got five minutes. Speak!"

I pulled the sandwich bag from my pocket and slid it across the blotter to him. He frowned at it and then decided he'd be better off frowning at me. "Explain," he demanded.

I related an abbreviated version of how I came to discover the hairs stuck to the tree. As I spoke, I watched his jaw working. My guess that he'd be pissed about my trespassing beyond the police tape appeared accurate.

He picked up the bag and eyed it warily. "Did you touch these?" he asked gruffly.

I told him how I used the inverted bag to retrieve the hairs. He nodded a grudging approval of my caution.

"Probably won't pan out," he said. "There were a lot of people traipsing in and out of those trees during the investigation." His tone, though gruff, held a hint of reluctant appreciation. Possibly even respect, though that might be overstating the situation.

"Worth a shot," I said. "At any rate, I promised to pass along any potential leads I came across, so that's what I'm doing."

"I'm glad to see being true to your word," Finley said as he toyed with the plastic bag. He squinted at it. "Are those bread crumbs?" he asked.

"It was all I had available," I said with a shrug.

The detective rolled his eyes and tossed the bag onto his blotter. "We may have a lead ourselves," Finley admitted slowly.

"Oh?"

"Had a guy in this morning. Nervous type,

obviously didn't really want to get involved with the police. Said he had been out walking his dog Saturday night. As he was passing by the Button place, his dog started barking at something. The guy says he thought he saw someone creeping along the trees. He was too far away to get a good view, but he figured it was a short guy. Said he didn't want to get involved and got out of there but, when he heard about the shooting, he decided he ought to speak up."

"Just another concerned citizen," I commented.

Finley shrugged. "Better than the ones who don't want to get involved no matter what."

"So your list of suspects has been narrowed down to 'a short guy'?" I asked. A smirk twitched my lips.

Finley's unblinking eyes were sharp as he glared at me. "I don't see you sauntering in here with the perp's name, smart guy! It's a process!" He waited a beat, then sighed. "I didn't say it was a good lead." He picked up the small plastic bag again and said, "Hopefully your little find will help us narrow it down further. I'll get this sent to the folks at the lab and see what they can come up with."

"Let me know?" I asked.

Detective Finley grunted. "Yeah, I suppose. You earned it."

The man was positively warming up to me. We'd

be BFF's in no time!

"Thank you, Detective," I said, standing. "I know you've got to be somewhere, so I'll let you go."

"Mr. Brady," Finley said in a low voice, stopping me in mid stand. I looked at him. "Any other leads you've dug up?"

I thought of Sarah Ooi, and of Vito Denato. I made my face as impassive as possible as I shook my head. Truthfully I said, "Nope, nothing I want to share."

"If you impede my case by holding anything back," Finley cautioned, "I'll make sure you're locked up and out of my way until my investigation is over. Do we understand each other?"

I resumed standing. "Perfectly," I agreed.

I left, feeling Detective Finley's steady stare sizzling against the sweat running down my back.

Chapter Twelve

The next day, Thursday the fifteenth, started out as most of the previous days. Angela and I met Tony at St. Luke's. We sat, ate a light breakfast – today was donuts and coffee – and talked about inconsequential matters while we waited for Regina to wake up. I wondered, only to myself, how long this cycle could continue before Angela and Tony finally started missing a day. If she was going to be in a coma for a long while, eventually, they would have to get on with their lives. Wouldn't they? I wondered what I would do if it was Angela laying there.

I had a plan for today. A goal anyway. Finley's vague description of the suspect spotted by the dog walker had stuck with me and I wanted to pursue it. But before I did that, there was something I wanted to ask Tony.

After we finished our donuts, Angela excused herself to go to the bathroom. I leaned in towards Tony and lowered my voice as I broached the topic. "I spoke with Sarah yesterday," I said. "Thank you for smoothing the way with her." He acknowledged the thanks, and the implication that I knew that he had spoken to her before I did, with a tilt of his chin. "She said one thing that I wanted to ask you about though. Were you and Regina having marital issues *before* you started having your affair?"

Tony glanced towards the closed bathroom door then whispered, "Truthfully, yes. I think that's what was causing most of my stress at the time. Well, that and Russell of course. But Regina and I had been drifting apart for several months. She just didn't seem…interested anymore. I don't just mean intimately. She just didn't care what I did. Sarah was kind and understanding and listened to my concerns. I'm not blaming Regina, of course, but if I had been getting that kind of attention at home, I never would have strayed."

I nodded. That jibed with Sarah's story. I was going to ask a follow up question but the toilet flushed and, after the brief running of water in the sink, Angela emerged, drying her hands on some brown paper towels. By the time she came out, Tony and I were sitting back again, sipping our coffee and looking innocent. I hoped. I gave her a smile and she gave my cheek a buzz as she passed me, resuming her vigil in the chair beside me.

"Anything new with the investigation?" she asked. Tony and I exchanged a glance. I told them briefly about hairs I'd found and delivered to Detective Finley. I also mentioned they had an incredibly vague description from a possible witness. And I mentioned

I'd spoken to a couple people including Tony's neighbor. I didn't mention Sarah Ooi to Angela.

"Where do you go from here?" Angela asked.

"At this point, my hands are still pretty tied by Detective Finley's orders. I thought I'd try talking to Russ and see if he can provide me anything useful."

Tony made a faint scoffing noise. "Doubtful," he said. "He's only been by to see his mother once since she was admitted. And it's not like he was anywhere near the house when it happened. What kind of information could you possibly get from him?"

Angela looked at me apologetically and agreed, "He's right, Patrick. I love my brother dearly, but he's pretty far removed from this. I don't know why you would talk to him about it."

I was hesitant to reveal my true reasoning – that he was the only one connected with the case that I would describe as a short man. "I won't know until I talk to him, I suppose," I said. I tried to choose my next words carefully. "Obviously he has his issues. Does he…benefit in any way if Regina was dead?"

I hadn't been careful enough. They both got the implication immediately.

"Wait!" Angela said, "Are you saying you suspect Russell of shooting Mom? That's ridiculous!"

"People do unexpected things under the

influence," I said gently.

"He's right," Tony nodded slowly. "It's not out of the realm of possibility."

"Daddy!" Angela demanded, her face aghast. She looked like she wanted to argue but as her father and I watched her placidly, acceptance gradually worked its way across her face. She looked down at her feet, her long auburn hair hiding her face. "I guess it's possible." She looked up at us with a hint of defiance and added, "I still don't believe it though."

"To answer your question," Tony said to me, "Not directly, no. Our wills are pretty simple. Anything happens to Regina or myself, the other spouse gets everything. Neither Russ, nor Angela for that matter, receive anything significant until we've both passed. They know that." Angela nodded confirmation.

I considered. The more this investigation proceeded, the more I realized how awkward it was investigating those who are close to me. Carefully I said, "There *were* two shots. And, if Regina hadn't moved at the last moment, one of them may have hit you."

Tony was silent, thoughtful. Angela's eyes sparkled wetly. "I don't like these questions, Patrick," she whispered.

I took her hand and gave it a reassuring squeeze. "I have to consider all the possibilities, Angie," I told her. "I know you want this to be a random act by some stranger. And maybe it will be. But all I can do right now is talk to the people closest to the situation. And that's mainly you and your family. You knew that when you asked me to look into the shooting."

Angela sighed. A tear dribbled down her cheek. "I know," she said, resting her head on my shoulder. I put my arm around her, inhaling the scent of her hair.

After the moment had passed, Tony shook his head. "The shots were pretty close together," he said. "Russ isn't a marksman of any kind. I can't see him being able to fire at both of us that quickly. Whoever was in those trees was aiming for one of us. Or a skilled shooter. I suppose he could have hired someone. But that probably requires more money than Russ has."

I thought of Russ bumming money from Angela at Thanksgiving and was inclined to agree. "I assume he and Regina were getting along? There was no way he'd benefit somehow other than financially?"

Tony and Angela exchanged a glance, but there didn't seem to be any hidden message passing between them. They both shook their heads. "Regina was probably his biggest supporter," Tony said. "Regardless of his shortcomings, she was his mother after all. He was the typical prodigal son and she would welcome back with open arms any chance she could." He shrugged. "Don't get me wrong. I love my son and I only want the best for him. But she was the one who insisted we help him when we can. If something happened to her, I think he'd see that as a negative."

"He's right," Angela agreed. "Russ has made some dumb decisions in his life, but he wouldn't kill the golden goose. Mom has always had a soft spot for him."

I nodded my understanding. "Maybe nothing will come from talking to him," I said. "But it can't hurt. And at least I'll feel like I'm doing something."

Tony took a small notepad and a pen from his breast pocket and scribbled down a phone number, passing it to me. "Russ's cell phone," he said. "Though I can't guarantee he'll answer, especially this early in the morning."

"Worth a shot," I agreed. "I'll be right back." I took the paper from Tony and made my way out to the lobby of the hospital. Russ's father was right about his son; after four rings, the call went to voice mail.

"Yeah, it's me. Leave a message. Or, you know, don't. Whatever." After the beep, I identified myself and asked him to give me a call. I left the reason for my call out of the message, hoping the omission might encourage him to call me back just out of curiosity. I returned to Regina's hospital room, just as a doctor was entering.

He greeted Tony and Angela with grim familiarity. "Good morning, Doc," Tony greeted him. The two men shook hands. "Think today might be the day?"

The doctor consulted the chart in his hand, running his finger down the page as he read, clucking his tongue. When he spoke, he directed his words at the clipboard rather than the patient's husband. I felt a chill. "As you know, Mr. Button, comas are tricky things. Like we've discussed, most patients recover in a matter of hours or days. I would have liked to see your wife alert and awake by now, but…" He spread his hands suggestively. "Looking at her chart," he continued, "your wife seems to have had a couple bouts of AFib during the night. She's stabilized now. But, I have to be honest." He found the courage to look at a spot over Tony's left shoulder. "I'm not feeling confident about her long term survival at this stage."

Angela let out a faint cry, clutching her father's hand. I took her other one, giving her a squeeze.

Tony was stolid. "What's your best guess for a timeline?" he asked tonelessly.

"Less than a week. Probably not more than a couple days at most," the doctor replied simply. Angela started to cry. Tony straightened his back so stiffly I thought he might snap it. "I'm very sorry."

"You and your staff have done everything you can," Tony assured him.

"We will, of course, make every effort to keep her comfortable."

Tony nodded silently. Angela sobbed. I shifted uncomfortably. The doctor bowed his head and with another murmured apology left us to our grief.

I hugged Angela for a moment while she cried, until she pulled away and held her father instead. I clapped a hand on the older man's shoulder and he nodded his thanks. His eyes glistened but he refrained from crying openly.

Finally, with a long last sniffle, Angela returned to her seat. To me, Tony said, "When you speak to my son, please be sure to let him know that, if he wishes to say good-bye, he should come by the hospital as soon as possible."

"I'll pass it along," I agreed.

As though on cue, my phone rang. I excused myself, stepping out into the hallway so the call didn't intrude on their grief.

"Hey, Jolly Green!" Russ's voice boomed when I answered. "How's it going?" He didn't wait for an answer and continued, "Returning your call. What's up? Sleeping beauty finally wake up from her long winter's nap?" His brashness sounded forced, his voice quavering just a bit.

"Thanks for the quick callback, Sprout," I said, soliciting a raspy chuckle from the shorter man. "Unfortunately, no, she's not awake yet." I took a breath and added, "In fact, the doctor was just telling us she's taking a turn for the worse. Your father says you should probably come visit sooner rather than later."

For a moment, there was silence on the other end of the line. I heard a long sniff then a sound like he was rubbing the tip of his nose brusquely with his hand. I felt guilty for wondering if he was snorting a line of something during our conversation. "Well," he said at last, all trace of frivolity absent from his voice, "that sucks."

"Yeah," I agreed.

"Yeah." He huffed and said, "Tell the old man I'll come by this afternoon. And why couldn't he call me himself and tell me? Or Angie for that matter? Aw, hell, how is Angie? She must be a wreck!"

I glanced towards the door to Regina's room. "She's holding steady for now. I think she's being strong for your father."

"She would be," Russell agreed. "She's a good at taking care of people." He sighed. "Yeah, I'll be by."

"They'd appreciate that, I know," I said. "As for why I called you, it's just a fluke of timing. I actually called for a totally different reason originally. I was hoping we could talk for a few minutes."

"You asking me for permission to marry my sister?" Russell asked, a trace of wryness returning to his voice. "Because your timing really sucks, if so. I'd probably give it to you anyway."

I smiled. "We aren't quite there yet," I answered. "But I appreciate your blessing."

"Yeah, well, you make her happy," he rumbled. "So what's up?"

"I was hoping to talk about the attack on your mother," I said. "But it can wait until you've had a chance to come and see her."

"Yeah, okay," he said. "I don't know what I can do to help but, yeah, sure."

I thanked him and we agreed to meet after his visit. I returned to the hospital room and informed Tony and Angela that Russell would be by in the afternoon. They appeared to have recovered their composure, though Angela was still holding her father's hand. She clutched a crumpled tissue in her free hand.

She smiled up at me sadly. "We're ok," she said, answering the question I didn't know how to ask. "I think we've kind of felt this coming all along. If you want to go, I know you hate hospitals. You can come back this afternoon and talk with Russ."

I gave her a grateful smile. "I'll stop by after lunch," I said. "Let me know if either of you need anything or if anything...changes."

We shared a lingering kiss good-bye and I left the hospital and drove to Balla's. My father's truck was alone in the parking lot when I pulled in so I knocked on his office door and stepped inside.

"What are you doing here?" he asked as I settled into the comfortable guest chair.

"I think I still work here," I answered.

"Did you find out who attacked your girlfriend's mother already?" Dad was eating a banana and tucked the bite into his cheek as he spoke. While he chewed, she used his knife to slather a shmear of peanut butter onto the next section of fruit.

"Not yet," I answered. "I've really got my hands kind of tied with the police limiting who I can talk to on the matter. I don't know if I honestly expect to solve this one, but I think having me doing the legwork reassures Angela. Unfortunately it looks like this may become a murder case, instead of attempted murder, in the near future." I explained about the doctor's visit and his lack of a reassuring prognosis.

My father shook his head. "I'm sorry to hear that. They're good people. You hate to see anything like this happen to a family like that. Or anyone really." He took another bite of banana and repeated the peanut butter slathering process. I agreed. "By the way," Dad continued, "you'll be hearing from someone from Hiram-Austin in the next couple days probably. Scott submitted the applications last night and interview committees were assigned. From what he says, it's going to be a close vote. There's a strong pro-merger faction forming in that Lodge and they know why we're joining. At any rate, make yourself available for the committee so they can vote on the twenty-eighth."

"Will do," I agreed. "I imagine it will be like the interview to join Acacia was?"

My father waggled a hand. "Expect it to be a little more confrontational.," he answered. "Mitch Svenson volunteered to be on both of our committees. I don't know if you've met him yet but he and I go back a ways. He an arrogant prick."

"That Lodge seems to breed that type," I suggested.

My father shrugged and finished his banana, tossing the peel in the garbage can behind his desk. "Breeds or attracts, the end result is the same. Svenson is in favor of the merger, he's been pushing it for a while already. I wouldn't be surprised if he put a bug in the District Deputy's ear that led to this discussion in the first place. Just watch your step with him." I assured him I would. He nodded. "Good. I'm glad you're here. You've got some bills in your inbox we need entered into the computer so I can start planning the cash flow for next month." January and February were always our leanest time in the construction business and had to be prepared for carefully so we could coast through til spring. Fortunately, the milder than normal winter had allowed us to stay busy this year.

"I'll get on that," I said and made a beeline for my office.

The routine and predictability of processing paperwork – some might call it monotony – was therapeutic. I was going through the limited motions I was allowed with the case surrounding Angela's mother and I didn't feel like I was getting anywhere. As I entered the bills we had accumulated in my absence into the computer and put together outgoing invoices, I began to feel in control again, productive. By the end of the day, I felt more confident in my ability to find Regina's attacker, though I still had no clear cut plan.

After work, I returned to St. Luke's and made my way to Regina's room. Angela was sitting beside her mother's bed, holding her hand. She had her head down on the mattress beside her mother's arm, not crying, but obviously exhausted. Anthony Button stood beside his daughter, stroking his wife's hair and looking down at her with resolute sorrow. Russell was pacing the floor at the foot of the bed, cracking his knuckles. As he turned, he looked up and saw me. "Thank God," he declared, "Gulliver's here." Angela and her father turned their eye son me as well.

"How's she doing?" I asked, crossing the room. I shook Russ's diminutive hand and put my arm around Angela who fell into my embrace like a desert wanderer at an oasis.

"Not good," she answered. "She's gone into A-Fib twice more this afternoon, and now her breathing is getting bad."

"Her lungs are starting to fill with fluid," Tony added. "Congestive heart failure." He seemed as out of sorts as I'd seen the man.

"She's dying," Russ stated, his voice edgy. "No one can do anything to stop it. They keep bumping up her morphine to keep her comfortable. Eventually either that or congestion or the A-Fib will kill her. Doesn't matter in the end which one gets her first. I just wish she'd hurry up and go."

"Russell!" Tony growled in a low voice. "That's the last time." I got the impression this opinion had already been expressed more than once.

"Why, Dad?" Russ snapped back. "She's going to die. They've already told us. Probably tonight. It's inevitable. And all this standing around and waiting for it happen is driving me fucking batshit."

"Imagine how those of us who've been sitting here for the last five days are feeling," Angela said. Her eyes were narrowed and her voice dripped with weary sarcasm. I felt the air in the room drop by several degrees.

"That's right, sis, twist the knife," Russell sneered. "Always the good daughter, here keeping Daddy company while you're sitting vigil. I'm just Russ the screw-up junkie, out getting stoned off my ass while his mother lays here dying! Appreciate you pointing that out again!"

Angela raised her head from my chest, glaring daggers at her brother. "If the shoe fits, Russ."

"That's enough!" Tony barked and his children immediately fell silent. "If these are to be your mother's last hours, I will not have them filled with petty bickering. We're all feeling the tension but I'll be damned if we're going to take it out on each other." He pointed a beefy finger at Russell. "Go take a walk, burn off some of that excess energy and attitude you've got."

"I'll come with you," I chimed in. I glanced at Angela to ensure she would be okay in my absence.

She read the concern in my eyes and gave me a faint nod.

"Yeah, fine," Russ said. He headed for the door and only my longer stride enabled me to catch up with him in the hall.

As we made for the elevator lobby, he jerked a thumb over his shoulder and said, "And *that* is exactly why I haven't been here much. Three hours in a room with all that and we're already at each other's throats. I have trouble sitting still and I have trouble with watching people die."

"And apparently you have trouble expressing those feelings constructively," I added.

Russ looked up at me sharply, but bit off his retort. He sighed. "You're probably right." We took the elevator down and followed the same hall I had walked with his father the day before.

"We all handle grief differently," I told him as we walked. I tried not to be obvious as I minced my steps so as not to outpace him.

"That we do," he agreed. He thrust his hands into his pockets as we walked. With that and the scowl on his face, he reminded me of one of the munchkins from the Lollipop Guild. This didn't seem to be the time to mention it.

"So how have you been dealing with it?" I asked.

Russ glanced up at me with a knowing look. "Is that your kinder, gentler way of asking if I've been shooting up all week?"

I shrugged. "I'm aware of your...addiction. And I know that addicts are more prone to use in times of high stress. And I couldn't help but notice the track marks at Thanksgiving." I paused and added, "And I can tell you're high now. Your eyes are bloodshot, you're jittery and you're wearing so much aftershave you smell like a French whore."

We took a few steps in silence. "You're pretty sharp there, Lurch," he said at last. "But not quite sharp enough. I'm clean now. Two weeks yesterday. I'm just tired, and worried about my mother. And I happen to like my aftershave, thank you very much." His voice still held a touch of belligerence.

"Fair enough. Keep up the good work. One day at a time," I told him.

"Yeah, yeah, I know," Russ said with a dismissive wave of his hand. "I've heard all the clichés. The rooms are full of them. Anyway, I used up the money Angela gave me to get my last dose of H. After the family festivities at Thanksgiving, I needed it! But after I finished that packet, I stopped. It was like Thanksgiving was a wakeup call. With all that crap with my parents, it just seemed like a good time to get my shit together again. I've been taking my suboxone as prescribed ever since then." He pulled a strip of medication from his pocket to show me and looked up at me, his jaw jutting out defiantly.

"I believe you," I said. "But I still contend you're high today."

Russell humphed and looked away. We reached the abandoned lobby and sat down. "So, I smoked some pot. Marijuana's a nothing drug! It's just to help me take the edge off my cravings for heroin. I don't know if you've heard but my mother's dying! I should get a fucking medal for not sitting out in my car right now with a needle in my arm!" He gripped the arms of his chair until his stubby knuckles turned white.

"I don't know about a medal," I replied. "But I'm proud of you for staying strong." He seemed surprised by my reaction. "It's not my place to judge you," I said. "I've done plenty of things I'm not proud of. We're only human. And it sounds like you're making an effort to get clean. I hope it works out."

"Well," Russ said, shifting uncomfortably in his seat. His feet didn't reach the floor. "I was really spoiling for an argument there, Bunyan. You kind of took the wind out of my sails."

I smiled. "Good," I said. "Then maybe we can move on to the other topic of discussion?"

"You mean the attack on my mother," Russ

surmised.

"I do. Any thoughts on who might have done it?"

"Well, the old man would have been my first guess if he hadn't been right there with her. Of course, we only have his word that they were walking into the house all happy and shit. No one else saw her get shot. So it could still be him."

"Interesting," I said with a raise of my eyebrows. The thought hadn't occurred to me.

"Why?" Russ asked. "You don't agree? You saw them going at it at Thanksgiving. I'm surprised he didn't plunge a carving knife into her chest then."

"I suppose it's possible," I conceded. "But you seem to be the first person connected with the case that is willing to say so."

Russ shrugged. "I'm sure they have their suspicions about me as well."

Reflecting on the conversation with Tony and Angela that morning, I admitted, "The topic came up."

Russ nodded knowingly. "You know," he said, "I was an A student. Well, B-plus anyway. An Eagle scout, too. Did you know that? I almost joined that Masonic youth group too."

"DeMolay," I inserted. "I was a member for a short time when I was in school."

"Yeah, that. I hold down a job. I donate to charity. Hell, I've even helped a fricking old lady across the street. I'm not a bad guy! But shoot some fricking dope into my veins for a couple years, and suddenly my family decides I'm capable of trying to kill my own mother. Makes me wonder why I bother trying to stay clean. They've already written me off!" He rested his chin on his clenched fist and stared out the window into the dusk. Or perhaps he was studying his own reflection. The winter equinox was a week away, so it was already dark outside even though it wasn't yet five o'clock.

"Angela believes in you," I told him. "She defended you. Your father doesn't even sound like he believes you did it. He just was more accepting of the fact that it was possible, especially if you were under the influence at the time."

Russ snorted. "Under the influence. I told you I been clean for two weeks." His gaze faltered and he added, "Funny thing is, I *was* high that night. Pot again. Good shit, too. My guy called it Big Red. We usually refer to weed as 'bubble gum' so people don't know what we're talking about. Anyway, this Big Red was pretty potent stuff. Knocked me on my ass and I'm no lightweight. No pun intended. Everyone was trying to get ahold of me after my mother was shot and I wouldn't answer the phone cause I was stoned out of my gourd. There's certainly no way I could have been out at my parents' house taking potshots at them."

"I don't suppose you have anyone who can collaborate that?" I asked.

Russ snorted. "Collaborate. You sound like a cop! No, no one I'm willing to throw under the bus. Picked up the bud from my guy around seven. But I'm not going to give you his name and, regardless, I was home alone by the time she was shot."

I steepled my fingers thoughtfully. I believed him and, as Tony had pointed out this morning, I doubted he had the money to hire someone. "I don't suppose you've ever sold drugs as well?"

His eyes narrowed as he looked at me across the dim room. With sky dark now, the only light here came from two illuminated exit signs. "You really *do* sound like a cop," Russ said.

I spread my hands innocently. "I assure you, I'm not."

Russ considered for a moment then said, "I've never sold the hard stuff, no. Pot, sure, from time to time. Maybe some pills And suboxone gets traded between addicts like baseball cards. But, no, I've never been a serious dealer. Why do you ask?"

"I'm wondering if anyone owed you a favor," I answered.

Russ laughed, his wide grin returning. "Oh, that's

droll!" I blinked. I was pretty sure he was using the word ironically. It didn't seem to fit in his mouth. "You think someone owes me enough that they can repay me by shooting my mother?" He laughed again. "Ain't no one out there owes me nothing. If anything it would be the other way around."

"Oh?" I asked casually. "So you could shoot someone if you needed to?"

"Yeah," Russ said with a smirk. "But fortunately I haven't had to. Yet."

"What kind of gun do you have?" I asked.

"It's a .40 caliber subcompact pistol," Russ answered. "Fully licensed, totally legal."

I wasn't sure what kind of gun had shot Regina Button; it occurred to me I ought to find that out. In the meantime, I asked, "Think I could see it?"

"Normally," Russ said, clambering to his feet, "I'd tell you to go screw. But I'm tired of sitting here in the dark with you, and I don't want to go back and deal with the family yet. So, yeah, come on. We'll take a ride over to my place and you can see for yourself." I stood and followed as we walked in silence to his car. As I folded myself into the passenger's seat of the Mini Cooper, he looked over at me and grinned. "We must look like a circus act," he confided. I smiled at the mental image.

It took about fifteen minutes in rush hour traffic to make our way through downtown Troy. We talked idly of inconsequential things. I did ask him when the last time he spoke to his mother had been. "I called her a couple days after Thanksgiving," he said. "The day I decided to get clean again. I wanted her to know what I was doing. She said she was proud of me. I'm not sure she was convinced I could do it, but no one ever is on that first day, especially when you've quit as many times as I have."

Russ's apartment was on the second floor of a three story white building, built into the side of a hill, right on the main drag in South Troy. It wasn't a great neighborhood, but the sidewalk was clean and no one tried to shoot us as we walked from the car to his door.

The apartment was immaculate. I admit to being surprised. Somehow, I expected bed sheets for curtains, dirty dishes laying around and other typical bric-a-brac of a poor, disheartened bachelor with a drug problem. "Nice place," I commented, looking around the large living room. Through a wide arch was a small dining room with a bedroom and a bathroom leading off to one side. At the far end, a door led into the kitchen.

He led the way into the bedroom. The bed was made and all the drawers in the long low dresser were closed. Russ opened the closet. A number of shelves lined one side. Standing on his tip-toes he pulled a lockbox from the center shelf and, placing it on the bed, turned the dials on the front with his thumb until he had the right combination. "My birthday," he mentioned, looking up at me. He opened the box with a flourish and said, "And, as you can see, my gun is…" His voice trailed off as he followed my gaze down into the empty box. "…missing." He finished numbly. "Well. That sucks." He looked up at me with what appeared to be genuine concern. "I swear, Patrick, I thought it was here."

I believed him, if only because he used my real name. "When did you see it last?" I asked.

Russell shrugged. "Right after Thanksgiving," he said. "I always brought it with me when I was buying heroin. Just in case, you know. I've never had to actually pull it out but you can't be too careful." He slammed the box closed, his initial shock wearing off rapidly. "Son of a *bitch!*" he shouted.

"Who else would have a key to your apartment?" I asked, "Or the combination to the lockbox?"

Russ shook his shaggy head. "No one. I mean Angie has a key, and my parents of course. But no one knows about the…well, no, actually my parents know about the box, too. I got it from them when I got the pistol. I remember my mother freaked out that I bought a gun. Figured I was going to shoot myself in the foot or..." He stopped and chuckled ironically. "Or that I'd shoot someone while I was high. Guess that belief runs in the family."

I felt a chill in my bones. "Anyone else?" I asked. "Anyone at all that might have had a passing knowledge of the box. Maybe they knew your birthday and knew that was the combination?"

Russell shook his head more enthusiastically. "No, no, no one. Just Angela and my parents." He paused, the realization finally sinking in. "So, you think one of them-?"

"It's too early to think anything," I said. "Report the gun stolen as soon as possible, and let the police sort it out. I'm sure there's a reasonable explanation."

"I hope you're right," Russell said, but he sounded as convinced as I felt. His distrust of the police was palpable.

We were saved from further disturbing contemplation by the ringing of my phone. Russell and I exchanged a glance as I answered.

"Where are you?" Angela demanded, her tense voice bristling with anxiety.

"We...just stepped out," I answered, "Is everything ok?"

"No, Patrick," Angela said, "my mother just had another attack. The nurses are upping her morphine again. She's going to go any time now. And I need my boyfriend here with me. And my brother."

"We'll be back in fifteen minutes," I said, gesturing to Russ for us to head back out. He closed the lockbox and returned it to the closet.

"Hurry," Angela pleaded and hung up.

Fourteen minutes later I stepped into Regina's hospital room one step behind Russell. Tony stood beside Regina's bed. Angela's face was buried in his chest, her shoulders trembling as she sobbed. The monitors over Regina's bed had been turned off.

"Aw, shit," Russell muttered. His father glanced over and the two locked eyes for a moment. Russ moved forward, to his mother's bedside. Tony put his arm around his son. Russ let him. Angela gave Russ a hug then looked at me. She wasn't mad that I wasn't here. She needed me now. I read it all in her eyes and in three strides, I joined them. She left her father and leaned into me and I held her tight.

"When?" I asked quietly.

"Five minutes ago," Tony answered. I held Angela with one arm and gripped his shoulder sympathetically with my free hand. He nodded his appreciation.

Russ's head had been bowed and I thought I saw his lips moving. He appeared to be praying quietly. I was surprised. After another moment, he swatted at his eyes with the back of his hand and steeled his shoulders, a homuncular version of his father. Through clenched teeth he hissed, "Some son of a bitch killed my mother."

Angela renewed her crying at his proclamation and I felt a cold hand clench my heart. But he was right. I was now investigating Regina's murder.

Chapter Thirteen

The next two days were a blur. The police came, of course, and there was an autopsy scheduled. Angela and her father and brother started to go through her affects and to discuss arrangements for her service. They each spent a fair chunk of time being interviewed by the police, especially Russell after he reported his gun stolen, a fact he neglected to let slip to his family. I gave them privacy when I could and was there to take Angela away and take her mind off things when she needed me to do so. Two days after Regina passed away, the four of us sat in a crowded office at the Courtland Brothers Funeral Home in Brunswick. Wayne Novello, Angela's uncle, was with us because things weren't already uncomfortable enough.

Raymond Courtland – "Call me Ray" – was a broad shouldered older man with thick, shockingly white hair, unnaturally straight teeth, a gravelly voice and a kind, sympathetic twinkle in his eye, probably the result of a lifetime spent working with the recently bereaved. He sat on one side of his desk while Tony and Angela sat across from him. I stood behind Angela, my hand on her shoulder protectively. Wayne made a point of lurking in the corner as far from Angela as the small space allowed. Russell took advantage of the remaining floor space to pace restlessly as the plans were being made.

"Yes," Ray said, "Monday afternoon and evening will work for the service. We'll have her prepared by then. You're welcome to come in the afternoon and make sure everything is how you want it. We'll have the pictures you provide displayed and, if you'd like, we can put together a CD with a memorial video of pictures and music. We can discuss those details shortly. We usually recommend receiving visitors by three or four, and then the memorial service proper at seven o'clock or so." He looked questioningly from Tony to Angela.

"That should be fine," Angela replied simply. Her father nodded.

"Very good," Ray said, making notes on his form. "Will Regina be buried or cremated?"

"Buried," Angela said.

At the same time, Tony answered, "Cremated."

The looked at each other, neither willing to engage in a disagreement over the issue.

"Your mother told me that she wanted to be cremated," Tony said simply.

"I don't like that," Angela responded. Her voice quavered as she struggled to maintain control. "I can't imagine her just…gone like that. If she's cremated, there's no cemetery to visit, no headstone to stand by when I want to talk to her or mourn her." She bit her lip, dabbed at her eyes with the rumpled tissue in her hand.

Tony exchanged a glance with his brother-in-law. "I understand, sweetie. And I get it." He squeezed her hand.

"Her cremains can still be interred in a plot," Ray Courtland added kindly. "She can be cremated and her ashes buried in a cemetery. With a headstone." He glanced up questioningly. "Unless she'd expressed a desire to be scattered?"

"No," Wayne replied. "Only that she be cremated. She didn't have any specific wishes."

"How would you know what her wishes were?" Angela hissed, glaring at him. "It's not like she would talk to you about anything. I don't even know why you're here."

Tony held up his hand before Wayne could speak. "He's here because he's family. Whatever might have happened before, he has a right to bury his sister."

"*You* were her husband!" Angela snapped. "*I* was her daughter! But not him, Daddy! *He* has no rights! *He's* a child molester!"

"Angela!" Tony barked. Ray Courtland blinked, set his pen down deliberately and settled back in his chair, suddenly becoming very interested in his cuticles.

For a moment we all stood and sat in silence.

"Holy shit," Russell whispered at last.

"Are you going to deny it, Dad?" Angela demanded. She raised a cold eyebrow and added, "Again."

Tony sat back as though she'd slapped him. Wayne stepped away from his corner and said, "Maybe it would be better if I left. Tony, I trust your judgement about what Regina would want."

"Good. Go," Angela said, looking down at her hands. "Good riddance."

"Perhaps," Ray suggested, his coarse voice slipping into the conversation like silk pajamas on satin sheets, "Miss Button would like to come with me for a few minutes to select a casket."

I squeezed my girlfriend's shoulder. "I'll go with you," I murmured. Angela stood wordlessly and we followed Ray out of the office and down a hall.

"I'm sorry for creating a scene," Angela told him as we walked.

He looked back at her with a wide smile. "Nonsense, my dear. This is a highly emotional time. And that was minor compared to some of the outbursts I've seen. No furniture was broken this time, so we'll chalk that up as a positive. Don't give it another thought." He entered a long room at the end of the hall, turning on the lights as we stepped in. Five coffins were arranged along one wall. A binder with glossy pages sat on a small table, probably for custom ordering. I wondered if anyone ever set out in life with the hopes and dreams of becoming a coffin catalog photographer.

"If you're looking for inexpensive, we do have this model," Ray said, presenting the first coffin. A surprised chuckle bubbled form Angela's lips as we exchanged a glance.

"No offense," she said, "but that looks like a huge hatbox." Even I could tell the coffin was of flimsy design. More concerning, though, was the fact that the entire thing seemed to be covered with a fabric resembling a dark blue corduroy.

"Has anyone ever actually bought that?" I asked.

Ray gave us an understanding smile. "It's not a looker, I know. But there are some who don't believe in spending a lot on something that's only going to be used once," he explained. "No, it's not a big seller, but it's enough to satisfy some people."

"I hope Tanya buries her father in something like that someday," Angela muttered to me. I patted her arm. To Ray, Angela said, "I think we can afford something a little more…traditional."

"Then allow me to show you these," Ray said smoothly moving on to the remaining caskets, which were all of the typical "glossy finished hardwood with shiny hardware" variety.

After a few minutes, Angela decided on a middle-range priced casket. I couldn't see much difference between them, except for details like the shade of stain or the finish on the hinges and handles. When she looked at me for reassurance on her decision, I smiled and nodded. "I'm sure your mother would love it," I said. She gave me a sad smile and nodded her assent to Ray Courtland.

As we returned to the hallway, Angela stopped, touching the funeral director on the arm. He turned and looked at her questioningly. She glanced at the floor then said, "I don't know if I can go back in there. My father can handle the arrangements. If you have any questions for me, he can give you my phone number. I hope you understand."

Ray nodded his snowy head. "Absolutely, my dear. For now, if you have any pictures you would like included in the video, you can get them to me any time in the next day or so." He handed her a business card. "You can email them to me if you'd rather. And if *you* have any questions, please don't hesitate to call."

Angela glanced at the card and nodded. "Thank

you. You've been very kind."

"It comes with the territory," he assured her. At the end of the hall, we headed for the exit and he returned to his small office.

Outside, we walked hand-in-hand to my trusty, if aging, Cavalier. "I don't want to go home," she said. "Not yet."

"My place?" I asked, trying not to make it sound too solicitous. I opened the passenger's door for her and walked around to my side.

"Actually," she said as I got behind the wheel, "maybe we could just grab a bite to eat. I don't have much of an appetite, but I know I have to eat something."

I drove us to Watervliet, to a diner on Nineteenth Street. The décor and atmosphere weren't much to write home about but I would be willing to punch a baby for a plate of their onion rings. I kept that observation to myself, as this was neither the time nor place to give in to such frivolity. I did order the onion rings, though, along with a medium rare bacon cheeseburger and a Diet Pepsi. Angela ordered a side salad and a water. I felt gluttonous and resolved to share the onion rings with her. Now that was true love.

"I'm going to go to work tonight," Angela said without preamble. She used her straw to idly swirl the ice in her water glass as she spoke.

"I thought Daniel told you to take as much time off as you needed," I answered.

"He did," Angela said with a sigh, "but I need to be doing *something*! I can't just sit around all night thinking about her. And the bills don't stop just because I'm in mourning. It's Saturday, so the money will be good. There'll be plenty of guys there wanting to put their hands all over me."

I frowned at the sneer in her words and tone. I made it a point not to think too deeply about what Angela did at work, particularly when she and a customer adjourned to the private couch dance rooms upstairs. In exchange, she made a point of not rubbing the duties of her job in my face. So to speak. The contempt with which she bit off the last words suggested that she wasn't trying to hurt me. In fact, I think she had someone else in mind that she would rather have seen hurt.

"You can't keep thinking about him," I murmured.

She stopped stirring the glass and stared up at me with a piercing gaze that made me wonder if maybe she *was* trying to hurt me as well. "I can't *not* think about him, Patrick! He's right here!" She tapped her forehead sharply with her fingernail. "And the only time I manage to stop reliving what he did to me is when I remember that my mother is dead!" Her lips trembled. "Patrick, honey, it's driving me nuts and I don't know what to do."

I reached for her hand. She pulled away, hugging herself, staring down at her slowly spinning ice. "I had...an accident the other night," she whispered. A tear dribbled from her eye and she swiped it away angrily. "I haven't wet the bed in twelve years! And now, he's back and my mother's dead and the nightmares are coming back and all my father can do is talk about Wayne's rights! Like nothing ever happened!" She shuddered, her self-control buckling. Fortunately, at mid-afternoon, the restaurant was mostly empty and as her voice rose with hysteria, there were not a lot of people to overhear.

I reached across the table and cupped her damp cheek and chin in my hand. She started to turn her head but my hand followed her. "Look at me," I said firmly but with compassion. She resisted. "Angela, please?" Her reddened eyes looked at me with a mixture of shame and wariness. "You are not in this alone, my love," I told her. "I am right here with you. And *we* will get through this. Together. Spend the night tonight. I will hold you all night and protect you from your bad dreams."

"And if I wet your bed too?" she whispered, lowering her eyes.

"I have extra sheets," I said. "And I know where the laundromat is."

She chewed her lower lip and slowly looked up again. Wordlessly she gave a small nod. I smiled at her reassuringly. "Good," I said. "I love you, Angela."

She leaned her head against my hand, turning a bit to kiss my palm. "I love you, Patrick," she said. "Thank you for everything you're doing."

"I'm always here for you," I told her.

"Forever and forever," she agreed.

Our touching moment was broken by the return of our waitress bearing a red plastic basket of hot, crispy onion rings. We sat back and, when the waitress left, I slid the basket towards the middle of the table. "Eat," I said. "You'll need your strength tonight." She took two small rings. I didn't begrudge her them.

I dropped Angela at her apartment after our late lunch, so she could shower, shave and get ready for work. Pulling a business card from my front pocket, I dialed a number on the cell phone while I watched Angela enter her building.

"Finley!" the Detective answered brusquely on the second ring. I had only spoken to the Detective once, briefly, the night that Regina had passed away. I hadn't been able to give him anything useful at the time and, while I was busy watching after Angela, I hadn't had an opportunity to do any more investigating. When I identified myself, his tone took on a surprisingly congenial tone. "Mr. Brady," he said, "how convenient you should call right now. I received the results from the tests done on the hairs you found and was just about to speak to their previous owner. You may as join me, since you did discover them."

"I can be there in fifteen minutes," I assured him, pulling away from the curb.

"Excellent," Finley said, ending the call as abruptly as it had begun.

At the State Police barracks, I identified myself to the desk sergeant and was directed to a small barren conference room. Detective Finley was there with another officer in uniform. He was around forty, a little over five feet tall but still in decent shape, with brown hair and a vaguely puzzled look in his brown eyes. As I entered, they stood and Finley introduced me to Officer Edward Carrigan.

"Turns out," Finley continued, as we all sat down, "it was Carrigan's hair you found at the crime scene."

I frowned. This didn't bode well. No wonder Finley had sounded almost happy. My potential lead had petered out.

"You must have been one of the investigators at the scene," I said to Carrigan.

The younger officer glanced at the Detective, who nodded, then Carrigan turned back to me and agreed, "Yes, sir. First on the scene actually. I was only a couple blocks away when the call came in." To Finley he added, "I remember slipping in the ice and mud under the trees. I barely grazed the trunk with my head. It never occurred to me that I may have contaminated the crime scene. I'm sorry for the oversight, Detective."

Finley waved a dismissive hand. "No real harm done. It would have been nice to have Mr. Brady's lead go somewhere, but we'll get to the bottom of things regardless." To me he added, "We are still following up on the lead of the man I mentioned to you the other day. That seems to be our strongest indicator now."

I nodded. "I understand. As you said, I'm sorry the lead was a dead end."

Finley could afford to be magnanimous at this point and he did so, saying, "I appreciate you bringing it to us regardless. If you find out anything else, I'm sure you'll do the same with that information."

"Absolutely," I assured him. I stood up and offered my hand to the officer, who shook it firmly. "I apologize for the inconvenience, Officer Carrigan."

Carrigan smiled sheepishly. "No trouble. Gets me off patrol duty for a little while," he said.

"If you gentlemen will excuse me," I said, "I'm going to try and visit my girlfriend at work this evening. She's had a pretty trying day, planning her mother's funeral and all."

"When *is* the funeral?" Carrigan asked. I don't know what it was about his tone. Perhaps he forced it to sound too casual, or maybe it was the fact that his voice was just a little higher than it had been. I felt my forehead crinkle as I looked at him. He returned my gaze directly, unblinking. Either Finley's ever-open eyelids were contagious, or Officer Carrigan was hiding something. I glanced sidelong at Finley. His head was cocked. Good, I thought, I wasn't the only one who heard it.

"The wake will be Monday evening. I think they're planning on the memorial service at seven," I replied, still gripping the officer's hand. "Did you know her?" I asked.

Carrigan looked like a scared horse, the whites of his eyes big and round as her looked from me to Finley and back again. He withdrew his hand and slumped into his chair. I sat as well. "Yes," Carrigan said in a tight voice. "Regina and I have crossed paths in the courthouse a couple times. She was a legal secretary, as you know, and we got to talking one day. She was a very intelligent woman. Funny. Charming really. I can't imagine why her husband would ever cheat on her."

Finley held up a hand sharply. "Stop. Right. There," he said, his face flushing as he chomped off each word. "You *knew* the victim? And what's this about the husband having an affair?"

"I...I thought you knew already," Carrigan stammered. "I guess it was over. I don't know. We...we didn't talk. Much. It's not like we were...you know, close or anything. But she mentioned a while back that she thought he was having an affair. I don't know any of the details." He spread his hands helplessly. I was half-convinced he was about to either cry or soil his uniform.

"Fine," Finley said, in a tone that implied it clearly wasn't. "And you didn't mention you knew her, why?"

"I was first on the scene, Detective," Carrigan said. His voice regained some of its strength. He was more confident in this answer. "I know it was wrong, but she was an acquaintance, nothing more. My knowing her had nothing to do with the case. I thought if I mentioned that I knew her it might look suspicious that I was there first as well." He gestured towards the report on the table in front of Finley and added, "Especially now that my hair was found there!"

Finley nodded, frowning. "I see. And you stick to your story of how that hair got stuck to the tree?" he demanded.

"Yes, sir." Finley squirmed in his chair. "I'm very

sorry, sir."

Finley regarded him in stony silence for a moment then turned his granite stare on me. I flinched. "What about you, Brady. Did you know about this affair?"

Now it was my turn to...obfuscate. Now that Finley knew about the affair, I had nothing to lose by saying anything. But I had made a promise. Finley would determine who the other woman was in due course, whether or not I told him, so I could keep my promise without impeding his investigation. It was a line finer than Carrigan's troublesome hair but it was the line I chose to rationalize along.

"There was an accusation last Thanksgiving," I said. "I think someone mentioned that to you early on." I didn't add that I had confirmed the allegation and, in fact, spoken with the woman in question. In my head, I heard my father admonish me that a lie by omission was still a lie.

Finley grunted. "If you're lying," he said, "you're better at it than he is." He gestured towards Carrigan with his chin.

"Thank you?" I asked.

"It wasn't a compliment," Finley replied. "Both of you get out of here." Carrigan and I headed for the door before Finley added, "And, Brady?" I turned back. "Let Mr. Button know I'll be coming to speak to him again."

I nodded and pulled the door closed behind me.

I brushed aside the heavy velvet curtain and stepped into the main room of Danny's as if my best friend owned the place. There were four guys scattered around the stage and one sitting at a table. Heather was straddling the last man, gyrating enthusiastically on his lap. She blew me a kiss over his shoulder. It was still early and Saturday night had not yet kicked into full swing. When I got to the bar, Sheila had a Diet Pepsi opened and ready for me. Her glossy brown hair was pulled back in a ponytail. I thanked her with a wink and a two dollar tip, and made my way to a table towards the back of the room.

One of the problems with hanging out at a strip club, owned by my friend, and where my girlfriend worked, was that eventually the novelty wears off. It's like eating ice cream every day; sooner or later you get sick of ice cream. Don't get me wrong; I'll never grow tired of looking at naked and scantily clad women. But now I knew them all as people instead of just nameless strippers to be objectified. I'd gotten to know about their lives. Angela and I had hung out with a few of them outside of the club. Seeing them naked now almost felt like a violation of that friendship.

Almost.

Ebony was on stage, already topless. Her deep brown skin was flawless, her full firm breasts were damned near perfect, topped with dark chocolate nipples. Her obsidian hair fell in loose soft waves around her shoulders. She had strong legs, as evidenced by the fact that she was currently hanging upside down from the brass pole by them. Her bright pink thong did nothing to hide her tight round butt cheeks that made an incredibly provocative and resounding sound when she slapped them with the palm of her hand. She claimed to be nineteen, but I was doubtful. If I didn't trust Daniel's extensive background check process before hiring anyone, I would have assumed she was no more than seventeen. Her age – be it seventeen or nineteen – and, of course, the fact that I was already dating Angela, with whom I was madly in love, were the only factors that prevented me from rolling over and begging like a dog trying to please his master every time she looked my way. For now I was content to sit at my small back table, nurse my Diet Pepsi, and watch her dance, hoping I spotted Angela before she had to come and wipe the drool from my chin. Yeah, it could be a *long* time before I got sick of this particular flavor of ice cream.

It was not Angela, but Heather, who eventually broke the line of sight between me and the stage. She stood there, in a pair of red pleather thigh-high heeled boots, and a matching red G-string and pasties. One of the older dancers in Daniel's employ, up close her makeup was thicker than I would have liked. She had her hand on her hip and gave me a cocky smile. "Hey, stranger," she said. "Care for a dance?"

I gave her a smile and sat back. "How can I refuse?" I smiled. She was about five and a half feet tall and had put on a few pounds since she quit smoking last summer. I had to admit I liked her better now that she didn't smell like an ashtray. Tonight her hair was platinum blonde. I knew it was a wig. I didn't care. As she straddled my left leg, letting her knee rub against me enticingly, she moved in close. I felt the warmth coming off her nearly naked body. I ran my fingers along her back, earning me a well-practiced purr in my ear. Her breasts pressed against my chest and the scent of her perfume wafted over us as she rubbed my nose with hers and we exchanged a laugh. She stepped back and repositioned, facing away from me so she could lay back against me, letting me look down her body as she reached back and ran her nails through my hair. As she moved I noticed a new tattoo of a pair of Indian feathers on her right shoulder.

"New ink," I murmured.

"Yep," she breathed in my ear. "You like?"

"Sexy as hell," I affirmed. She ground her ass against me in appreciation.

As the dance finished, I slid a five dollar bill into her garter. I always made a point to tip well, since they were friends and we all knew I wasn't going upstairs with any of them.

Heather moved off in search of less pleasant, but more profitable company. A new patron was standing just inside the curtain separating the main room from the entryway. Thick black hair swept back from his broad forehead, a broad nose, sharp eyes that darted around the room. Wide shoulders, not tall but solid. Heather approached him, running her hand along his chest and pressed her mouth to his ear, no doubt whispering something enticing. His mouth twitched into a smile and he shook his head, saying something briefly to her. She gave a nod and a shrug and moved on. His dark eyes turned my way and he crossed the room to where I sat. When he stopped at my table, I looked up at him questioningly.

"Mr. Brady," he said. It wasn't a question. "Mind if I join you?" That was a question but he didn't wait for an answer before seating himself beside me at the table. Over the thumping of the music, I thought I detected a bit of an accent. He sat silently for a moment, appreciatively watching Ebony, now fully exposed, jiggling her perfect derriere inches from the face of one man at the edge of the stage.

"Something I can help you with, friend?" I asked. I sipped my soda to disguise my discomfort.

"You are trying to find Regina Button's killer," he said. Definitely an accent. Definitely not a question.

"I'm a friend of the family," I said evasively. "Obviously they would like to find out who shot her."

"You are going to cease your investigation," the stranger said. It was the same neutral tone he'd used in his first two statements, but it had the weight of a directive. He continued to watch Ebony, his eyes not even flicking my way.

"I'd hardly call it an investigation," I remarked. "The family asked me to make some inquiries is all."

He turned his head towards me slowly and his gaze was penetrating. "Then you will cease your *inquiries*," he said. He rested his folded hands on the table.

I copied the move, casually brushing my soda out of the way. If this got physical, I wouldn't want to spill the soda and add to Daniel's cleaning bill. "And why would I do that?" I asked mildly.

The man gave me a cold smile. "Because I'm asking nice. This time." He let that blatant threat hang in the air for a moment and added, "It will hurt the family to learn the truth." He leaned in closer and added, "And it will *definitely* hurt you if you keep asking questions."

I took the threat seriously. He seemed like the

type who would follow through. I hid my fear well, I thought. "Just one more question, if you don't mind," I replied. "Is your name Vito? Vito Denato?" I shrugged. "I guess that's two questions."

The man's grin gained some warmth. "So. I see my reputation precedes me. Tony must have mentioned me."

"Your name came up," I agreed.

Vito nodded, looked away again, thoughtfully watching the blank stage. Ebony had gathered her clothes and was leaving the stage. The DJ reminded everyone that the girls danced for tips and encouraged everyone to be generous. He introduced the next dancer. Vanessa was twenty-five, with fine brown hair in a pixie cut and brown eyes. Five-four, about a hundred and thirty-five pounds. She had a butterfly tattooed on her left forearm and a fleur de lis "tramp stamp" peeking out over the back of her thong. Curves in all the right places, including a nice round butt and a set of 38C breasts. Obviously I was spending too much time getting to know these women. I also knew, from our interactions outside the club, that she had a black boyfriend who was taller and broader than me and could probably beat the batsnot out of any guy in the place. Including Vito, if it came to that.

"How will knowing who killed Regina hurt the

family?" I asked. "I would think not knowing the answer would be harder."

Vito's jaw worked. He probably wasn't accustomed to having his directions questioned and he didn't seem to fond of the rare experience. "You would be wrong," he said.

I nodded, sipped my soda. "Sounds like," I suggested, "you know who the killer is."

"It's no longer your concern," Vito neither confirmed nor denied.

I made a disappointed noise with my mouth. "Here's my problem, Vito. I'm dating Regina's daughter. We may actually go the distance. She's asked me to find her mother's murderer. I'm going to have to give her a really good reason why I'm not doing that."

Vito gave me the glare again. "Because if you keep at it," he said, "she's going to lose someone else she loves," he said.

With those menacing words, he stood and strode out of the club. I watched him go. He didn't look back. Cocky son of a bitch.

"Who was that?"

I glanced up. Angela was standing beside me and I wondered how Ebony or Heather or Vanessa could make any money at all when they had to compete against her for customer's attention. She was currently wearing an outfit that screamed slutty schoolgirl. A red and black plaid skirt that was no more than two inches long. A loose white shirt that had no hope of ever buttoning across her breasts and was just tied closed above her pierced belly button. White knee high socks and a pair of white and black high-heeled saddle shoes completed the look. I remembered fondly that she had brought the costume home more than once and modeled it for me. It had led to a number of memorable nights. She smirked when she realized I was staring, momentarily distracted from her question.

"Just…a friend of a friend," I answered absently.

She sat sideways on my lap, draping an arm around my neck, content to let one of her breasts press against my cheek. I wrapped an arm protectively around her back. Her perfume smelled like vanilla. "How are you doing?" I asked.

She gave me a sad smile. "Okay," she said. "Everyone's been great. Rumor has it Danny and Jane are getting more serious than he let on, by the way. And you know I love dancing. It's actually cheering me up. The other stuff," she shrugged, "it's a necessary evil to make the money. But I'm glad I came in tonight."

"Good," I said, giving her a squeeze. I savored the weight of her body on my legs, the scent and texture of her skin against mine. I stayed for a couple hours. I kept her mind off her mother's death. She kept mine off Vito's threats.

Chapter Fourteen

We slept in the next morning, Sunday. I'd gotten home about one and Angela kept her word and spent the night at my apartment, getting there and slipping into bed beside me. She wore a plain white T-shirt and a loose-fitting pair of sweatpants, but I didn't mind. She still smelled nice. Half-awake, I wrapped my arm around her, holding her close. She gave a contented moan and that was the last thing I remembered until the sun finally woke me up around ten. I eased out of the bed, careful not to wake her, noting with satisfaction that her sweatpants and the sheets were still bone dry. For one night, at least, the nightmares had been held at bay.

I had no real plans for the day. I wanted to talk to Tony eventually and let him know that the police knew about his affair. But I suspected he already knew that. I also wanted to tell him that I'd had a run in with his good friend from the past. I wondered if he knew that as well. I also wondered what Vito's real motivation was. I could guess, but I didn't like that answer so I remained optimistic I'd find a different one eventually. My main focus of the day, though, was the company I had coming that evening.

I was frying up some bacon when Angela came

into the kitchen, still wearing her sweats, her auburn hair all mussed up with sleep, face still made up and glittery from work the night before. "Mmmm," she murmured, "I love waking up to a man in his boxer shorts making breakfast." She came to my side and we kissed. She put her arms around me and rested her head on my shoulder while I flipped the bacon. It sputtered and spat a drop of hot grease onto my chest but I ignored it, in quite a manly fashion I thought, and continued letting her hug me as I cooked.

"I could get used to waking up with a beautiful woman in my bed every morning," I agreed.

She looked up at me. "Once school is over," she said, "That's what we planned."

I nodded. Bacon flipped, I turned and gave her my full attention, wrapping my arms around her waist. "I know," I said. "But it's nice to think about."

She smiled. "I agree."

More kissing ensued.

When we separated, the bacon was sizzling away and I hurriedly grabbed a couple paper towels on which to drain it. She excused herself to take a quick shower. I removed the bacon to the towels and drained the grease into an old pickle jar kept beside the stove for just that purpose.

I gave the pan a quick wipe to remove the excess

greasiness then put it back on the stove with a pat of butter. I had diced half an onion and a red pepper before Angela joined me and I dumped these in, letting them sauté for a few minutes. Four eggs joined them and I whisked them together with some heavy cream before they had a chance to become over easy. In the shower, Angela was humming. It felt very homey and comfortable and I smiled to myself.

After a few minutes the eggs had fluffed up with just a thin layer of uncooked yolk on top. With a deft flip of the wrist I flipped the omelet and caught it again. It was a near perfect maneuver and I regretted that no one was there to see it. I probably couldn't have gotten it right again if I'd tried. Since I am averse to anything but very well cooked eggs, I let the omelet go for a moment while I retrieved some leftover shredded mozzarella from a homemade pizza night we'd had sometime in the past month. Sprinkled the mozzarella on one half of the omelet and folded it in half. I turned off the burner letting the residual heat melt the cheese while I grabbed a couple plates from the cupboard. Two pieces of bacon for her, three for me. Cut the omelet in half and had them on the kitchen table with a glass of orange juice for both of us as the bathroom door opened and Angela stepped out, amid a cloud of steam, wrapped in my black satin bathrobe. It was an improvement over the sweatshirt. I noted she was still wearing the sweatpants underneath.

Baby steps, I guess. When she sat across from me at the table, the robe revealed the narrow valley between her breasts and she made no attempt to cover up.

She took a bite of omelet and moaned with delight. "You don't know how glad I am to have found a man who can cook."

I shrugged. "I just threw stuff in the pan. The flame did the hard part."

We ate in companionable silence, talking occasionally of inconsequential things. I told her about the visit I expected later that afternoon.

She gave me a patient smile. "I don't get all that," she said. "Aren't you all supposed to be Brothers and friends? Why does there always seem to be some kind of drama or political maneuvering going on?"

I finished gnawing on a piece of bacon, savoring the combination of chewy, crispy and salty as I contemplated my response. "It's human nature, I think," I said after swallowing. "You get more than three people in a room and you're going to have different opinions. And if a lot of them happen to be dominant personalities, there's going to be constant shuffling for position. We have a common goal of charity and brotherly love and, honestly, I think most people, on either side of any given issue, are doing what they feel is in the best interest of the fraternity. It's just that we can't always agree on what that is."

"So instead of discussing it like grownups you try to covertly take over each other's Lodges and bend them to your will?" Angela asked, staring at me steadily over the rim of her glass.

"Well," I said, averting my eyes, "yeah. Basically."

"I see," she countered with a smile. "So what happens if they don't vote to let you join Hiram-Austin?"

I spread my hands. "I don't know. The vote to merge has to win by a simple majority in each Lodge. If we can't stop H-A from approving it, the battle will have to be fought in Acacia. Though I think Acacia is pretty much against the merger, so the H-A fight might not even be unnecessary."

"Fighting battles in your own fraternity. Brother against Brother. Like a civil war. Sounds real fraternal," she remarked. She bit into a piece of bacon.

"Are you saying I shouldn't join Hiram-Austin?" I asked.

She shook her head. "No, I'm just wondering if you're doing what you think is right for the fraternity, or what your father thinks is right for them."

My brows slid up my forehead. "You think I'm just going along with this to make my father happy?" I asked. "Maybe it's just that I agree with him."

"Maybe," she conceded. "But eventually you are

going to have to show that you're your own man. If everyone continues to see you as just 'Sean's son', you'll never go as far as you could otherwise."

"Meaning what?" I asked.

She shrugged. "Sooner or later you're going to have an opportunity to make a name for yourself, aside from just being your father's son, and, if you take it, you could go far in the fraternity. I don't know what that opportunity is or when it will happen. But it's bound to happen."

"Something to think about," I agreed.

After breakfast, Angela left for home to look for pictures of her mother for the funeral home. I did my dishes and straightened up the apartment. I couldn't help but think of the interview that had followed my petition to join Acacia Lodge. My father had given me the nuts and bolts of what to expect – three men from the Lodge would come to my house, answer any questions I had, tell me a little about the fraternity in general and the Lodge specifically. Kind of a chance for them to get a feel for me and vice versa before they reported back at the next meeting and, based solely on their favorable or unfavorable report, the Lodge would vote on my membership. Obviously I had made a favorable impression that time.

In a way this impending interview felt both easier and more difficult. Easier, because I'd been through the process already. I had a couple years of Masonry under my belt now and I didn't have any real rookie questions. More difficult, though, because whereas my initial interviewers had wanted me in the Lodge, or at least had started out neutrally on the topic, the Brothers interviewing me today were, according to my father, somewhat more skeptical. My admission into Hiram-Austin Lodge, and with it the probable future of both H-A and Acacia Lodges, hung in the balance.

Around five o'clock there was a knock at the door. The apartment looked better than it had in a long time and I'd had time to shower and put on some clean clothes. Button down shirt, a pair of grey slacks. You know, lounging around the house on a Sunday afternoon clothes. I didn't feel it was necessary to wear a tie like I had for my interview with Acacia.

Three men stood in the tiny hall outside, two of them relegated to standing on the narrow staircase that ran up the center of the building. I knew two of them by sight. The man just outside the door, Mitch Svenson, was about fifty-five, five-seven, tending towards round in the middle and had a thick head of salt and pepper hair. His mouth had a tendency to pucker, as though he was persistently sucking lemons. His brown eyes held no warmth.

At the end of the line, I was surprised to see

Victor Van Rensselaer. The twenty-three year old was a newer Brother of the Lodge, only having been a member about as long as I had. I couldn't think of a time I hadn't seen him in the company of Scott Tisdale. It was interesting that he was on my interview committee. I assumed that, as Scott's friend, he was planning to vote against the merger, which meant I had at least one ally interviewing me. He had shaggy blond hair, wide green eyes and a stocky build. Around his right wrist was a tribal tattoo.

The third man was tall and thin, about Svenson's age with a heavily receded hairline. He was a gray man. His hair was silver, his skin pale. Even his eyes were grey, but not unkind.

"Brother Brady," Svenson said, his voice a sonorous tenor, "this is an opportunity we have long sought!" A wide smile that failed to reach his eyes stretched across his face and he held out his hand. I shook it, half expecting the electrical jolt of a joy buzzer. He gestured to his companions and added, "This is Len Tempel. And I think you already know Vic Van Rensselaer from your short-lived experience with the bar."

About a year ago, an effort had been made, on the parts of Hiram-Austin and Acacia Lodges, to have the bar in our mutual meeting hall opened for business on non-meeting nights, as a way of bringing in additional revenue for the maintenance of the property. At the time I was a Steward in Acacia Lodge and Vic had been a Steward from H-A, so we were two of the Brothers in the rotation to man the bar when it was open. Sadly one of our patrons had an unfortunate encounter with a tree on his way home one evening and the bar was pre-emptively shut down. Fortunately, no liability issues had cropped up following the accident, but the bar remained closed, except for meeting nights, for the time being. From Svenson's tone, I got the impression he hadn't been sorry to see the endeavor fail.

I shook hands with each of them and allowed them in, guiding them through the small apartment to the living room. I offered them drinks. They declined. Len sat on the rattan couch and, after giving the room a dubious look and deciding it was his best bet, Mitch sat beside him. Vic took the recliner. I dragged a chair in from the adjoining kitchen and joined them.

"So, Patrick," Mitch began, crossing his legs and folding his hands over his knee, "you're Sean Brady's boy. And you've been a member of Acacia Lodge about a year and a half, is that right?" He had the exact tone of someone who was trying not to sound condescending but not really caring if he succeeded or not.

"Yes," I answered, playing along. "I was raised a year ago last March. Just before St. Patrick's Day." It had been a memorable occasion for more than one reason.

"So it's safe to say you're still relatively new to the whole Masonic experience?" he asked, feigning innocence.

I shrugged. "I suppose that's true."

Mitch Svenson nodded as though I'd said something significant and glanced at the other two men. "And so why do think now is the time to seek dual membership with Hiram-Austin? Especially when you've barely gotten a taste of things in your mother Lodge?"

I gave him an ingratiating smile and was pleased to see his own saccharine grin dim a watt or two. "That's precisely why, Mitch," I answered. "I'm still new and I'm eager to see not only how my Lodge works, but how others operate, so that I can get a better grasp of the bigger picture."

"Have you visited any other Lodges in the District?" Len Tempel interjected. His voice, like his body, was thin and reedy.

"I've been to a couple District Deputy visits," I said, "but I haven't attended any regular meetings of other Lodges, no."

"The official visit of the District Deputy Grand Master to a Lodge," Svenson pontificated, occasionally emphasizing seemingly random words, "is a special occasion." He steepled his fingers, tipping his head back in thought. "It might be compared to the difference between going to a friend's house for Thanksgiving versus dropping in on them unexpectedly on some random Thursday night. For the District Deputy's visit, everyone is dressed up, the Lodge is on their best behavior, and the room is full of visiting Brothers. None of the routine business of the Lodge is conducted, the business of the night being solely that of the DDGM. It is *completely* different than a regular meeting, where the officers might be in jackets and ties or even more casually dressed, the tone of the meeting is more laid back, and the business of the Lodge is of a more commonplace nature. If you truly want to get the feel for the personality of a Lodge, you really *must* visit them on a regular meeting night, not just on special occasions." He tilted his head back down and looked directly at me, leaning forward. "It would also be wise to visit more than one Lodge, and to do so more than once, before you decide to petition them for affiliation. That way you can be sure they are a good fit for you. And, you for them." The cold smile returned. "And I don't recall ever seeing you at Hiram-Austin."

I felt myself flushing but ground my teeth and spread my hands innocently. "This is true. I haven't had the pleasure yet. But the Lodge comes highly recommended. My father has undoubtedly been to more than a few of your meetings over the years. You must have made a good impression, since he is petitioning for membership. It seemed like a good time for me to do so too." Inwardly, I winced, hating to sound like I was just following along behind Daddy, especially in light of my recent conversation with Angela.

"Oh, I know your father," Svenson said. "He's a smart man and, *generally*, a good one. I thought it was interesting that, after all this time, he decided that now was the right time to affiliate with *us*. In fact, it appears to be a very popular move. In addition to the two of you, two other Brothers from Acacia put in petitions at our last meeting."

"Interesting," I said. I left it at that.

Mitch and I regarded each other for a moment. Vic shifted uncomfortably. Eventually Len cleared his throat. "Some have made the suggestion," he said, "that Acacia may be stacking the deck in some sort of coup attempt."

I let my eyebrows slide up my forehead. "To what end?" I asked.

Mitch glanced at Len, who turned back to me. "There are rumors of a merger being proposed between our two Lodges in the near future," he explained. "It's a contentious issue. It would not be a unanimous decision by any count."

"And," Mitch added, "an influx of new members who might feel one way or the other about it could *sway* the vote. It's a manipulative tactic and not in the best interest of the peace and harmony of either Lodge." He held up a piece of paper that I recognized as the petition I had submitted. "So let me ask you, Patrick. Are you really sure *you* want to do this?"

I met his gaze with my own, ignoring the uncertainty gurgling in my stomach, and said, "Absolutely. I think it will be a great learning experience."

"Just remember," Mitch intoned, "experience can be a cruel teacher."

There were a few more questions, routine things – would I be available for the Lodge meetings on the second and fourth Wednesdays of the month, how did I think the Lodge would benefit from my membership, and so on. Nothing that sounded like it was meant to trap me or expose my role in the coup d'état that was brewing. When they left, I was sure I hadn't persuaded Mitch Svenson of my sincerity, but I felt like Len and Vic were willing to give me a chance. Overall, I considered the interview a success.

After the door closed behind them, I called my father. I was surprised when he answered the phone instead of my mother. At least until I realized he was chewing something. The phone was near my parents' refrigerator. Apparently so was my father.

"Hey, Dad," I said. "Just wanted to let you know the interview committee just left. Miraculously, I'm still alive."

My father swallowed his food and said, "Always good to hear. How'd it go?"

"It was fine," I said. "Mitch Svenson was subtly antagonistic like you suggested he would be, but the other two were fine. I was surprised to see Vic Van Rensselaer on the committee. And the other guy, Len Tempel, was innocuous."

My father scoffed. It turned into a hacking cough. I waited until he cleared his throat. Then he said, "Kid, if you thought Len was innocuous, you weren't paying attention. Think of him as the Hiram-Austin version of Cliff." Clifford Everett was the senior member of Acacia Lodge. Though he didn't hold any office, very little happened in the Lodge without his awareness and approval. In retrospect, it occurred to me that Len had raised the valid point about my lack of attendance at other Lodges, as well as addressing the concerns about a possible coup to prevent the merger. Otherwise he was content to let Mitch do all the grandstanding, barking like a dog on a chain, while his handler kept an eye out for the real danger. It bothered me that I had misread the situation.

"I'll keep my eyes and ears open a little more next

time," I promised both my father and myself.

"Wise move," Dad chewed, soft crunches forming verbal parenthesis around his words.

"They mentioned that there were two other members affiliating," I said. "Any idea who?"

"I know Clifford is one of them," Dad replied.

"Really?" I asked. "At lunch after the DD visit he sounded like he was in favor of the merge."

Dad burped quietly and said, "We talked some more after that. You've been busy so I didn't want to burden you with all the politics. He still thinks we will end up merging eventually. But he wants Acacia to have every chance to survive on its own first. We still have time before we reach a critical point. Merging now is premature and Cliff realizes that. He'll vote against it this time. It's no guarantee he'll do so next time the issue comes up. And trust me, it *will* come up again."

"So do you think we'll have the votes to stop it?" I asked.

"Cliff's opinion will carry some weight as a Right Worshipful; it might sway a vote or two our way. But honestly? We're just going to have to wait and see."

We ended that conversation on that less than positive note.

Angela was planning to sleep over again tonight. With her mother's memorial service scheduled for the next day, she wanted the added security of me beside her as she slept. I was happy to oblige. I decided to throw together a meatloaf and some mashed potatoes for dinner; the comfort food would do her well. The ground beef was still browning in the pan when my phone rang. I turned the burner down and answered on the third ring.

"Mr. Brady," Detective Finley said. His voice was as close to happy as I'd heard it yet, which really wasn't saying much.

"Detective," I said, "what a nice surprise. I'm guessing this isn't a social call?"

"You guess correctly. Since you've been playing fair with us on this investigation, I thought I'd return the favor." I rolled my eyes. "Our prime suspect was just arrested. They found him South Carolina. The boys down there are shipping him back here so we can have a few words with him. He should be in our custody by tomorrow evening."

Chapter Fifteen

The knowledge that Regina Button's alleged killer had been arrested did less than I would have thought to lighten the mood at her memorial service. I'd passed the news on to Angela over dinner the previous evening and she had called her father afterwards.

She had spent the night again. Aside from one bad dream from which I woke her and after which I held her until she fell back to sleep, the night passed uneventfully. We arrived at the funeral home about an hour before the viewing hours were scheduled to begin. Her father was already there, standing in the foyer speaking softly with Ray Courtland, the funeral director. Anthony seemed grateful to see us, relieved to have people by his side for this difficult day.

"I was just telling your father," Ray explained to Angela after the usual pleasantries had been exchanged, "everything is in place. You can go in whenever you're ready and have some private time alone with her. We've started the video playing on a repeating loop if you'd like to watch that before people begin to arrive. If there is anything either of you need, you have only to ask."

Angela thanked him and turned to her father.

"Any word from Russ yet?"

With a sigh, Anthony shook his head. "Hopefully he will be here soon. Do you want to wait for him?"

"No," Angela replied after a moment's consideration. "We may as well do this."

She took her father's arm and together they passed through the archway from the lobby into the viewing room. I followed solemnly behind them. Eleven rows of folding chairs had been set up. The room was chilly and smelled of the various arrangements of flowers that were displayed on either side of the polished coffin at the front of the room. The casket was open and Regina lay within, appearing to be nothing more than sleeping. The funeral home had done a fine job with her make up as near as I could tell.

The breath caught in Anthony's throat as he stood gazing down at his wife's body. Angela rubbed his back and rested her head against his arm. I snatched up a couple tissues from a conveniently located dispenser. I stood behind her and slipped them into her free hand. She nodded her thanks and dabbed at her eyes.

"I don't know if we would have made it," Anthony said eventually, breaking the quietude, "but I would have liked the opportunity to find out." He sighed. "We always said we would grow old together."

He lapsed into silence again. There didn't seem to be an appropriate response.

The front door of the parlor opened and I glanced out towards the lobby, expecting to see Russell sauntering in. Outside the bright morning sun was beginning to succumb to gathering clouds, more appropriate for the occasion. Despite winter officially starting in just a couple days, the daytime temperatures continued to linger in the upper thirties and lower forties. There was a chance of some showers tonight but overall, I anticipated a less than white Christmas.

Instead of Angela's brother, a young woman entered. Mid-twenties, a thick head of wavy ebony hair cascading back between her shoulder blades, disappearing against the matching black of her blazer. A dark skirt landed just above her knees and the white satin blouse strained to contain her breasts. She had a round face and big eyes. There was something familiar about her but I couldn't place it.

Immediately behind her, Wayne Novello entered the funeral parlor. I felt my spine tense. This was an occasion I had not looked forward to.

I touched Angela's elbow and leaned in to her ear, whispering, "Maybe we should go look at the memorial video for a few minutes."

She glanced back at me, then at the new arrivals. "Daddy?" she asked her father. "Let's give Wayne and

Tanya a few minutes." Anthony nodded.

Angela and I moved away, towards the flat screen monitor standing against one wall of the room. As we got close, I could hear an instrumental version of *Greensleeves* coming from the speakers as the video cycled through pictures of Angela's mother at various stages in her life, each picture lasting four or five seconds before transitioning into the next. Before following us, Anthony greeted the newcomers, shaking Wayne's hand and giving the younger woman a hug and saying a few words to them both. The girl looked our way and I gave her a nod in greeting. Angela kept her back to them, purposely walking towards the video screen without looking back. Anthony joined us a moment later.

The video was seven, maybe eight, minutes long. At various pictures, Angela and her father would let out an "Awww..." or a chuckle. I even made an appearance in the background of one or two of the more recent shots, taken at family functions over the last couple years. There were a few pictures of her at her office in Albany. One in particular caught my eye. It appeared to be Regina's birthday, judging from the cake in front of her and the pointy hat she was wearing. I felt my skin prickle and the back of my brain desperately trying to make me conscious mind aware of something in the picture but the scene changed before I was able to figure out what it was. I'd have to try and catch it on a subsequent loop.

The video ended, some brief credits rolled and, a moment later, it started over again, depicting a photo album with Regina's name inscribed on the cover and the funeral home's name printed discretely and discreetly below. The album opened with the visual effect of the first picture unfolding from its pages and the slideshow began again. In due course, the pictures began repeating. I could sense Angela's reluctance to turn away and risk making eye contact with her uncle at her mother's side, as well as her relief when the young woman joined us and greeted Angela with a broad sad smile and a long, tight hug.

"I'm so sorry I couldn't come up sooner," she said into Angela's hair. "How have you been holding up, hon?"

"It's been tough," Angela conceded. "Real tough." She glanced at me and said, "But I think it's almost over. They apparently have someone in custody."

"That'll help," her friend agreed with a nod, "but you'll still miss her for a long time. Trust me, I don't think that ever goes away. But what do I know? I've had abandonment issues for half my life."

Angela nodded and turned her hand towards me, "By the way, Tanya, this is my boyfriend Patrick. Patrick, this is my cousin Tanya. *His* daughter. She lives about an hour and a half south of here. We were like sisters growing up though!" To Tanya, she added, "Patrick's been great through all this. I don't know if I could have gotten through it without him."

Tanya and I shook hands and she said, "Good to know someone is looking out for the old lady."

Angela smiled and explained, "I'm nine and a half months older than Tanya. A fact she rarely lets me forget."

"Just making up for grade school, when she always teased me because she was a year ahead of me," Tanya countered. The two women shared a laugh and, for a fleeting moment, I saw a glimmer of the Angela I knew before the attack on her mother.

Wayne had left the casket and was talking quietly with Anthony. The two men were working their way back to the video display. Angela's eyes flicked in their direction. "Do you still smoke, T?" she asked, putting a hand on her cousin's elbow.

"Only when I'm stressed," Tanya grinned. Her eyes crinkled. She had seen Angela's attention shift as well. "Why don't we step outside and catch up for a bit?"

"I thought you'd never ask," Angela said. To me she said, "We'll be back in a few. Keep an eye on my father please?"

I assured her I would. I was surprised to hear the suggestion that they were going to smoke. Last I knew, Angela hadn't had a cigarette in two years. I suppose if there was ever a time to start again, this was it. I watched them go, then took a seat where I could see the pictures rotating through the screen again. I wasn't trying to eavesdrop, but the room was quiet and Wayne and Anthony really didn't seem too concerned if I heard them.

"I appreciate you including me," Wayne said.

Anthony shrugged. "You're Regina's brother," he said. "You were still important to her and I'm sure she would have wanted you here."

"I'm sure Angela doesn't agree," Wayne said. "I'm sorry I'm causing her so much distress." He sounded genuinely concerned. My stomach twisted.

Anthony continued watching the pictures of his late wife scrolling across the screen. "My daughter is resilient. But having you around has been pushing that to her limits. It's probably damaged my relationship with her." He turned his head just enough to look sideways at his brother-in-law. "After this is all over, I expect you to go back to Newburgh…and I don't want you to contact either of us again."

I arched my eyebrows in surprise but didn't comment, becoming very interested in my shoelaces for a moment or two, should either of them happen to look my way.

Wayne nodded silently for a moment. "I never meant to hurt –" he started.

Anthony to face him full on, his face hard. "Don't," he said with a voice like iced steel. "I mean it, Wayne. I see you again after this…I'll kill you myself."

Anthony may have never become an active member of the mob, but any other eavesdropper wouldn't have been able to tell that from the sincerity in his voice.

I felt distinctly uncomfortable as the two men faced each other down. After a moment, by unspoken consent, they turned away from each other and went their separate ways. Wayne went to stand by the casket. Anthony sauntered around the room, checking out the different floral arrangements, reading each card. I glanced over at the video just in time to see the picture changing to the one that had caught my eye earlier. There was Regina, with the party hat and the cake and her co-workers. Beside her, his hand on her shoulder stood a man in his late thirties with brown hair and eyes. I knew him. It took the full four seconds but, as the picture was dissolving, it came to me. I had met him a few days earlier in a conference room at the State Police barracks.

Before I could consider the picture further, a voice broke my train of thought. "Hey, Bunyan. Is it just me or is it really tense in here?"

He spoke quietly, at least for him, but I noticed both Wayne and Anthony glance our way when Russ spoke. I hadn't heard him enter the building.

"Glad you could make it, Russ," Anthony said before returning to his study of the flowers.

"Wouldn't miss it, Dad!" Russ replied to his father's back, raising a hand in greeting. He shrugged and turned back to me. His eyes glistened feverishly. He was clean shaven and wore a dark blazer over a dark button down shirt that was threadbare around the collar. He squirmed under my gaze, blinking rapidly.

I waited.

"What?" Russ finally demanded gruffly. "Why are you just looking at me like that, Jolly Green?"

"Because, Short Round," I answered, "you seem jittery."

"It's my mother's memorial service," he snapped. He tried to glare at me with his moist reddened eyes but couldn't quite meet my gaze. He scratched his right forearm self-consciously. I shifted my gaze to the itch, then gave him a questioning look.

Russ let out a heavy sigh, glancing around before lowering his voice and leaning closer before letting loose with a hissing torrent. "Fine! I need a fix! There was no way I could get through something like this without it! And save your breath, Lurch. I know it's wrong. I know I fucked up. I know it'll probably kill me some day. Maybe I'll get clean again tomorrow. Maybe not. But it's my choice. And I can do without your self-righteous criticism, thank you very much!"

I gave him a patient smile as he sat there with his chest heaving. "I'm not judging you, Russ," I said truthfully. "I'm wondering if there's anything I can do to help you."

"Sure," Russ scowled, "you got fifty bucks I can borrow? And, by 'borrow,' I mean I probably won't get it back to you."

I hoped my look didn't convey pity; that wasn't what he needed right now. "No," I said. "But if you decide you want to get clean again and you need someone to vent to or to help you stay on the straight and narrow, I'd be glad to be a sounding board."

Russell frowned. "You're a good man, Patrick," he grumbled.

I smiled. "So are you, Russ." He scoffed. "Don't sell yourself short," I chided. He looked up at me. I shrugged. "So to speak." That netted me a chuckle and a grin.

Angela and Tanya returned. Russell and I joined them as they entered the room. Tanya and Russ exchanged pleasantries and hugged. Russ nestled his head against her chest for a second. I suppose it was one of the advantages of his stature. Tanya laughed. "That's the most attention I've had since I broke up with Mike last month," she declared.

At ten minutes before four, Ray Courtland corralled us together at the front of the viewing room, explaining the wake would start shortly. The family lined up, Angela and one end and Wayne at the other. I stood by Angela, providing tissues as needed and nodding and smiling as she introduced me to family members I may or may not have met over the last year and a half. Some smiled sympathetically, some were solemn. Angela hugged friends and family as they went through the line, or let them grasp her hands as they extended their sympathies, all the while a neutral smile plastered on her face, demonstrating strength in the wake of adversity. For my part, I was grateful when a Mason I recognized showed up in support of Tony, and I was able to introduce them to Angela for a change. Many of them raved about how they remembered her when she was just a girl running around during the summer picnic. She laughed and blushed.

Around five thirty, my parents came through the line. Mom hugged Angela tightly and told her she could always come to her for motherly advice. Angela smiled and thanked her. My father hugged her briefly as well, but refrained from offering fatherly advice.

When he shook my hand he asked, "Ian been here yet?" His eyes twinkled.

"No, is he planning to?" I asked.

"Said he was," Dad said.

"I'll keep an eye out for him," I promised.

Dad nodded and smiled. "Ask him what's new," he advised before moving down the line. Angela introduced them to Tanya and Russ.

The line of guests continued to parade past us, expressing their condolences. At one point, Officer Carrigan, dressed in street clothes, appeared before us. He seemed surprised to see me. I shook his hand and thanked him for coming, introducing him to Angela.

"I-I was a friend of your mother's," he said, glancing at me. I watched him impassively. "I knew her from her job."

"Thank you for coming," Angela said. "There are a few people from her office here already. It was kind of you to come by."

He nodded his acknowledgement. "I'm sorry for your loss," he said before moving on.

Ian arrived about half an hour later. He managed to clean up nicely, wearing his good jeans. He shook my hand and slapped me on the shoulder and hugged Angela. She thanked him for coming.

"Dad told me to ask you what's new," I said to him. My parents were still across the room, talking with Stuart Humphrey, current Master of Acacia Lodge, and his wife. My mother looked prim and properly bored. To be fair, so did Stu's wife.

Ian laughed. "Yeah, he would," he said. He glanced towards our parents before giving me a sheepish grin and saying, "Dad finally convinced me to join your little club."

I blinked. "You're going to become a Mason?" I asked.

Ian shrugged. "He made a convincing argument. He knows I've been looking for something more in my life and he thought maybe Freemasonry might point me in the right direction." The argument sounded vaguely familiar.

"He offered to pay your initiation fee and life membership, didn't he?" I asked drily.

"That too," Ian smiled.

"Well, whatever the reasons, I'm glad to hear it," I told him. "I look forward to participating in your Degrees."

"I'm sure you do," Ian said. "Whatever that means."

Angela glanced towards the line of waiting attendees and, with a patient smile, she smoothly interjected, "Ian, this is my cousin Tanya."

Ian turned towards the dark haired woman, opened his mouth to speak and hesitated. Then he grinned. "Nice to meet you," my brother said. "I'm sorry it's under such tragic circumstances." He took her hand, shook it, held it for a lingering moment.

Tanya's fair skin reddened as she blushed under Ian's attention. She glanced downward, chewed her lower lip and said, "Well, thank you. Nice to meet you too. Maybe we'll meet again on a more…pleasant occasion."

"I certainly hope so!" Ian's grin widened.

Russell leaned in between Tanya and Ian and remarked, "Move it along, Romeo. You're holding up traffic."

"Maybe we can chat again later," Tanya said as Ian finally released her hand.

"Count on it," he replied. As God is my witness he even winked at her. She fell for it though, giving a girlish giggle.

Ian moved on, shaking hands with a bemused Russell before he greeted Anthony.

Tanya and Angela exchanged a knowing glance. I looked briefly heavenward wondering what slice of hell was about to enter my life.

By seven fifteen the line of visitors had diminished. Everyone took a seat. Russ, Tony, Angela, Tanya and Wayne took the front row. I sat beside Angela, rubbing her shoulder encouragingly. Ian sat behind Tanya.

The pastor from Anthony and Regina's church gave a eulogy. He was a professional public speaker, probably an occupational benefit, but I had the impression he didn't have any particular connection with Regina. Twice I saw him glance down at a paper on the podium prior to mentioning her by name.

After the service, the forty or so mourners said their final good-byes and offered their condolences once more to the various family members that they knew best.

My parents bid Ian and I farewell. I thought Ian might leave with them. He didn't.

Officer Carrigan, who had been lingering and watching the pictures scroll by on the video, made his way to us and said a hasty good-bye. He seemed more broken up than a co-worker should be. I was unsurprised. Angela didn't seem to notice.

As the crowd thinned, Angela and I stood with Russ and Tanya and Ian. We were discussing post-memorial service plans, most of which included alcohol, when Wayne Novello stepped up beside his daughter. "Honey," he said, "I think I'm heading out.

Are you ready to go?"

Angela became very interested in studying any section of the viewing room that didn't contain her uncle.

Tanya glanced at our little group, eyes lingering on Ian. He gave a faint shrug. "No, Dad," he said to Wayne. "I think we're going out first. I'll meet you back at the hotel later."

"Ok," Wayne said, leaning in and kissing her cheek. He shook hands with Russell, who regarded him with indifference. "Good night, Angela," he said to my girlfriend's back. "I'm sorry for…everything."

I saw her back stiffen, felt my own jaw clench.

Wayne glanced at us, uncomfortably. Very soon, I knew, he wouldn't be around anymore to make Angela so unhappy. Something told me we weren't going to make it to that deadline.

"Angie," he said. He reached out and rested his hand on her arm. "Seriously, I –"

In an instant Angela turned into a whirling dervish as the tension erupted from her. Spinning away from him, eyes wide, she let out a shriek of banshee proportions. Her chest heaved as she panted and stared at him, hands balled into fists that she flailed against his chest in a frantic barrage.

"You don't get to call me Angie!" she shrieked.

"You don't get to be sorry! I wish it was you lying there, not her! I wish you were fucking dead!"

To his credit, Wayne didn't touch her again, didn't try to restrain her flying fists, though he did back away. We had, of course, caught the attention of the entire room. Anthony was striding towards us. Ray Courtland was scurrying in from the foyer. I reached out to take Angela's arm, to whisper words of reassurance to her. Tanya stepped between us with a brisk shake of her head in my direction, putting her arm around Angela's shoulders and whispering in her ear. Gradually Angela's anger subsided and she dropped her arms to her side and began to sob uncontrollably. Tanya took her in her arms, rubbed her hair, whispered something and guided her away from us towards the ladies' room.

Seeing the situation subside, Ray took up a sentry position outside the archway to the viewing room. Anthony reached us as they departed and we menfolk stood their somewhat awkwardly for a moment. That's our go to reaction when a woman erupts into fits of emotion. "What the hell was that about?" Anthony demanded.

"I was just saying good-bye," Wayne said, holding up his hands defensively.

"You grabbed her arm," Russell pointed out, glaring up at him. "I oughta punch you right in the nuts."

"I didn't *grab* her arm," Wayne said quickly. "I just touched it. To get her attention."

"It's time for you to go," Anthony said. "And you better stay gone. *Capice?*"

"I was just leaving," Wayne said, trying to regain some sense of dignity. None of us seemed willing to let him have it.

"I'll see you out," I said coldly. The offer wasn't for his benefit. I wanted to ensure Angela didn't cross paths with him again in the foyer.

As we crossed the foyer, I could see the flush rising in the back of Wayne's neck. Embarrassment? Anger? I didn't care. I just wanted him gone. He mumbled something under his breath. "I'm sorry?" I snapped.

He turned a baleful eye towards me, pausing just inside the exterior door. "I said, I wish Regina had been brave enough to leave Anthony months ago when she found out about his affair. She said she needed the money but I told her she already had plenty. If she'd listened to me, maybe none of this would have happened. Ward could have…"

I cut him off. "All this," I growled gesturing in vague circular motions with an open hand to indicate the scene that had just occurred, "had nothing to do with anything except you raping Angela all those years ago."

The look that crossed his face was indecipherable. I saw shame and regret, but there was a smirk and some cockiness. I felt like I was looking through the magic mirror on Romper Room with all the different faces I saw him go through. In a low voice, he said, very distinctly, "I never raped her. What happened between us was consensual. It was only afterward that she called it rape."

Every once in a while, a person experiences a truly satisfying moment. Slipping under a warm comforter on a cold winter's night. Taking off the too tight shoes after a long day on one's feet. Maybe the first savory bite of a favorite meal.

Each of these pales in comparison to the satisfaction I got when my right fist, almost of its own volition, landed squarely in Wayne's left eye socket and he dropped to the ground like a sack of proverbial potatoes.

I crouched down and got right in his face as Ray Courtland led the parade coming to see what the latest uproar was about. "You *ever* say something like that again," I hissed, a drop of spittle landing on his already swelling cheek, "and I will castrate you with my bare hands." As the family members gathered around us, I glanced up at Tony then back at Wayne. "*Capice?*" I demanded.

Looking genuinely scared, Wayne nodded. I stood, dragging him to his feet by the lapels of his jacket. He staggered. I made an exaggerated show of straightening his collar and flicking an imaginary fleck of dust from his shoulder. "Have a nice night," I said.

Wayne left without another word. I ignored the questions and curious looks. No one seemed too broken up by what I had done. Ian slapped me on the shoulder and said, "That was a nice solid punch, Bro. I didn't know you had it in you!"

Russ agreed. "No one was more deserving."

Even Anthony gave me a knowing smile. "He's had that coming for a long time."

The ladies returned from the bathroom. Angela's eyes were bloodshot and her nose was red and congested but she wasn't shaking anymore. "What's going on here?" Tanya asked, running a suspicious look over us.

By mutual unspoken consent, we kept mum. Even Ray wandered into the viewing room to avoid getting involved. "Your father is gone," Anthony said at last. To Angela he asked, "Are you okay, sweetheart?"

She gave him a sad smile. "No," she said. "But I will be." To me, she said, "I'd really just like to go home, if that's okay?" I agreed.

Ian turned to Tanya. "How about you?" he asked. "Wanna grab a drink?"

Tanya smiled. "I thought you'd never ask." She looked down at Russ. "Do you want to come along?" Her tone made it clear what her preferred answer was.

Russ waved a dismissive hand. "Are you kidding me? Do I want to be a spare wheel sitting there while you two make enough sugary goo-goo eyes at each other to put me in a diabetic coma? No, really, thanks, but I'll pass." He waggled a pudgy finger at Ian. "You just watch your hands with my cousin there, loverboy."

Ian smirked. "I intend to."

We donned our jackets, stepping out into the mild overcast evening, and went our separate ways, each of us no doubt relieved that the service was over.

Ray Courtland quietly closed the door quietly behind us.

Chapter Sixteen

The next morning was grey and overcast. A fine mist, almost unworthy of the name rain, coated everything. We were fortunate that it was just not quite cold enough to turn to ice. In all, the gloom was the perfect weather for the day.

At the funeral home, the family said their final farewells to Regina. I lurked in the lobby, close enough to step in if needed for emotional support, but giving them some space to grieve and pay their last respects in private. Russ was the first to leave the casket and, after a few whispered words to her father, Angela followed. The three of us watched and waited patiently as Anthony spoke to Regina. I held Angela close. Even Russ, who appeared to be clean and sober that day, remained respectfully silent. There was no sign of Wayne.

Ray Courtland explained that Regina would be brought to the crematorium that evening and Anthony could pick up her ashes the next day. He reminded us that, when the family was ready, the cremains could be interred at the cemetery, but there was no rush.

As we left for our cars, I spotted Wayne behind the wheel of his car across the street. I assumed he was waiting until we'd left to have his own opportunity to say good-bye to his sister. I excused myself as Angela got in the car, and crossed the street. Wayne rolled down the window just enough so we could speak. His left eye was puffed out and red and, despite feeling fully justified in doing it to him, it still physically hurt to look at the bruise.

"I don't want any trouble," he said tentatively.

During the night, when replaying the scene in my head, I had realized that my emotional reaction had blinded me to a salient detail. It was fortuitous that I'd seen him today, so I could follow up on it. The social norms indicated that I should smooth the waters first by apologizing for punching him. But I didn't feel apologetic and if social norms didn't like it, I was tempted to pop them one too.

I asked, "Who's Ward?"

"What?" he demanded. I suppose he had a right to be snippy given my circumvention of social norms and all.

"Right before I…interrupted you last night, you were saying something about someone named Ward. Who is Ward?"

Wayne laughed humorlessly but the gesture caused him to wince and he stopped. "You really think I'm going to answer your questions? After all this?" He gestured towards the situation with his eye.

I shrugged. "I had hoped we could move past our difficulties, yes," I said. "Besides, if it helps to find your sister's killer, why wouldn't you want to help?"

"The cops already have the guy," Wayne sneered.

"They have a suspect. Until he's charged, tried and convicted, we can't really know for sure."

He glared at me in silence for a few more beats.

"I'd rather not give you a matching set," I said, looking towards his right eye.

"You caught me off guard," Wayne muttered, "I could take you in a fair fight."

"Hopefully we don't have to find that out."

Whether it was the veiled threat of more violence or he was just sick of my voice, Wayne finally spread his hands and said, "Well, fact is, I can't help you much anyway. Ward was just some guy she'd mentioned at one point. Guess he was a friend of hers. It sounded like there might be more there but she never said. Don't know anything about him, last name, where he lives, what he looks like. Nothing. So there you go."

"Well," I said with a shrug, "that's not very helpful. But I appreciate your candor."

"Yeah, sure," Wayne grunted. "Candor."

There was a small luncheon at Tony's house that day, to have a chance to interact with and thank those who had attended the memorial service. Relatives came by, ate casseroles and lunchmeats and meatballs and paid their respects once more before departing. Wayne didn't make an appearance, but Tanya showed for a while. Ian was with her. I was less surprised than I should have been, I suppose.

Around one forty, as Angela, Tanya and Russ were cleaning up from lunch, I touched my girlfriend on the shoulder and told her I had to go. She nodded, gave me a hug and a kiss on the cheek and thanked me for everything. She didn't ask where I was going; I'd warned her that morning that I had an appointment at two.

Five minutes early, I strode into the State Police barracks. Detective Finley was already waiting for me. The secured door to the sanctum sanctorum buzzed and Finley led me inside without a word. Once in the hallway beyond he said, "Got him here and processed a couple hours ago. I let him sit for a while. Maybe that will loosen his lips."

He opened a door, allowing me to enter before him. We were on the see-thru side of a one-sided mirror, in a small room. A speaker hung on one wall. "Stay in here," he said. "You're here as a courtesy, Mr. Brady, nothing more. Frankly, I'd rather have you here where I can keep an eye on you than have you running around out there plucking hairs off of trees and stirring up trouble while I'm trying to interview a legitimate suspect."

I gave him a wan smile. "I appreciate your generosity." He made a gruff harrumphing noise and pulled the door closed.

A moment later I saw him enter the adjoining room on the other side of the mirror. I pressed the power button on the speaker and glanced around for a chair. There was none. I stood. Finley sat with his back to me and spent a moment or two reviewing the file folder he'd brought with him. I was sure he already knew what was in it and was just making the kid sweat some more. I looked past the back of his closely cropped cinnamon and sugar hair at the suspect in custody. Lean and short with a thick head of black hair. Hispanic and somewhere in between Angela and myself in age, at a guess. His hands were cuffed and chained to the table but he sat slumped back in his metal chair watching Finley with well-feigned indifference and arrogance. I could see he was sweating and I'm sure the fact wasn't lost on the detective either.

Finley closed the folder at last, clasping his hands on top of it and faced the accused. "Jose Roberto Ramos," he drawled, rolling his r's in an exaggerated fashion. "Welcome back. I hope you enjoyed your trip."

Ramos lifted one shoulder in a carefree shrug. "Seats were comfortable and the company wasn't very talkative. But it was aight. So why'm I here? I didn't do nothing."

Finley gestured vaguely with his hands. "Well, that's good to know. Maybe we can get this cleared up quick then, be out of here in time for a siesta." Ramos chuffed and turned his face away from the officer in disgust. "See, Jose, we have a dead woman on our hands. And you happen to fit the description of a suspect spotted near the crime scene."

"Man, that's bull," Jose huffed, "I didn't cap no chica. Believe me. I done it, you ain't never of caught me." His left eye twitched. I was sure Finley saw it too.

"Well, if that's the case," Finley said still in a tone that was both taunting and mild, "you got nothing to worry about. But maybe you might want to know about her death anyway. Seeing as you knew the family and all."

My eyebrows rose. That was news to me. Jose seemed discomfited by the revelation as well. "Who was it?" he asked. The confidence was slipping from his voice.

"Woman named Regina Button," Finley said. "Seems your family and theirs were near neighbors during your formative years, back when you were just a teen getting busted for drug possession and B-and-

E's."

Jose made a show of thinking for a moment before saying, "Yeah, yeah, I think I remember her. Nice lady. Shame she dead. Still got nothing to do with me."

"I heard," Finley pressed, "you were good friends with their daughter before you started your life of crime." Finley's head turned just a couple degrees to the right. I could see his eyelashes, eyes open and steady as usual. "You ever tap that?" he asked. I froze.

Jose laughed and wriggled in his chair, looking away again. "Man, what the hell kinda question is that? Ain't none of your business where my dick's been. Let's clean up this murder BS and get me outta here."

Finley spread his hands again. "Indulge me," he said. It wasn't a request.

Ramos looked like he was going to refuse again but finally shrugged and relented. "No, she wasn't down wit dat. She had a cousin, though, pretty hot and liked to party. Satisfied?"

I was, though I resolved not to mention Tanya's history to Ian. To be fair, he had a string of casual encounters behind him as well. I glanced over as the door to the room opened abruptly. Officer Carrigan stepped in, closing the door behind him and stopped when he saw me. His face went white with surprise.

"Officer," I greeted him mildly.

"Mr.…Mr. Brady," he said, recovering quickly. "I didn't realize the Detective was allowing you in here to listen in."

"So I gathered." I tipped my head towards the window. "Come to watch the show?"

"I…yeah," he said sheepishly. "I know I'm not really on the case, per se, but she was my…my friend. And I want to see the guy who killed her with my own eyes."

I nodded. "There he is," I said, gesturing with my chin. "Allegedly." We both turned to face the window.

Finley was asking, "Did Regina know you… partied with her niece? Or that you wanted to do so with her daughter?" Carrigan's hands tightened into fists.

Jose shifted uncomfortably again. "I don't know what she knew, man. Probably. Girls, they talk to they moms about shit like that, I guess."

"Maybe she didn't approve," Finley suggested, his tone slipping from casual to cold as he concluded, "Maybe that's why you killed her."

For a moment Jose was still and the two men locked eyes. Then, with a cocky smirk, Jose leaned forward. Finley held his ground. "Man, if that's what you think, you barking up the wrong tree. Regina approved of me aight! You know what I'm saying?"

Finley tipped his head to one side. Almost too quietly he asked, "I think so, but why don't you spell it out?" He paused for a beat. "Did you... party with Regina too?"

A low guttural sound came from Officer Carrigan's throat. I ignored him.

"Maybe I did," Jose replied in a tone that resounded with yesses. "Maybe I saw her at the courthouse a few months back. My cousin was being arraigned for something he didn't do and I saw her and she came up and said hello. She remembered me, asked if I was staying outta trouble. Small talk bullshit, you know? But all the while she be given me this look like she could eat me right up." He grinned broadly enough for me to see he was missing a molar. "So later that day, she did."

Carrigan slammed a fist against the wall. Jose Ramos looked up towards the glass. Finley threw a disgusted look over his shoulder, probably assuming I was reacting harshly to the punk's violation of my sainted mother-in-law.

I glanced sidelong at Carrigan, who was pacing the tight room in an aggrieved manner. "That must be tough to hear," I murmured, "Given that you were in love with her."

He stopped and looked at me in surprise. "What did you say?" he demanded.

Instead of answering, I turned and faced him full on and asked, "How long were you together, *Ward?*"

His jaw worked for a moment, then his shoulders slumped. "How did you know?" he asked.

"Aside from the fact that you've been walking around like a man with nothing left to lose since I've known you?" I asked. "Her brother mentioned you. Loose lips sink ships." I glanced toward the interrogation room and, though I felt dirty saying it, I prodded, "They apparently do other things too."

He let out another groan and turned away, then spun back to face me, speaking feverishly. "Look, you can't say anything to anyone. Yes, Regina and I were in love. It started last September. We were already acquaintances from when our paths crossed for work. We were talking and she broke down, crying and talking about her husband having an affair. I took her for coffee. We talked. It grew from there. We were in love." He looked at me plaintively, "She told me she loved me and I believe her." Gesturing towards the mirror he said in a bewildered voice, "Now. Now I'm not sure what she felt. If any of it was real. She told me she was going to leave her husband. After the holidays. She wanted to be with me. That's what she said."

I gave him credit for not bursting into tears.

Having your heart broken by a woman is never easy. But, given his current emotional state, I had to ask. If he was ever going to confess, it would be now. "Did you kill her?"

He looked at me with genuine surprise in his eyes. "Of course not! Until now, I thought everything was great between us! I had no reason to kill her! We were going to be together!" He lowered his voice and turned away, repeating, "We were going to be together."

"What the hell is this?" Finley's voice rang out sharply and we both spun towards the sound. I admit, even though I'd done nothing wrong, just the accusation in his voice filled my heart with guilt.

Fortunately, he was still in the interrogation room and not speaking to us. I assumed he had continued questioning Jose Ramos, trying to approach from different verbal angles until the suspect slipped and said something that incriminated himself. I regretted not being able to listen in during my conversation with Officer Carrigan. Especially now that the interrogation appeared to have come to an end.

A young female officer stood just inside the adjoining room, holding the door open and looking apologetic. A large, well-dressed man with slick grey hair and a slicker suit strode in purposely. He slapped a briefcase onto the table, deftly popping the latches and pulling out a piece of paper. He pointed a stubby finger at Ramos and barked, "Don't say a word." To Finley, he added, "My client is done here."

"Your client?" Finley demanded skeptically. The female officer quietly slipped away, pulling the door closed. "Who are you?"

"Vince Capaldi. I'm Mr. Ramos's attorney."

"Man, you my lawyer?" Jose asked. "Dayum!"

"What did I just say?" the lawyer snapped at Jose before thrusting the paper into Detective Finley's hand. "You got nothing to hold him on. That there's a judge's order remanding him to my custody. This party's over."

Finley scowled at the written order while the lawyer waited impassively, arms crossed across his broad chest. "Wait here," he growled, heading for the door.

"And, Detective," Capaldi added. Finley turned back and the lawyer gestured towards the mirror. "Make sure there's no one listening in on my *private* conversation with my client."

Finley didn't answer, but left the room, slamming the door behind him. Carrigan was already leaving our room and met him in the hall. I hurried behind him. If Finley seemed surprised to see the officer there, he was too distracted to comment.

"Detective," Carrigan said, "you *can't* let him go. He killed her. We both know it."

"Stand down, Carrigan," Finley barked. He waved the paper angrily. "They got a judge to sign the order. A crooked judge, no doubt. Crooked as that sonofabitch lawyer's weasley smile. But a judge all the same. Our hands are tied."

"But, Detective…"

"Carrigan, you're too close to this. Whatever torch you were carrying for the victim, your head isn't in the game. Get the hell out of my sight. We'll get the guy, I promise." Carrigan wanted to argue some more but Finley spun on me. "You recognize that guy?" He jerked his thumb over his shoulder towards the interrogation room.

"Ramos?" I asked, "No, never seen…"

Finley shook his head fervently. "No, no, the lawyer. You know that sleazeball?"

I blinked. "I can't say that I do."

"Yeah," Finley growled, "well, I recognize his name. He's pretty well known down in the city. Especially with the mafia types."

"He's a mob lawyer?" I asked. "How does a guy like Ramos afford that?"

"*He* doesn't," Finley confirmed. "But I'll bet we

know someone else can. And if they can afford a mob lawyer, they can probably afford a hitman too, one they don't want questioned any further by the cops. Know anyone like that?" He gave me a significant gaze. I knew what name came to my mind but I ground my teeth refusing to give credence to Finley's suspicions. He smiled coldly. "I know you're thinking what I'm thinking, Brady," he said. "I'd advise you to keep your mouth shut about it when you leave here. If I find out you gave anyone a warning, I'll arrest you for interfering with an investigation."

"My lips are sealed," I agreed glumly.

"Good," Finley said. He whirled towards the female officer who had admitted Capaldi to the interrogation room and pointed at her. "Slingerland! I started a full trace on this Ramos guy yesterday when I found out he was being shipped up here. Follow up on those. I want phone records, bank records, gun possession records, everything. Have we got a warrant to search his place yet?"

Officer Slingerland stiffened her back, stood her ground under Finley's barrage. "We should have the warrant in the next thirty minutes," she replied. "No phone records; he probably uses a burner. He has a registered Smith & Wesson M&P 15-22 Sport." She grimaced. "Button was killed by a .40 caliber round," she added.

Finley grunted. "If there's one gun, Slingerland, there's bound to be more. We can stall this guy and his lawyer with paperwork for an hour, maybe two. Soon as that warrant comes in, I want any guns found and down to the labs to have ballistics run on it."

When Finley turned back to stalk towards his desk, he spotted me and stopped short. "What are you still doing here? The interview is obviously over."

"If he's the killer," I asked, "what's his motive?"

"Love affair gone bad, maybe," Finley said. He didn't sound entirely convinced. "I'm more inclined to believe he was hired by someone. I think we both know who."

"Will you let me know what you find out?" I requested.

Finley showed his teeth in a wolfish smile. "Trust me, Mr. Brady," he said. "If this shakes out like it feels it's going to, you'll find out soon enough."

That didn't bode well. I thanked him and left the barracks.

I returned to Tony's house. Angela and Tony were the only ones still there. The house felt empty. Angela asked me about my visit to the police station. I hedged. I couldn't tell them what I was afraid was coming, no matter how much I wanted to. I saw nothing wrong with talking about the suspect though, especially since he'd lawyered up.

"Jose?" Angela sked, frowning. "I remember him." She looked at her father and reminded him, "You remember the Ramoses, Daddy. Jose mowed your lawn a few times. He was a year or two ahead of me, maybe even in Russ's class. He came over once in a while."

Tony shrugged distractedly. "I can't picture him," he said. He asked me, "The police are convinced that he's the one who killed Regina, though?"

"He seems like Finley's prime suspect right now," I agreed.

"But why?" Angela asked. "I don't think any of us have seen them since my parents moved out here. What motive would he have?"

I shrugged. I doubted both of Finley's theories on the topic and saw no reason to cause either of them pain by repeating them. "He didn't give me a good explanation," I hedged.

"Well, at any rate," Tony sighed, "if they've got him in custody, maybe this nightmare is almost over."

I rubbed my nose and huffed. This thin line I was treading between family and the police was getting so fuzzy it was making my allergies act up. "I'm sure," I said at last, "Finley will get everything worked out in the end. He seems pretty competent when it comes down to it."

"But?" Angela asked. She knew me too well.

"But…I don't know how long Ramos is going to remain in police custody," I admitted. "Someone hired him a slick New York City lawyer and got a judge to sign an order releasing him. At least for now."

"Who hired him a lawyer?" Angela frowned.

"I don't know, but he seems pretty good," I answered watching Tony. "Name's Vince Capaldi." The sudden tension in Tony's jaw and back were subtle but they were there. He recognized the name. Angela must have noticed it, too. She was looking at her father with a puzzled look. I patted her on the shoulder, distracting her. "I wouldn't worry, though," I told her. "Finley will build his case and they'll have him back in custody soon enough."

"It might be soon," Angela remarked, her father's behavior forgotten, "but I wouldn't call it soon enough." I conceded the point.

There was a heavy knock on the door.

The three of us exchanged glances. Tony's gaze lingered on mine for a moment. Something unspoken passed between us. He knew who was there and he knew I did too. His eyes had the look of a caged animal who has given up trying to escape. With a heavy sigh, he climbed to his feet.

"Detective," he greeted Finley in a flat voice as he opened the door.

"Anthony Button," Finley said formally. He held up a pair of handcuffs. "You're under arrest for conspiracy to commit murder."

Chapter Seventeen

Tony was arraigned on one count of conspiracy to murder the next day. Angela and I sat in the gallery and watched the proceedings. They were straight forward. Tony pled not guilty. The judge remanded him to custody on half a million dollars' bail pending trial and banged his gavel, sealing the deal. Angela wept but didn't throw herself on the bar separating our seats from the main section of the courtroom as her father, dressed in State-issued drab green garb, was escorted back out of the room.

I put my arm around Angela's waist and escorted her out into the hallway. "What do we do now?" she asked me. She sounded like a lost little girl.

"He'll probably be kept in RCJ pending trial," I said. "I'll see if I can pull some strings and get us in to see him." Derek Beckham, the Chief of Police in Troy, where Rensselaer County Jail was located, was a fellow Mason. I didn't like to abuse that connection, but in this instance I was pretty sure Derek would be willing to make a call to get us in, even outside regular visiting hours.

"Give him my regards," a gruff voice said behind us. We stopped and turned.

Vito Denato was leaning against the wide Doric marble pillar we had just passed. He wore a black leather jacket and white shirt, blue jeans and boots. The corner of his mouth twitched in a hint of smirk as I recognized him.

"Brady," he said. He dipped his head to my girlfriend. "Angela. You've grown into a good looking woman. I'm sure your old man is proud."

"Thank you," Angela said with a puzzled frown. "Who are you?"

"I'm a childhood friend of your father's," Vito replied smoothly. "Heard about his arrest, happened to be in the area."

Angela nodded slowly, sliding a look from the mobster to me and back again. "And you were chatting up my boyfriend at Danny's Place a few nights ago," she said.

Vito's grin broadened. "Perceptive, too. Sharp broad."

"I'm surprised to see you're still here," I remarked. "I had the impression you were headed back to the city."

The smile faded as he turned his piercing eyes towards me. "And I had the impression you were putting an end to your…inquiries," he said. "Was I mistaken?"

"The police arrested a suspect without any assistance on my part," I replied a touch defensively.

"Relax, Brady," Vito said, clapping a meaty hand on my shoulder. I managed not to flinch. "I know you had nothing to do with Jose's arrest. Or Tony's for that matter."

"Good to know," I said. "Along the same lines, can I assume you had something to do with Jose being released?"

Denato's bushy eyebrows rose. "Me? I'm just a businessman. What do I know about lawyers or judges?" he asked with blatant insincerity.

Angela had been watching our exchange with a frown. She chimed in. "Wait a minute. *You* hired the lawyer to get Jose out of jail? Why would you do that?" she demanded.

Before Vito could answer, I spoke up. "He thought he was protecting your father," I told her. Turning to the so-called businessman, I asked, "Isn't that right, Vito? You made sure Jose was sprung from police custody for the same reason you tried to deter me from my investigation. You think Tony's guilty!"

Vito's jaw worked for a moment. His lips twisted and writhed around his face for a moment as he glared at me. Finally he conceded, "It's certainly a possibility."

"It absolutely is not," Angela snapped. "If you really knew my father, you'd know that's not in his nature."

To her, Vito replied, "Sorry, kid. But if *you* really knew your father, you'd realize it is."

"Regardless," I interceded, "I think we need to go on the assumption that he's innocent until we see proof otherwise. Any chance the same judge that sprung Jose will work his magic for Tony as well."

Vito looked peeved. "Sadly, that judge has decided he can't repeatedly interfere with an ongoing investigation. If we were in the City, it would be a different story, but up here my connections are… limited. I would have liked to keep Tony out of jail altogether. But, if Tony is going to get out any time soon, you'll have to prove his innocence."

"Believe me," I said, "I have every intention of doing so."

Vito nodded. "If you need any wheels greased, you let me know," he said.

"I'll keep that in mind," I agreed drily. I glanced at Angela, knowing what I wanted to ask, but wondering which one of them would respond more vehemently. "And what happens if it turns out he's guilty?"

"Do you really believe that?" Angela asked, staring at me aghast. She pulled her arm away from me, hugging herself.

"I don't believe the police would have arrested him unless they had *some* kind of justification," I answered. "Hopefully we can find out what that is, and then we can work to disprove it. I *believe* he's innocent, love. But that's not going to be enough to get him out. We'll need proof."

"Your old man is a good guy, Angela," Vito chimed in. "And your boyfriend is sharp. If your dad is innocent, we'll find a way to spring him." He turned to me. "And, to answer your question, if he's guilty… well, we'll have to burn that bridge when we get to it."

"Don't you mean we'll cross that bridge?" I asked. Vito stared at me without comment, his silence speaking volumes. I nodded. "I see," I said at last.

"Give Tony my regards," Vito reiterated. He dipped his head at Angela and walked away, his hands in his jacket pocket.

"Who was that man?" Angela asked me as we watched him go. "And how does he know my father?"

"You'd have to ask your father," I replied.

She looked up at me. "I'm asking you," she countered.

I swallowed. "Like he said, they were friends when they were younger. Anything more than that, you'd have to get from your father directly."

She stared at me, using that "silence to force the other person to spill his guts" trick on me. I grit my teeth, calling on all my fortitude to not say more. Finally she turned away. "Fine," she muttered. I'd won the battle, but she wasn't happy about it. I tried to take her arm, but she pulled away and walked two steps ahead of me as we left the courthouse.

Derek Beckham was hesitant to use his position to get us in to see Tony but he knew Tony and agreed with my assessment that he was probably innocent, so he said he'd make a call and let me know. He called back about ten minutes later. "You're good to go. He'll be back at RCJ after lunch; I let the guard on duty at the window know you'd be stopping by."

I thanked him and, around one o'clock that afternoon, Angela and I were parking in the large empty lot in front of the jail.

The County Jail sits on a broad plain in the southern end of Troy, between the city transfer station and an abandoned ironworks factory. To the west, the Hudson River made a pretty effective barrier. I'd been a temporary guest of the county at this facility a little over a year ago, due to a misunderstanding and my knack for being in the wrong place at the wrong time. I hadn't returned here since, except for one time. Last June, several of the local Masons marched in the Flag Day Parade. As the home and final resting place of Uncle Sam, Troy boasts the largest Flag Day Parade in the country. I don't know if that's accurate. All I know is that our contingent – at 300 plus marchers and three floats, the Freemasons had the largest group in the parade - used the long road that ran beside the jail (outside the barbed wire topped fence of course) as a staging area. I made every effort at the time to ignore the building.

I steeled myself and Angela and I entered. We spoke to the guard behind the thick Plexiglas barrier and identified ourselves before putting all our valuables in a locker and taking a seat in a pair of hard plastic chairs while we waited to be admitted. I wondered vaguely what law enforcement locations had against comfortable seating. Fortunately the wait was a brief one and the guard admitted us through a set of two secured doors before we were directed into the large concrete, windowless visitation room. I remembered this room from a different angle, when my father had come to visit during my stay. We selected a pair of stools about halfway along the winding counter that separated freedom and imprisonment. The stools, metal and bolted to the floor, were even less comfortable that the chairs in the hallway. A few minutes later, Tony was escorted in.

He look tired, but resilient. His back remained straight and he thanked the guard who was escorting him by name. As Tony sat the guard retreated to a respectful distance where he could probably still overhear the conversation without being obvious about it. He tried not to look directly at us but there really wasn't anything else interesting in the room. He seemed relaxed but I knew if Tony suddenly got the urge to jump the table and make a run for freedom, the guard could whip out his Taser and have Tony on the ground in a matter of seconds. I sincerely doubted any of that was going to happen.

"Hi, Daddy," Angela said, smiling. She was determined to stay upbeat, if only for him. Tony and I exchanged a nod of greeting.

"Hey Dumpling," he said to her. "How are you holding up?"

"I'm okay," she answered, "but how are you?"

Tony shrugged. "It's county," he said philosophically. "Mostly drug dealers and thieves. I haven't been here long so I haven't really had a time to make friends yet." He gave a half-hearted grin.

"Is there anything you need?" I asked.

Another shrug. "I'd like to get out of here. But I imagine that will happen in due course." He gave Angela an earnest look. "I *am* innocent, Angie," he said, "I hope you know that."

She smiled. "Of course I do, Daddy." She glanced my way. She still wasn't thrilled with me but was starting to soften up again. "We both do. And Patrick is going to get you out of here real soon."

"I appreciate your efforts," Tony told me.

I accepted the gesture with a dip of my chin and asked, "Do you have any idea what kind of evidence they have?"

Tony frowned. "I'm not sure. That Detective, Finley, he had a lot of questions. He's a clever one. Kept asking me for details, made me retell my story three or four times, always trying to trip me up. Hell, a little longer in there with him and I might have started to think I was guilty myself! But there seemed to be two main points that he was focused on that I couldn't help him with. One had to do with a bank transfer, and the other was a gun."

"Was it a .40 caliber subcompact pistol by any chance?" I asked, furrowing my brow.

"Actually, yes," Tony answered surprised. "How did you know?"

I shook my head. "Just a hunch," I lied. "What was the deal with this bank transfer?"

Tony spread his hands helplessly. The guard noticed the movement and tensed almost imperceptibly. "I really have no idea," Tony replied. "He kept asking me about twenty grand. Where it came from, why I withdrew it, where it was now. He didn't believe I had no idea what he was talking about."

"Have you made any transfers or withdrawals?" I asked.

"Nothing out of the ordinary," Tony replied. "Maybe took a thousand out of the Christmas club account but that was as extravagant as we got."

"But you have other bank accounts?" I pressed.

Tony's jaw worked for a moment. "I do," he agreed. "Regina and I each had a checking account and a savings account, plus we had a joint savings for big expenses – saving for a new car, for example. But I didn't touch any of them."

I glanced at Angela then asked, "What about Russ?"

Tony frowned. "What about Russ? We had a savings account set up in his name when he was a child. Did that for both of them. But we let them take them over when they were twenty-one. I'm sure Russ's account is empty by now."

"I meant did Russ have access to any of your accounts?" I clarified. Angela turned to look at me but said nothing.

"No," Tony said firmly. "Those accounts only had mine and Regina's names on them." He leaned forward with a scowl. "Are you suggesting Russ stole the money from one of those accounts?"

"I don't believe that," Angela chimed in. "Yeah, Russ has been known to steal money or little things that he can sell or pawn to get some quick cash, but he rarely takes more than he needs to get his next fix. Or whatever he needs money for at the time. He'd never write a phony check or anything that would be so easily traceable or for so much money. That's just not his style."

"I agree," Tony said. "He's a petty thief at best. I doubt he's ever written a check, fraudulent or not, in his life."

"You could be right," I said noncommittally. "Did Finley suggest anything else that might tie you to Jose Ramos?"

"No," Tony answered. "But he must have felt he had sufficient evidence. He made a point of telling me that they'd found the gun you mentioned in Jose's apartment, and alluded to a large deposit he'd made, and told me I could expect to see Jose in here tonight because he was putting out another warrant for him. He said it like he was hoping to get a reaction out of me. Said something like we'd be reunited or something along those lines. But, of course, since I barely remember the kid, let alone conspired with him to kill my wife, I think he was disappointed by my response." Tony chuckled. "He sneered at me before he left the interrogation room."

I nodded. "That sounds like the detective," I said. "He sneers a lot."

We were quiet for a minute. "So how are we going to get my father out of here?" Angela asked me finally.

I gave her a thoughtful look. "The evidence sounds pretty damning," I said. "Personally I think it damns too many people for him to be able to pin it on you. Anyone could have written a check from one of the accounts and scribbled a signature. The gun concerns me because I think it's Russ's." Angela and Tony exchanged a look. "The problem is, I don't really want it to be anyone that could have had access to the gun and the checkbook. Because that pretty much narrows it down to your father, your brother...or you."

It's possible I could have slapped Angela across the face and gotten a less explosive reaction. She stared, stunned for a moment, then scooted backwards off the stool, staggering before regaining her feet. The guard went on instant alert, taking two steps towards us, hand hovering over his now unbuttoned holster.

"Are you *fucking* serious?" she shouted at me. In the year and a half we'd been together, a time frame that included a brief time when she thought I was having an affair, Angela had screamed at me exactly three times. It was not a pleasant experience.

"Ma'am," the guard intoned warningly. "I need you to sit down."

She remained standing, glaring at me for another moment. "Angie," Tony said gently, "please." Grudgingly she sat, leaving an empty stool between the two of us, and folded her arms over her chest, turning towards her father. The guard relaxed his stance again. "We asked Patrick to look into this and he's doing the best he can under the circumstances. And he's not wrong. The evidence is pretty damaging. Looked at from the outside, any of us *could* have hired Jose to shoot your mother. I don't believe – and I don't think Patrick believes – that any of us did, though. We'll get the money thing figured out and, more importantly, once they have Jose back in custody and they question him, sooner or later, he'll break. And he'll tell them that he did it of his own volition."

I remained silent but looked apologetic. It was a rookie relationship move, suggesting that my girlfriend could have conspired in her mother's murder. I had, as Anthony had explained, meant that it could have been interpreted that way from the outside. In retrospect, I still should have kept it to myself. Unfortunately, I was less confident about the rest of his statement. I hadn't told them about the relationship between Jose and Regina. Thrown into the mix and Tony had the motive, means and opportunity. Russ did, too, since it was his gun, but only if he had managed to steal a check from his parents. I doubted Angela was culpable; she would have had to know about, and steal, her brother's gun *and* a check from her parents. Too many if's there. Besides, I'm sure there were other people higher on her "to kill" list than her mother. Her mother's brother, for example.

"Fine," Angela said in response to her father. To me, she said,. "Just do whatever you have to to get my father out of here. Preferably without landing my brother here…or me." She raised one eyebrow archly, her mouth a thin line.

"I'll do my best," I promised, "to find the truth without causing any of you anymore pain."

"That's not the same thing," she pointed out.

"I know," I agreed.

"Speaking of people doing whatever they have to to protect you, Daddy," Angela said, turning to her father, "we ran into a friend of yours today. Vito Denato?" Apparently Anthony was going to catch some of the shrapnel from Angela's anger at me.

Tony tried to hide his surprise but was not entirely successful. "Oh?" he asked.

"Apparently he was the one who hired the lawyer that got the guy that probably killed Mom out of jail," she said. "Good company you're keeping."

"I'm sure he had his reasons," Tony said

reluctantly.

"He claims he did it to protect you. Apparently, he thought you were guilty to and was trying to protect you." She looked around. "Fat lot of good that did."

Tony sighed. "Vito's a good guy but his brain isn't always as big as his heart," he said. After a moment, he turned to me and changed the subject, "We have a First Degree tonight. Obviously I'm not going to make it. Please pass along my apologies. I'd prefer you not tell them why I was...detained."

"My lips are sealed," I promised.

Angela grunted. "You're actually going to Lodge tonight while my father sits in jail?" she demanded.

I opened my mouth but Tony held up his hand to stop me. Good choice. It would carry more weight from him at this point. "Angie," he said, "I'm going to be fine. I can hold my own in here. Patrick has a responsibility at Lodge tonight and there's no reason my situation should keep him from fulfilling that. I'm sure he'll make every effort tomorrow into getting this resolved."

The both glanced at me. I crossed my heart and held up three fingers, pledging scout's honor. "You'd better," she told me sullenly.

We wrapped our conversation and said our goodbyes. Angela wanted to hug her father and the guard reluctantly agreed, standing nearby and keeping an eye on their hands. We waited until the guard had escorted him back within the confines of the jail, then we left.

Tony had been right about one thing. I did have a responsibility at Lodge that night, albeit a minor one. It was one of my first opportunities to perform some of the Masonic ritual. As Senior Master of Ceremony, my job for Degree consisted of one paragraph of memorized ritual (which I had been practicing for weeks and had letter perfect), preparing the new candidate for the Degree with the assistance of the Junior MC, and some floorwork, which mostly consisted of marching around the Lodge with my staff, following the person in front of me. On the whole, not a difficult night but my inner thespian, who often wished I'd gone into acting after my time in the high school drama club, was looking forward to busting loose.

The meeting was opened in due form. We had a good turnout. All the officers' chairs were filled, except for the obvious absence of our Treasurer. On the sidelines were Cliff Everett, my father and Dick McAlistair, an elderly member of the Lodge who, according to his doctors, should have been dead a year ago. They sat on the south side of the Lodge, between the Junior Warden's station and the Secretary's desk. Across the room from them sat our two visitors for the evening – Right Worshipful Luke Grey, our District Staff Officer, and Very Worshipful David Johnson, the Assistant Grand Lecturer. David and I had sat together during dinner before the meeting, to my father's delight. Right Worshipful Randall Simmons, the District Deputy who had created all the hubbub with his talk of merging Lodges, was conspicuously absent.

After the Lodge was opened and Stu Humphrey, the Master of the Lodge, asked if anyone knew of any sick Brothers or any in need of assistance, I stood, self-consciously straightening my tuxedo jacket, and made the sign of fidelity, a gesture of respect when addressing a higher ranking officer. "Worshipful Master," I said when he called on me, "Worshipful Anthony Button is indisposed this evening and asked me to pass along his regards."

The Worshipful Master nodded his head solemnly and I sat. His mustache fluttered as he said, "I would imagine he is. Brothers, for those of you who haven't yet heard, our Treasurer's wife was shot outside their home a couple weeks ago and passed away this past week. Brother Secretary, I'd like to get a sympathy card out to the family." He paused.

Gerald Wight, the Secretary, rose abruptly and saluted. "Yes, Worshipful Master," he said, "I'll get right on that, okay? I should have a couple here, okay? So if everyone can come up to my desk when we have a break and sign the card that would be, you know, great." The Master nodded and Jerry sat back down and began rooting through his briefcase.

From there, the Worshipful Master moved efficiently through the couple of minor business issues we had for the night. It being the night of a First Degree, any non-pressing matters were held over until a later meeting, so as to give the Degree the time it deserved. There was one issue that required attention.

"Brother Secretary," Stu asked, "do you have petitions or reports on petitions?"

Jerry stood and saluted and replied, "Yes, Worshipful Master. You know, I have a petition for membership from Mr. Ian Brady, okay?" He read briefly through the questions and my brother's responses and Stu asked for volunteers for the Interview Committee. I raised my hand. So did my father. Stu smiled and asked if there were any non-family members interested in being on the committee. In the end a committee led by Cliff and including Stephen Hill, our Junior Warden, and Harvey Mann, our Junior Deacon, was appointed.

Jerry stood again and reported, "Okay, Worshipful Master, also the committee to interview Bro. Scott Tisdale, a candidate for affiliation has reported favorably."

The Master nodded and rose, announcing that the committee was dismissed with the thanks of the Lodge and moved smoothly into the balloting process. After the ballot box had been examined and placed on the altar for the votes, the members of the Lodge filed up and cast their ballots. In my turn, I reached in, felt for one of the small balls in the reserve portion of the box, then dropped it into the slot, voting in favor of Scott's membership in the Lodge.

After the votes had been cast, the ballot was again reviewed by the Wardens and returned to the Master. After checking the results, he glanced around the room with a frown and conferred for a moment quietly with the Chaplain. Phil Ballard, who sat to the Master's left, had been Master of the Lodge the year before. Stu nodded once and faced the Lodge. After confirming the results with the Wardens, he announced that the ballot was clear and Scott Tisdale had been duly elected to become a member of the Lodge. From his momentary confusion, I suspected the ballot had been not been unanimous. It took three negative votes – represented by black cubes instead of a white ball like I had used – to reject a petitioner. In older days, we used black balls, instead of cubes, to reject someone. Hence the origin of the phrase "to black ball someone." But in the dimly lit Lodge rooms of yore, it was too easy to mistake the color of the ball and, since it only took one negative vote at that time to reject a petitioner, the balls were replaced by cubes. Since Scott's petition passed, I assumed only one or two people had voted against Scott. I wondered who the detractors had been.

When the rest of the routine business had been dispensed with, Stu moved on to the First Degree. When he addressed Jared Lawson and myself, we stood, staves in hand, and saluted. He asked how a candidate would be prepared for the Degree and I launched into my one and only line. I felt myself flush as I missed a word, then tried to go back and replace it, breaking my rhythm and causing myself to lose the entire line. I paused, took a quick breath, started from the beginning and repeated the line like I had done multiple times in the shower and in the car earlier in the day. The brief embarrassment was a lesson on the importance of practice, not to mention avoiding getting overly cocky about my performance.

We were directed to the preparation room to prepare the candidate. Jared and I saluted at the altar and left the room through the Inner Door.

Our new candidate, Samuel Byler, was sitting on a bench in the preparation room, waiting for us. He was in his early twenties, tall and lean, dressed in a simple dark suit. He had brown eyes and a thick mop of curly dark blonde hair that merged with the bushy sideburns on his chins. He stood as we entered and leaned our staves against the wall.

I greeted him, having had a chance to meet him briefly during the dinner before the meeting. "So," I explained, "part of the first part of Degree requires you to wear a ceremonial outfit. They probably mentioned that during your interview." I paused questioningly.

"They did," Sam confirmed. He had a heavy accent. German, maybe, possible Dutch. I wasn't sure.

I directed him to the enclosed stall in one corner of the room and explained how the different pieces of clothing were worn for the Degree. He went in, closed the door and begun to change.

"So," I asked, making conversation, "what brings you to Freemasonry?"

"I met Donald Florence about seven years ago," Sam explained, referencing our Senior Warden. "He was one of my first friends during my rumspringa. After I left the Church, I roomed with him for a while. He has suggested to me for a while that I should join, so I decided to see what it was about."

"I'm sure he wouldn't recommend you if he didn't think you'd be a good match," I said. "He takes the customs and protocols of the Fraternity pretty seriously." I tilted my head. "So, you mentioned rumspringa and the Church. You're Amish, then?"

"I was raised Amish, yes," Samuel replied. "Out

west, in Ephratah. I left after my rumspringa and have not been a part of the community for two years now." He sounded like he had doubts about that decision.

"I'm sorry to hear that," I offered. Jared was quietly getting the footwear together for Samuel. "It must have been a difficult decision to leave your family."

"It was not," Sam replied to my surprise. "But not because I don't love my family. It was not a difficult decision because I made the choice too hastily, without really considering all the consequences. However," he added with a sigh, "life goes on."

I shifted back to more immediate matters as Samuel exited the changing area. As I adjusted his outfit and we did the few remaining things necessary to prepare him properly, I reassured him, "I know the outfit seems kind of odd, but just bear in mind it has a symbolic purpose. Keep your ears open. You're going to hear a lot tonight and you probably won't remember most of it, but that's normal. Just absorb what you can; you'll learn the rest as you continue in Masonry. Just remember, everyone in that room has gone through the exact same process you're about to, so there's no reason to be self-conscious. And despite whatever you might have heard, there are no goats and no one has ever died as part of this ritual."

"What about that guy out near Batavia back in the

1820's?" Jared piped up. "We killed him supposedly."

The man doesn't say a word the whole time, until he pipes up with this. I shook my head slowly. "Nothing was ever proven," I assured both him and the candidate. I didn't mention that I'd had a distant relative who had been close to the William Morgan case, so the whole affair held a bit of fascination for me.

When Sam was prepared, we alert the Lodge and the First Degree was conferred. It went relatively smoothly. Any missteps were quickly corrected or simply overlooked in the interest of keeping things on track. My father made a point, afterwards, of telling me to relax and focus on the work at hand in order to avoid tripping over my tongue as I had during my one piece. I thanked him for being the only person to bring it up, but took the advice to heart.

It was just a tick past ten o'clock when I left the hall. The Degree had ended around nine thirty and Stu briefly wished everyone a happy winter holiday of their choosing before closing the Lodge. There was dessert after the meeting and I'm not usually one to pass that up, so I briefly indulged in the cake, decorated to congratulate our newest Entered Apprentice. It gave me a chance to meet up with Sam again and see how he enjoyed the Degree. He looked slightly dazed but said he'd enjoyed it and got a lot out of it. I empathized, remembering the sensations of my own

First Degree a year and a half earlier.

In the car I turned on the radio to catch the news. I was hoping there was nothing about Anthony's arrest. I'd been careful not to let word of that slip. I pulled out of the parking lot from the Lodge and headed towards Waterford and home as the national news ended and the local anchor ran down the top stories.

"Topping the local news tonight," the newscaster said, "A shooting outside Rensselaer County Jail tonight leaves one man in St. Luke's Hospital. Jose Ramos, himself a suspect in the death of Regina Button, was being escorted into the jail when an unknown gunman opened fire. Troy Police say they have a suspect in custody but are not releasing any details at this time. Ramos's condition is unknown. Stay tuned to WGAU for further details as they become available."

Chapter Eighteen

After listening for a couple minutes to see if there were any more details forthcoming – there weren't – I snapped the radio off and started to dial Angela's phone number. I stopped, hung up and dialed Russ instead. If he answered, I could tell him about the attack. If he didn't…at the back of my mind I wondered if he already knew about it, perhaps before it occurred. After four rings, the call went to voice mail. Not conclusive, but I hung up without leaving a message. Following a second hunch, I dialed the number Vito Denato had given me. He answered before the first ring had finished. "Mr. Brady," he intoned. "I thought I'd be hearing from you."

I forced myself to not think about the fact that he recognized my phone number, despite my having never given it to him. "Then you've heard?" I asked.

"It was on the television news at six o'clock," Vito answered. "I'm surprised it took you so long to call and see if I was accounted for."

I bristled. "I've been in a dinner and then a meeting all evening. I only just heard on the radio. You were my second call."

"Who was your first?" he asked with genuine

interest.

"Russell Button," I responded after a moment's consideration.

"I see," Vito replied. He paused then asked, "How did he take the news?"

"He didn't answer," I muttered.

"Mmm hmm," Vito hummed. "Interesting."

"Do you think it was him?" I asked.

"I think it's at least a reasonable possibility," Vito replied.

I sighed. "Me too."

"Well," the mobster said smoothly, "you're the one with the connection to the police chief. Maybe you can get some information from him."

"That's call number three," I agreed.

I hung up and dialed Derek Beckham. The news had said the Troy Police had a suspect in custody. I hoped that was still the case and that the State boys hadn't taken over jurisdiction, citing a connection to their ongoing investigation.

"Patrick," Derek said when he answered, sounding like he'd aged ten years since I'd spoken with him that morning. "I really can't talk right now."

"Just a quick question," I said hurriedly. "Maybe

two."

"I can't tell you anything about the investigation," Derek said apologetically. "It's still ongoing and you are too close to it." He lowered his voice. "Finley's here, too, by the way. We're working in tandem at the moment."

"Do you have the shooter in custody?" I asked.

A pause. "Yes."

"Are you sure it's him?" I asked.

"Yes." No pause.

"Is it Russ Button?" I asked, briefly closing my eyes as I idled at a red light and silently praying my gut was wrong.

"I'm sorry, Patrick," Derek said, sounding like he meant it. "We aren't releasing any information yet about the shooter. To anyone."

"Derek-" I started.

"To anyone," he reiterated. "Is there anything else? I really do need to go."

"What's Jose Ramos's condition at St. Luke's?" I asked, changing the topic.

"He's in critical condition," Derek said. "He's technically in State custody so they have a State trooper guarding his room."

"No chance I can get in to see him?"

Derek let out a toneless laugh. "None."

"Alright," I sighed. "What about Tony?" Can I get a visit with him?"

"Sorry," the police chief replied, "I pulled strings once. Now with this, there's no way I can put my neck on the line a second time so soon. You might be able to get a regular visit with him if you call and schedule one in the morning. That's the best I can tell you."

I nodded to myself. "Thanks, Derek. I understand. Please let me know when you can tell me anything else?"

"You'll be my first call," he promised and hung up.

I tried Russ again. It rolled over to voice mail. I hung up, disgusted. Something felt off about the whole thing and I just couldn't pinpoint what it was.

Finally I called Angela. She'd heard the news. She seemed remarkably stoic about the whole thing. "I think I'm just numb," she explained when I commented. "It's been such an emotional couple of weeks. Part of me thinks I should be glad that he got shot the way he shot my mother. Part of me thinks it's unfair because we'll never really know what happened if he dies. Mostly, though, my brain is just full. I can't process any more at this point. I'm actually going to bed right now and I'm going to do my best not to think about any of it."

After asking if I should come over and being told no, because she'd probably be asleep by the time I got there, I wished her pleasant dreams and drove back to my place. I must have been emotionally drained, too, because sleep took me quickly.

The next morning, after failing to reach Russ again, I drove to Sarah Ooi's house. It was a long shot really. No one who could tell me anything was being helpful, so maybe it was time to talk to those who couldn't and hope something new jogged loose.

She seemed surprised to see me when she came to the door. She blinked up at me. "Mr. Brady," she said tonelessly. "This is unexpected." She didn't sound pleasantly surprised.

"I hope you don't mind my stopping by unannounced," I said. "I was hoping you could spare a few minutes to talk."

She considered, then shrugged, turning away from the open door. I took that as an invitation to follow her inside, closing the door behind me. "Actually you're lucky to catch me at home," she said over her shoulder. "I took today and tomorrow off from work so I could spend an extended holiday weekend with family. Another half hour or so and you would have missed me." There were two suitcases by the door, confirming that story. Sarah led me to the kitchen where she gestured vaguely towards the stool at the counter. She stood on the other side, like a television chef preparing for a cooking demonstration. "So what can I do for you?"

"Did you hear about the incident at RCJ last night?" I asked.

"I was busy packing last night and went to bed early, so I haven't seen any news. What's happened?" Her voice took on a tone of concern.

I gave her a thumbnail sketch of the events as I knew them – the main suspect in Regina's death had been caught and was shot on his way into the jail by a suspect already in custody.

She shook her head. "I don't know what this world is coming to," she remarked, "but I'm not sure what your question is. It sounds like everything has been wrapped up. The police already have both Regina's killer and the guy who shot him. What else is there to investigate?"

"Tony was also arrested," I answered. "Allegedly he hired Jose Ramos to shoot Regina."

Sarah frowned and shook her head decisively. "That's completely wrong," she said, matter of factly. "He had just dumped me a few days before because he was trying to make things work with her. Why would he do that if he was just going to turn around and have her shot?"

"That was my question, too," I agreed. "Unfortunately, the evidence appears to be piling up. There was a cash transfer and the gun that was used was owned by a family member."

"Christ," Sarah breathed. All trace of her displeasure at my presence had faded. "It doesn't make sense though," she said.

I concurred. "I don't suppose Tony ever said anything to you about Regina having an affair?" I asked.

She clucked her tongue thoughtfully. "I'm not sure how to answer that," she said. "Will it help Tony?"

"It can't hurt at this point," I said.

She dipped her head in acknowledgement. "It was just pillow talk. Seems weird, I know, talking about his wife right after we had…you know. But it's not as uncommon as you might think. Anyway, he confided in me back in October or November that he thought she was seeing someone. They fought about me and she had made some reference that maybe she should leave him for someone else too. Words to that effect. He got the impression she was seeing someone too. But again, after Thanksgiving or thereabouts, she had decided she wanted to make things work. He complained about that a lot – Regina was never able to commit to a course of action. Personally, I think she decided to stay because she couldn't live without the money. Not that I'm speaking ill of the dead," she hastened to add. "After all, it served her well, I suppose. In the end, he was with her, not me."

I nodded solemnly. "I don't suppose he mentioned any issues between Regina and Russ?" I asked.

"The son?" she asked surprised. "Not that I know of. He rarely mentioned Russ. I got the impression he wasn't around much."

"Probably true," I said. I couldn't think of any other questions so I asked, "Is there anything you can think of that might shed some light on things?"

She spread her hands. "I wish I could. I don't believe Tony had any part of this. He had no reason to do so. I wish I could help prove his innocence."

I nodded grimly. "Hopefully something will come to light. It's possible that, now that he's been shot, Jose Ramos may be a little more forthcoming. If he says who hired him, that would get Tony off the hook." I was trying to encourage her so I didn't add the concern that he might die before that confession was made.

She glanced subtly at her watch and I stood. "I need to get on the road," she said. She scribbled on a piece of paper and slid it across the counter to me. "That's my cellular number. If you have any other questions or I can do anything to help Tony, please let me know."

I assured her I would, wished her a safe journey, and took my leave.

As I was driving home, my phone rang. It was Russ. I breathed a sigh of relief. "Don't you ever sleep?" he demanded when I answered. "I woke up this morning and I had three missed calls from you!"

I wondered if he had been sleeping or passed out, but decided not to press the issue. I was just relieved he wasn't in jail for shooting Jose Ramos. Sadly, I still wasn't sure whether or not he was involved with his mother's death.

I asked if he knew about the attack on Ramos. He groaned. "Yeah," he said. "I saw it on the news. That was just fricking crazy." His tone was subdued, almost guilty. "I ended up using. I just didn't want to think about the whole thing anymore," he admitted. I nodded to myself.

"Well, if it makes you feel better," I said, "I'm glad you aren't the one who shot Ramos."

"Me?" Russ asked, genuinely surprised. "Is the air

too thin for your brain up there? It was probably whoever hired him to shoot my mother. Why would I...wait a minute! You don't think *I* paid off Jose?"

I hesitated. "The thought has crossed my mind," I confessed.

Russ laughed. "That's pretty rich. Like I could afford that." He let the chuckle die away and said, "Look. I'll be honest with you, because you seem to be a decent and rational guy. Usually. I knew Jose from school. And, honestly, I get some of my dope from him sometimes. One of my last bags before I got clean this last time came from him. But I haven't seen him since then and we never talked about my mother. Well, except for his bullshit jibes about wanting to bang her. But we took potshots at each other like that all the time."

I considered telling Russ that Jose had finally followed through with getting involved with Regina, but I didn't see anything productive coming from that. "I'll take your word for it," I assured him instead.

My call waiting beeped and I glanced at the display on the phone. "Russ, I have to let you go. Talk soon!" I hung up without waiting for an answer, picking up the incoming call. "Derek!" I proclaimed.

"Hey, Pat," the police chief said by way of greeting. "I can talk to you now about last night's incident. Come down to my office?"

Glancing at my watch I said, "I can be there in fifteen minutes."

"I'll see you then," Derek confirmed and rang off.

Chief Beckham was waiting for me when I reached the police station. He was in a low conversation with another officer at one side of the anteroom, and held up a finger to me to wait as he concluded. When done, he gestured for me to follow him to his office. He closed the door behind us and I took a seat across the desk from him.

Derek looked weary, his broad shoulders sloping more than usual. His thick dark hair was greyer than the last time I'd seen him. Though we were from different Lodges, we had gotten to know each other when my godfather had been killed. He folded his thick hands on the desk and I noticed the indention where his Masonic ring usually was. He took it off while at work, probably for political purposes. His deep voice was scratchy when he spoke. "Sorry about this morning. I've been up all night, dealing with this thing and working with Finley on it. We're both none too cheery right now, as you can imagine."

"I would think not," I said sympathetically. "So what can you tell me?"

"The important details will be on the news, no doubt, but I can give you the whole story as I know it." He leaned back in the chair, staring at the ceiling.

"To your question earlier, no, the shooter was not Russell Button, or anyone else connected to Regina Button's murder, near as we can tell."

I breathed a sigh of relief. I didn't mention I'd heard from Russ.

"Jose Ramos was actually shot by Edward Carrigan," he continued tonelessly.

"Wait," I interrupted, "A *cop* shot Ramos?" I sat up straighter.

"Now you understand why we've been playing this so close to the vest. He was waiting there for him. We have him on a number of video and traffic cameras. Probably thought he was being slick, parking a couple blocks away and then slipping down into one of the abandoned buildings across the way. But the whole place is monitored. There's no way it wasn't him."

I shook my head in disbelief. "Why, though?" I asked. "What was his motive?"

Derek sighed. "Same old story," he said. "Jealousy and revenge." He glanced at me more directly and asked, "You're aware Carrigan was having an relationship with your vic?"

I nodded.

"Well, apparently she was getting a little side action from Ramos. Between that and the likelihood that Ramos ended up killing her, well," he shrugged expansively, "Carrigan just snapped. He didn't even try to make it back to his car after the shooting. Just kind of sat down and started bawling like a baby. He was devastated that she had cheated on him and that Ramos had killed her."

I nodded, taking it all in. "And you're sure that Carrigan wasn't involved in Regina's death?" I asked. "Maybe this other stuff is just a smokescreen and he's really the one who hired Ramos to shoot her?"

Derek frowned. "He vehemently denies any connection to Regina's murder. He freely admitted to the attack on Ramos, maybe because it was undeniable, but he was steadfast that he had nothing to do with the first case. Kept repeating how much he loved her. And crying." Derek sounded vaguely disgusted. "Unfortunately, every indication we have is that Ramos was hired by someone in the Button family. The money that changed hands, her son's gun used in the crime, the phone calls. Honestly, I think they've got Tony dead to rights on this. Finley's probably going to press formal charges today or tomorrow, and there's enough evidence to get it to stick. He's at the hospital now. Ramos is in critical condition and Finley wants to get a confession out of him before we lose him. That will seal the deal." He must have noticed the look in my eyes and he added, "I'm sorry, Pat. I know this is the last thing you or the family will want to hear."

I nodded my thanks. "What phone calls?" I asked. "I've heard a little about the money and the gun, but the phone calls are new."

"Someone from the Button household has been calling Ramos a couple times a week for about two months now. Presumably that was Regina, carrying on their affair. The calls became more frequent in December, as though more than one person was in contact with him. In the two days before she was killed, there were nine calls, all of them unanswered. The first time he was in custody, Ramos had said he'd lost his phone. According to Finley no phone hs been found yet. So maybe that's why she couldn't reach him. Or maybe it was Tony calling him. Probably both."

"But," I said, "you really can't prove who was making those calls, can you? So it's circumstantial at best."

"By itself," Derek agreed, "yes. But combined with the other evidence…" He let the sentence trail off, the implication hanging in the air between us.

"This doesn't look good," I said at last.

"No," Derek agreed. "It doesn't."

"Anything else I should know?" I asked.

Derek shook his head. "That's pretty much all the

salient information I have." He leaned forward confidentially. "I'll say this, though, Pat. The media is going to be all over this thing like flies on shit. Any time a cop is involved in a killing they eat it right up. And it won't be hard for them to start digging into Regina's case looking for connections. There's going to be a lot of pressure, and I mean a *lot* of pressure, from above to get both these cases cleared up as quickly and smoothly as possible. *If* Tony is innocent, you probably don't have a whole lot of time left to prove it."

I agreed. We waxed Masonic for a few minutes. He was interested when I told him about Sam Byler's degree. He hadn't heard of a Mason coming from an Amish background before, but he was sure it must have happened. I also asked his opinion of the possible merger between Acacia and Hiram-Austin. Since he was a member of Spindle City Lodge in Cohoes, and not involved in the merger at all, he could be impartial.

"I think," he said, seeming relieved to talk about something other than murder and rogue lovesick police officers, "it depends on the strength of each Lodge. Not just financial, but the membership, too. Are both Lodges bringing in new members regularly? Are the active in the community and in the District? Do they have a good turnout at their meetings? And, yes, can they afford to continue to operate under the status quo? Those are all factors. Spindle City was the result of a merger between Waterford and Latham, many years ago. It's not a seamless process, and there will be members lost in the shuffle. But now enough time has passed that we're a coherent body. It took some time and some work, though. Sometimes it's better, especially in your case, for the two Lodges to stay independent, but start doing more joint events. If you do end up merging, there may be fewer hard feelings down the road." He gave a shrug. "It's an unfortunate sign of the times, I guess, with declining membership. Hopefully we'll be able to reverse that trend someday."

On that point we agreed.

That afternoon, Angela and I headed to the mall to do some long overdue Christmas shopping. She had already picked up a few things before the attack on her mother, but, due to my high amounts of testosterone, I had neglected it until nearly the last minute.

"Do you think your parents will be upset if I don't come with you on Sunday?" Angela asked quiet as we drove.

I glanced sideways at her. "Just not feeling the Christmas spirit this year?" I asked.

"Can you blame me?" she retorted with an arch look.

"Not at all," I replied smoothly, turning into the parking lot and slowly cruising the aisles looking for an empty spot or someone headed to their car. "And I'm sure my parents would understand too. But you will be missed." I reached over and gave her leg a squeeze. She didn't flinch. The longer her uncle was gone, the more she was getting back to normal. "Especially by me," I added.

She gave me a wan smile. "We can exchange gifts in private afterwards," she promised, with a glimmer of the old sexy, seductive smile I knew so well. I was so distracted by it, I almost didn't see the BMW backing out further up the lane. I sped up enough to reach the spot before any of the other vultures circling the lot fell upon the carcass. The spot was tight but I managed to maneuver the Cavalier in without doing any serious damage.

As we were getting out and locked the car, the phone rang. I slipped one arm through Angela's and answered the phone with the other.

"Mr. Brady," Detective Finley gave his usual gruff greeting.

"Detective," I replied. "How is everything going?"

"Swell," he grumbled. "I needed to speak to you briefly. Something has come up that, I'm sure you'll be glad to hear, but it pisses the hell out of me."

"Sounds intriguing," I admitted. Focused on the conversation, I started walking slower. Angela patiently kept pace.

"I know you're up to speed and talked to Beckham this afternoon. I wasn't thrilled that he talked to you without me, but technically the Ramos shooting is his jurisdiction. Regardless, it's water under the bridge now." He sighed, not sounding like he was particularly ready to let it go. "At any rate, as you know, I spoke with Ramos this afternoon. The doctors aren't sure yet if he's going to pull through. He's got a collapsed lung and one of the bullets grazed his bowel. If he lives he'll have a colostomy bag for the rest of his life probably. They got him on some pretty good pain meds, though. I don't know if it was the drugs or the looming threat of death, but something finally loosened his lips a little bit. He was a bit delirious, gloated a bit about his sexual exploits with Mrs. Button. But then he finally gave me something interesting to work with."

"And what is that?" I asked. We paused checking to see if any cars were coming before crossing from the lot to the mall entrance.

"Apparently, Regina Button wasn't the target."

I stopped dead. Bad choice of words. Nevertheless, I stopped, staring straight ahead, quickly processing the new information. Finley was right. All along, we'd been looking for someone with motive to kill Angela. But if *Tony* was the target, not only did that free him from the conspiracy charge, but it also meant we had to reconsider everything.

"Did you hear me?" Finley demanded as I remained still and silent.

"I...yeah. Wow," I said intelligently. I was quickly going through my list of players, wondering who might have wanted Tony dead. Russ? Possibly. Sarah Ooi? I didn't think so. I found myself wondering about Vito Denato and his seemingly endless desire to hang around the area while this whole thing played out.

"Patrick!" Angela yelped suddenly, calling my attention back to the present. We had stopped in the middle of the road and a teenager in a Hyundai had just turned the corner in our direction. Angela threw herself in front of me pushing me back towards the parking lot, out of harm's way. In true holiday spirit, the teenager flipped us off as he cruised through the space I had occupied a moment before. I barely noticed.

I was staring at Angela and she was looking up at me. "Are you okay?" she asked. In my ear Finley was asking the same thing, demanding to know what was going on.

"I'm fine, I'm fine," I told them both hastily. "Did he get you?" I asked Angela. She shook her head.

Something clicked in my head.

"Brady, what the hell's going on over there?" Finley demanded.

Looking into Angela's eyes, my stomach twisted. Into the phone, but speaking to them both, I said, "I think I know what happened."

Chapter Nineteen

Angela didn't like my answer. Neither did Finley, for different reasons. Truth be told, I wasn't thrilled about it either.

Angela and I sat just inside the mall entrance as I put Finley on speaker and explained my theory to both of them. Finley said he'd go back to the hospital and see if he could get some confirmation from Jose Ramos. Angela and I quickly did our Christmas shopping, feeling far from jolly. While she was off getting a gift or two for me, I purchased a silver tennis bracelet that she'd had her eye on for some time.

As we were driving back to Angela's apartment, Finley called me back and, in clipped tones, reported that Jose had confirmed my theory. He grudgingly congratulated me on figuring it out. I accepted the praise gracefully, but it didn't feel like much of a win.

Two hectic days later, I joined my family for an early Christmas dinner.

I hugged my mother, buzzing her cheek, and shook Dad's hand, wishing them both a Merry Christmas. Mom asked about Angela and I explained that she just wasn't feeling very festive. As anticipated, they were understanding and sent their best wishes.

I sat at the counter, letting the warm, fragrant smell of the turkey in the oven melt away the tension of the past year. Dad and I picked at the shrimp cocktail set out as an appetizer and talked about the First Degree earlier the week and about the merger while Mom bustled around doing cooking things and occasionally chiming in. We paused at one point and Mom told me about that morning's church service and who they had sat with. "You remember Beth Fowler?" she asked me.

"No," I answered around a mouthful of shrimp.

"Yes, you do," Mom cajoled, "she was your Sunday school teacher for a while."

"Oh, yeah," I said, "Her." I didn't have the heart to tell her I still had no idea who she was talking about. Maybe it was because I often ditched Sunday school and sat in the garden that surrounded our church. Once I heard the adult service ending, I would slip back inside and join the crowd. I just felt closer to God in the garden than in Sunday school. Of course, it was possible that I couldn't remember this person because I hadn't been back to the church in about fifteen years.

Regardless, Mom went on to tell me about Beth Fowler's daughter, who was going to college now to be a doctor. I nodded with vaguely feigned interest. "She may have been closer to Ian's age, come to think of it," Mom remarked at the end of her story.

Through the window, I saw Ian's truck pulling up behind my Cavalier. "You should be sure to tell him all about it," I told her. "I'm sure he remembers her."

My mother slid me a shrewd look, apparently picking up on my playful sarcasm. Dad smirked but refrained from commenting, lest she turn on him.

A moment later the door opened and Ian strode in, a broad smile on his face. He'd shaved for the occasion, his usual scruffy appearance abandoned in favor of a smooth, ruddy complexion. We shook hands and, looking over his shoulder, I realized why he was looking so happy and well groomed. Tanya Novello walked in behind him, looking a little uncertain. She smiled at me as our eyes met.

"Merry Christmas, bro!" Ian said.

"Back at ya," I agreed. He moved past me to greet the parents and I hugged Tanya. "Nice to see you again, especially under better circumstances," I told her.

"Thanks," she said, lowering her voice. "I wasn't sure I'd be welcome, just coming along with Ian like this, unannounced."

I opened my mouth to reply, but my mother, who hears all things, said, "Of course you're welcome." She moved forward, taking Tanya's hand and drawing her further into the kitchen. "Tanya, isn't it? I think we met briefly the other day."

Tanya dipped her head and smiled. "I remember. Thank you." She gestured towards Ian, who was studiously avoiding my questioning gaze. "Ian said you wouldn't mind but I still told him he should call ahead and let you know."

My mother's eyes flicked towards her other son. "I must have missed his call," she murmured. Ian grabbed a shrimp and crammed it in his mouth in response.

"I wish I'd known you would be here," I commented, also glancing at my chipmunk-cheeked brother. "Angela might have come if she'd known. She didn't feel up to it, all things considered."

"I don't blame her," Tanya agreed. "I'll give her a call and let her know. Maybe she'll come over after all." Cell phone in hand, she excused herself and stepped outside. We all watched her go, then turned towards Ian. With all three of us watching him, his options were limited.

"What?" he demanded around a mouthful of shrimp. "After the whole thing with her father, she wasn't quite ready to go home again. She decided to stay in the area for a week…or two." He shrugged, staring fixedly at the shrimp and picking up another one.

"And where is she staying?" Mom asked. She moved to the oven to take the turkey out, but she spared a moment to give him a pursed lip gaze.

Ian's response was muffled by partially masticated crustacean. I leaned in, putting a hand to my ear. "Sorry, I don't think we heard that," I said. Dad chuckled.

"With me, okay?" Ian replied louder, glancing towards the door. "She's staying with me but it's not what you think. We seem to have this real... connection, I guess. You know? Like the first night, after the memorial service, we went out, had a couple drinks and went back to my place. And then we stayed up most of the night talking. Talking! When was the last time I wasted time doing that with a woman?"

"Not in recent memory," our father answered. "Impressive. You're showing signs of maturity."

"It had to happen sooner or later," I told him. Dad nodded in thoughtful agreement.

We all looked towards my mother, who closed the oven door very deliberately and wiped her hands on a towel. "Well," she said, "obviously I don't know her very well. Yet." She smiled and we three wise men all began to breathe again. "But so far, I like her." While not necessary, Mom's approval made things so much easier. Not just in relationships but in all things.

"I'm glad to see you taking it slow," I told him. "Though it's weird seeing you in a relationship with a woman you haven't slept with yet."

Ian gave a cocky grin. "I said we stayed up talking *most* of the night," he reminded me.

"Ian!" Mom snapped at him.

My brother shrugged and laughed. "Come on, you don't expect me to change completely, do you?"

My father, with an eye on the window, cleared his throat sharply and, when the door opened a moment later, we all looked like we hadn't just been talking behind Tanya's back.

Tanya announced that Angela had agreed to join us for presents and dessert a little later. We finished setting the table in the dining room and Dad carved the turkey. We gathered around the table for dinner. I could hear Burl Ives singing from the stereo in the den at the far end of the house, providing mood music. Perhaps as penance for his premarital sexual activities, my mother asked Ian to say grace before we ate. He fumbled his way through in a way that had the two of us snickering like children by the time he had finished. We began to pass the food around and load up our plates and, as we settled into eating, my father asked the inevitable question.

"So, Patrick," he said, pouring gravy on pretty

much everything on his plate, "regale us with the tale of how you figured out what happened with Angela's mother."

I looked at Tanya questioningly. I'd already gotten Angela's permission to discuss the case in her absence; we both knew it was bound to come up. Tanya waved a dismissive hand. "Go for it," she said, "I'd love to hear it myself."

I nodded, took a bite of turkey as I framed the story in my head, swallowed and explained, "As often happens, I just got lucky. I was just in the right place at the right time for several things to click into place for me." The turkey was really good. I wanted more, but everyone was already listening attentively.

"Regina's death was culmination of a number of unfortunate decisions that she and Tony made in their lives," I began. "You all know the gist of what happened at Thanksgiving but, really, that was just the tip of the iceberg. Sadly, things between the two of them have been going sour for some time now. Unfortunately, I believe they really did love each other. They lost their way over the last few months but maybe there's some comfort to be found that they were in the process of healing their relationship when Regina was shot."

I paused for another bite or two. Everyone, aside from Ian, had been eating slowly, watching me with interest. Ian was also listening, but that didn't stop him from chowing down.

"Last summer, Tony started seeing someone on the side. The marriage had hit a bumpy patch and maybe it was inevitable, but that doesn't excuse it. He and Sarah Ooi began to get serious. During the fall, Regina somehow found out that he was being unfaithful and confronted him about it. Her initial reaction was that she was going to leave him. If she had, it's likely none of this would have happened. But, as was recently pointed out to me, Regina wasn't good at sticking with a course of action. And that was the real character flaw that got her killed. She may also have stayed because Tony made more than her. I'm not convinced of that, though; she would have made out very well in a divorce. For whatever reason, she stayed."

"You're going to drag this out, aren't you?" Ian demanded around a mouth of mashed potatoes. There seemed to be a lot of talking with our mouths full lately.

"Oh, baby, let him tell it his way," Tanya teased him. Ian flushed. My parents exchanged a surreptitious glance.

"Sorry," I said, "I didn't realize you had somewhere to go. I'll try to move it along." I took a sip of my Diet Pepsi, making a point of linger over it like my glass was filled with a fine wine. My brother grunted and smirked. I swallowed and continued, "Maybe the reason she stayed was because she'd found someone else, too. Edward Carrigan, a police officer she had met a couple times during the course of her work. It sounds like things were actually okay for a month or two. Both Tony and Regina were in relationships with other people, so they were less likely to argue between themselves. That changed when Regina crossed paths with Jose Ramos.

She remembered him from when he went to school with Russ. I don't think she realized that Jose was also Russ's occasional dealer. I also don't know if the idea occurred to her after she met up with Jose, or if he was the unlucky first person to cross her path after she'd decided to find someone to kill her husband."

I paused dramatically, letting that statement sink in. I took a casual bite of stuffing. It was pretty good.

"Holy shit," Ian breathed, finally putting his fork down.

My mother frowned, both at Ian's language at the table and at what I'd just revealed. "What do you mean?" she asked, "*She* hired the person who killed her?"

"That's what he said," my father murmured.

"Basically," I answered. "Not intentionally, of course. She had access to the joint bank accounts with Tony so it was easy enough for her to transfer the money. She knew her son had a gun, not to mention the combination to the case it was locked in. I'm reasonably certain that she intended to frame Russ for the attack. With his history and the murder weapon being his gun, it would have been a strong case. She could have talked about how the father and son never really saw eye to eye." Tanya smirked at me. "No pun intended," I assured her. "And if anyone did realize Ramos was the shooter, she'd claim that Russ must have gotten the account number sometime when he was stealing some other trinket to pay for his addiction."

"How could she be sure Ramos wouldn't turn on her?" my father asked. His reddish brown eyebrows were high on his forehead as he listened with interest.

I shrugged with a grimace. "Sex, of course," I said. "That, and promises that the two of them would be free to be together. Maybe even the promise of another payoff after the deed was done. For all I know she would have killed him too. We may never know."

"I'm still confused," my mother remarked. "Why did he shoot her instead?"

"It was an accident," I replied. I tilted my head to one side and amended, "Well, sort of. More of a tragic sacrifice. See, after she started seeing Jose, things got worse with her and Tony again, probably contributing to the scene at Thanksgiving. Tony realized he was in danger of losing her and was determined to heal his marriage. He broke things off with Sarah Ooi and began to give Regina his love and attention again. They were working things out. On that fateful night, he's even said they were like their old selves again. And, as we know, Regina didn't excel at sticking to a plan. As she and Tony began to improve their relationship, she reached out to Jose to call off the attack. Unfortunately, he'd lost his phone and never got the call. That's why she was so skittish those last couple of days. Jose confirmed that they had agreed she would have no idea where or when the attack would take place. It would give her plausible deniability. For two days, she was paranoid that he would show up at any time. So she stuck close to Tony. As she and Tony were walking into their house, she must have spotted Jose hiding among the trees and she did the only thing she could – she threw herself in front of him." I gave a sad smile, adding, "Angela did pretty much the same thing to me the other day, and, along with the news that Regina hadn't been the target, that brought everything into focus."

We ate silently for a few moments, absorbing the tragedy of the whole situation.

"You probably know the rest of it from the

news," I said after a while. "The police got a lead that led them to Ramos and they caught him down south. He ran when he realized he'd shot the wrong person and everything had gone awry. They brought him back here to question him and a...friend of Tony's got him a good lawyer, afraid that Tony might be implicated. That only made Tony look guiltier, so he was arrested. Of course, he's been released now and the charges dropped, but it was touch and go for a while there. When they were bringing Ramos back to jail, Edward Carrigan, in a fit of jealousy and wrongfully believing that Jose had killed Regina on purpose, took a shot at him. Carrigan's career is over and he'll probably do some time. But it may have been a good thing, at least for Tony. If he hadn't been shot and close to death, Jose may never have admitted that Regina was the one who hired him, and Tony would have gotten tried, and probably convicted, on the conspiracy charges. Last I heard, Jose's condition had been upgraded to stable. He'll probably live to have his day in court."

My mother clucked her tongue. "What a shame," she said. "I would never have guessed any of that was going on."

We all made murmuring agreement noises as we ate. There didn't seem to be much else to say on the topic and when my mother turned to grilling Tanya about what she did for a living, where she went to school and the full gamut of new relationship questions, I was relieved to be done telling the story.

Angela arrived as we were finishing cleaning up from dinner. She smiled brightly as she greeted everyone, and I saw only a glimmer of sadness hidden in her eyes. We kissed and I gave her a hug and she clung to me just a little longer than usual. I put my arm around her as we filed into the living room to start opening presents. I leaned towards her and said, "Merry Christmas, love."

She rewarded me with a genuine smile. "Merry Christmas," she agreed.

Chapter Twenty

New Year's Eve. In a few short hours, 2011 would be over. Neither of us would be sorry to see it go.

In the wake of the revelation that Angela's mother had died as a result of conspiring to have Anthony killed, her remaining family members had begun to come together. So far the overtures had been tentative and uncertain. Nonetheless, they drew strength and comfort from each other. The whole family had had secrets revealed about themselves or old wounds scraped open during the course of the investigation and, emotionally, they were each raw and drained. By unspoken consent, they had decided that none of their respective issues trumped what her mother had done so, for now at least, her brother's drug use and her father's connections and the details of her own trauma were all set aside. Wayne Novello had not been seen or heard from since the memorial service and I knew Angela, for one, was relieved by his absence.

Neither of us really felt like ringing in the new year by staying up until midnight, but we had agreed on an early dinner at a halfway decent restaurant, to regroup and to try and return to some semblance of normality. And, for when we returned to my apartment, Angela had casually mentioned that she brought home the schoolgirl uniform from work. I had invited Ian to join us for dinner, suggesting that he could bring Tanya with him. He said they already had other plans to end the year with a bang and waggled his eyebrows at me suggestively. I tried to take some small comfort that at least one good thing had come out of this whole affair, but the poor choice of words made me wince.

I was enjoying a steak with garlic blue cheese and a side of thick creamy mashed potatoes. There was also a vegetable that I was studiously avoiding. When the new year came, I would make my inevitable resolution to get healthier but for the next six hours, butter and steak were still my foods of choice. I found myself chewing slowly, not really tasting my food. Angela had ordered salmon and there was still more on her plate than she'd put in her mouth. She sat staring into her glass of white wine as she swirled it slowly and thoughtfully. My brain cautioned me to leave well enough alone, but my heart ached at her distraction and urged me to try and restore peace to her troubled mind. As usual, my heart won out.

I swallowed a well masticated piece of meat and said, "Nickel for your thoughts."

She raised her eyes to mine, a slight pucker furrowing between her eyebrows. "Don't you mean a penny?" she asked.

"Inflation," I shrugged. "Besides, your thoughts are especially valuable to me." I reached across and took her free hand. "What's wrong, my love?"

She grimaced and was silent long enough that I thought she might not answer. Finally she sighed and said softly, "I can't remember the last words I said to my mother."

"Oh." I nodded sympathetically. I squeezed her hand. "Well, you're in luck. Because I know exactly what they were."

She looked up with surprise and hope and bewilderment in her eyes. "You do? How?"

"It was two days before she was shot," I explained. "She called, looking for suggestions for us for Christmas because they were going shopping that weekend. I didn't hear the conversation, but you told me about it. And you've always ended phone calls with your mother by telling her you loved her." I gave her a reassuring smile. "So the last thing you said to your mother was…'I love you.'"

Her eyes glistened and a tear dribbled down her cheek, but she smiled at me and nodded. "You're right. I remember now. That *was* the last time I spoke to her. And I did say that."

We went back to our meals in companionable

silence for a few moments. In time, she commented, "For what it's worth, I think your sterility may be a blessing in disguise."

I blinked at the shift in subject. We hadn't broached the topic in over a year and her attitude surprised me. "How so?" I asked cautiously.

"Families are messy," Angela said. "Parents are flawed. Hell, I know you and I are both damaged goods. What makes us think we have the ability or the right to bring more people into this world and subject them to its horrors?"

"That's pretty dark," I commented.

With a cool gaze, Angela responded, "You know my mother tried to have my father murdered and ended up being killed herself, right? I think I'm entitled to a dimmer view of the world for a while."

"Valid point," I agreed, raising my hands defensively. I proceeded slowly, picking my words as carefully as I would pick my way through a minefield. "But I think…it's like those investment shows on the radio say…Past performance is not an indicator of future results." The frown between her eyes was back. I elaborated. "Just because your family had their tragedies, just because we've got our own crosses to bear…that doesn't mean we wouldn't be good parents. In fact, we might even be better parents. We've had a lot more experiences than some people; I like to think it's made us stronger, not just harder. Or darker."

She took a dainty bite of salmon and considered my words before shrugging dismissively. "It's a moot point anyway. Whether we decide someday to have children or not, it's not really up to us. Our wishes aren't going to make your...parts work any better."

"There are options," I said. "We could adopt. Or artificial insemination, for example. If we want it, we can make it happen."

"Maybe," she said, sounding unconvinced. I was inclined to leave the topic alone. We weren't at a point where we were ready to have children yet anyway. If we ever got married and were thinking about kids, hopefully the dark cloud hanging over Angela would have passed, or at least thinned significantly. If I continued to press her now, it could just as easily lead to an argument. I was just putting together the words for a verbal tactical retreat when she changed the topic.

"So," she asked, "now that you and your father are members of Hiram-Austin Lodge, does that mean I'm not going to see you at all on Wednesdays?"

Three days earlier, the four petitions for affiliation at Hiram-Austin had been balloted upon. Although discussion of a vote is strictly forbidden in Freemasonry, people often find roundabout ways to skirt the regulations, and I had been informed that my father and I had each squeaked by with two black cubes against each of us. We hadn't attended the meeting, but I was sure Mitch Svenson cast one of the negative ballots in both cases. I suspected Len Temple may have cast the other, but I wasn't positive.

"No," I assured her, "I may have to attend H-A a few times over the next couple of months until the merger discussion dies down, but I don't plan on being a regular participant. I want to focus on going through the line at Acacia."

She hummed and nodded. "And I assume the conspiracy to prevent the merger is proceeding apace?"

"Looks like we'll have the votes to block it," I agreed. Having pretty much licked my plate clean of meat and potatoes, I bit into a hesitant forkful of broccoli and shrugged. Another pat of butter and it wouldn't be too bad.

"I'm sure your father is happy about that," Angela remarked drily.

I ignored the arch tone behind her comment. "He is," I said noncommittally. I knew I wouldn't always be able to follow in my father's footsteps. Sooner or later, he and I would disagree on something Masonic. Whether or not that led to better opportunities for me in the fraternity, I didn't know for sure, but it was inevitable. For now, I was content for our ideals to be aligned.

"Where have you been?" a gruff voice demanded. We turned, as did a couple people at other tables, toward the man who had spoken these words. He was in his mid to late twenties with two days growth of facial hair. He seemed the type who was not accustomed to dressing up but who had made a half-hearted attempt to dress appropriately for the restaurant. His hair was slicked off to one side and still looked wet and greasy, grey streaks already lightening the brown. His face was pockmarked and weathered. Life had not been kind to him. He was missing an incisor. He was addressing a girl of about six. She wore a simple white dress, not fancy and not quite her size, probably a hand me down from an older and larger sister. She had the proverbial button nose and thick honey brown hair. Big, soulful eyes that looked at the man with a mixture of fear and defiance, as though she wasn't sure how much she could get away with, but she was determined to find out. She took a step away from him as her advanced toward her.

"The bathroom," she answered. Her voice was low and quavered a little and had a hint of "remember, I told you that's where I was going" in it. She glanced around as though seeking an escape route. I watched as she and Angela locked eyes for a moment. Rather than look away, the two stared at each other, some silent communication occurring that I was too obtuse to perceive or understand. The girl stuck her thumb in her mouth, sucking nervously. She should have outgrown that habit by now, and the action made her look even younger.

The man took her thin arm in one hand. His fingers sunk into her flesh and she winced but didn't give him the satisfaction of crying out. "You've been gone for ten minutes. You got your mother all worked up now. Come on." He began to pull her back the way he had come. She didn't resist but she didn't walk any faster than he forced her to either.

Uncomfortable with the scene, many of the diners who had been first attracted to the pair became focused on their meals. I continued to watch. The girl looked at Angela, eyes pleading, for another moment before turning to the man and saying, "I'm sorry, Daddy!"

"Of course you are," the man grumbled. "You're always sorry, Phoebe. It's never your fault. I swear to God, sometimes you just drive me up the wall." The rest of the conversation was lost as Phoebe and her father returned to the next room and, presumably, their table.

"Well," I murmured, returning to my vegetable and my girlfriend, "that was awkward. Talk about people who shouldn't be parents. I…" I paused. Angela wasn't listening. She was watching the arch through which the man and daughter had passed. Her eyes gave the impression her mind was far away, her lips parted as though entranced. "What?" I asked. There was no response. I placed a hand on her wrist and the contact seemed to shake her free from her reverie. She turned and looked at me.

"Foster care," she said.

"I'm sorry?" I asked, not mentally limber enough to keep up with her train of thought.

"We can do foster care," she explained. It wasn't a suggestion or a question, but a forgone conclusion. Seeing my bewilderment, she swallowed and shifted uncomfortably before continuing, "It's just a…feeling."

"A feeling like you know what's going to happen?" I asked. I kept every ounce of skepticism from my tone.

"Yes," she said, still aware of my doubts. "I know you don't really understand, but I'm telling you. We're going to do foster care." She gestured towards the archway again. "I think we're going to help that little girl, that Phoebe."

"We aren't even married yet," I pointed out with a nervous chuckle.

She smiled back. "We will be."

"Um…"

"Patrick, I'm serious," Angela insisted. "When she looked at me, there was a…connection. I knew. And, it was weird. I…I think she felt something too. I don't know how or when. But we are going to see her again. We're going to help her…." She trailed off, lowering her eyes to her Riesling again.

"And?" I prodded.

Her eyes, when she raised them, were sad. "And…I think it might destroy us."

ABOUT THE AUTHOR

Jason is reasonably sure that most people don't even both to read this section. I mean, sure, I suppose if you're a friend or a relative, you might read this to see if I say something amusing, or if I mention the cats, Cora and Fat Ass. But really, if you don't already know me, do you even bother? And, if so, why? Does it make you feel closer to me somehow, like we're friends or something? That's kind of stalkerish, don't you think? Not like "boil my bunny" stalker, but more like "fanboy showing up on my doorstep unannounced on a Sunday afternoon when I'm sitting around the house in my underwear" kind of stalker. If that's you, please don't come knocking. I appreciate the sentiment, honest I do. But, really, don't. Just don't. Email (jasonedzembo@gmail.com) or Facebook (facebook.com/jasonedzembo) works just as well. Honest.

Made in the USA
Middletown, DE
01 October 2017